FOR A SONG

FOR A SONG

Peggy Hogan

FOR A SONG

DOUBLE DRAGON

CHAPTER 1

Blat (an unfortunate name for a singer) sang one of his favourite ballads as he led the plough horse around and around the field.

The song began with the story of a poor orphan boy mistreated by his so-called caretakers. This part always made Blat cry a little and he let the emotion help his voice warble at the end of each line. One day the boy was adopted by an old wizard who claimed he needed an apprentice. The boy soon learned that he had traded one type of misery for another. Invoking the despair of shattered hope, Blat transformed his voice from the relief that the boy had finally found a home into the horrible realisation that he was worse off than before. In the final and triumphant verse, the boy realised that he understood the language of the arcane spells that the wizard invoked to keep him docile and subservient. His newfound power burst forth and he hurled a vengeful spell at his abusive master. Aflame with righteous anger, Blat let his voice ring with indignation.

With a secret smile, Blat launched into a fourth verse, one that he had added to the song himself. He felt in his heart that the orphan boy was capable of forgiveness. Instead of crushing the old wizard as he lay helpless on the ground, the boy relented and to his amazement, the wizard was reduced to tears, only then realising that the boy was his long-lost son. Whenever Blat sang this verse to his younger brothers, they rolled their eyes and groaned. Blat didn't care - he loved happy endings.

He brought the ballad to a close with a flourish of joyous notes.

Slow steady applause startled Blat and he felt himself blush. He shaded his eyes and looked up. Dusty boots dangled from beneath a dusty cloak. The sun was behind whoever it was that straddled the fence and he couldn't make out any features.

"Boy, you are wasted, wasted, wasted at this menial labour! Come closer." It was the voice of a woman, with a tone as imperious as the village headman when he got himself into a snit. She impatiently tapped her heel against a fence post as Blat dropped the horse's reins and shuffled over to where she sat. She leaned over and rudely took his chin in her hand and turned his head this way and that.

Blat was stunned. He had been taught to respect his elders, but did that mean that he had to put up with this kind of handling? From a stranger?

A small smile curved her lips. "That last verse. That was yours?"

Does she also mock me? thought Blat. A flare of anger blazed in his green eyes.

Her smile widened. "Take me to your parents, boy."

He considered refusing. Who was this not-very-polite woman anyway? It was a warm day; perhaps a few hours on that hard, wooden seat would teach her some manners.

"I have to finish ploughing this field," he declared with what he hoped was authority.

She shrugged and promptly stretched out on the sun-warmed top rail. It was barely wide enough for

6

her, but she didn't seem to care. She clasped her hands at her waist, crossed her ankles, and was snoring softly before Blat had retrieved the slack lead rope.

So much for his moment of defiance.

The sun was low in the sky when Blat nudged the woman awake. She came instantly alert, vaulted from her perch, and landed nimbly beside him. She gathered her things and they walked down the lane in silence.

Their boots kicked up a choking dust and Blat stifled a sneeze. The earth was baked hard this year, harder than Blat could remember. Of course, at fourteen, there weren't that many years to remember. From the talk, this was the worst one ever, but then again, every year had been declared the worst one ever. His father was worried, though, and Blat hated to see him fret.

Just before they reached the path that would take him home, Blat stopped. "Who are you and why do you want to talk to my father?" His anxiety made him speak a little sharper that he intended and he also knew that he was out of line; grown-up business was for grown-ups. But this woman bothered him.

She turned to him in surprise. "You don't know what I am?" She shook her head at his blank stare and muttered to herself saying something about how everybody should know and what was the world coming to anyway.

"Come." She took his arm. "I'll tell the tale but once to both you and your parents."

7

Blat let her propel him towards the house that was visible through a gap in the hedgerow. "I should tell you," he said, "that my mother is dead these past six years."

She squeezed his shoulder.

He did not want her sympathy and shrugged her hand off. He climbed the pair of stairs to the porch, pushed the door open, and walked in, leaving it ajar for her to come in or not. He didn't care.

Blat's father was an ordinary man - average height, average build, brown hair, and brown eyes - with the look of farmers everywhere in his thickly muscled forearms and deeply tanned face. He was in the midst of ladling out bowls of stew to a small tribe of children. "Ah, Blat. Did you finish the…" He stumbled to a halt. The boys had gone quiet - a marvel in itself - but it was the stranger in the doorway, a female stranger, a minstrel female stranger, that had brought the interrogation to an abrupt end.

"Good evening, sir. My name is Sarah Tucana. Please excuse my intrusion during your mealtime; I'll come back later." She turned to go.

Blat's father remembered his manners. "No, no. Please join us. We would be honoured."

Blat's brothers had not moved, some with spoons halfway to their mouths. Their father turned his attention back to his brood. "Alvin, Michael, Stuart. Slide down to the end of the bench, there's good lads. Robert, Raymond," Tomias Raike continued his orders, "fetch another bowl and spoon, clean ones mind." With that, Blat's father

8

unburdened their guest of her pack and cloak, and gestured for Sarah to seat herself.

Blat took the momentary shuffle to step out to the rain barrel and splash some water on his face and hands. Robert and Raymond had manoeuvred themselves next to Sarah leaving him at the far end of the table. His twin brothers quickly lost their shyness and plied Sarah with question after question. Who was she? Where did she come from? How come they had never seen her before? What was she doing with their stupid brother Blat?

Sarah calmly ate her stew and smiled at them. Tomias eyed his two youngest boys but knew it would be worse if he tried to quiet them. His other boys contented themselves with staring at her between gulps of food.

When supper had been devoured - and that was exactly the right word for the voracious appetites of this many growing boys - Tomias meted out instructions for the clean-up of both the supper dishes and of the hands, faces, and teeth of his sons. With the usual grumbling, they trooped off to their duties while he invited Sarah to sit by the hearth for a cup of tea which Blat quietly prepared and served. Tomias joined her when he was fairly certain that his orders would be carried out. He sat with a sigh and closed his eyes for a brief moment. "Ah, but it's a good thing that I love them."

"I know just what you mean," she interjected before he could be embarrassed by his unguarded remark. "I have a fair knowledge of children myself." And they were off discussing the great variety of parental headaches.

In a brief lull in the conversation, Tomias ventured the question that had been niggling at him. "So what brings you to my humble home?"

Sarah cleared her throat. "May I first thank you for a most cordial welcome and for the fine meal. I know that it is the custom in these parts to treat strangers with kindness, but you have gone the extra step of making me feel genuinely welcome." She paused to sip her cooling tea. "As you know, I am a Touring Minstrel and it is about Blat that I wish to speak." She glanced at the boy sitting just beyond the reach of the firelight.

"A minstrel," Stuart blurted. The children had quietly gathered around the two grown-ups, some sitting on the hearth and some on the braided rug. They had learned that if they were not heard, they might not be seen and hence allowed to stay. But Stuart had ruined it. Now they would be sent to bed.

Alvin and Michael turned on their brother. "Now you've done it!" they said in unison. You would think that they were the twins instead of being eight and nine years old respectively. Stuart, at ten years old, should have known better. Even the twins had kept quiet.

Sarah smiled. "Yes, a minstrel. Do you know what that means?"

"A minstrel sings songs," Michael offered.

"Yeah, but so does stupid Blat and he's no minstrel," Robert piped up. "Blat, Blat, Blat, Blat, Blat, Blat," he mock-sang in a high, squeaky voice.

"Well, you should talk," Raymond entered into the fray, "you screech almost as much as he does."

10

"Do not!"

"Do too!"

"Do not!"

This could have continued to the inevitable scuffle and tears, but Sarah chose that moment to pull out the small pipes that she carried on her person and began a sprightly tune. Robert and Raymond instantly settled to enjoy the first 'real music' (as they would later call it) in their house. She then sang stories of magical beasts and heroes, of strange lands and even stranger people, of impossible feats of strength, and of beauty beyond compare (the younger boys made faces during these ones). Sarah spotted the first stifled yawn and played a lullaby; several sets of eyelids began to droop. Tomias gathered the twins, one under each arm, and Blat followed, gently coaxing the other three, into the boys' communal bedroom.

"This was an evening they will not soon forget," Tomias said when he returned from tucking his young children into bed. "And I thank you for it." He opened a cupboard well above the reach of curious hands and poured them a drop of the whisky that he saved for special occasions.

Sarah sipped. "Now that's a fine thing," she said, admiring the golden glow of the spirit in her cup.

They drank in companionable silence for a few moments.

"So Tomias, if you don't mind my asking, wherever did you get the name 'Blat?' It's the first time I've come across it and I've come across many a name."

Tomias smiled. "It was a bit of a mix-up, really, at first. Marie and I had chosen 'Bartholomew' for the lad. It was her father's name. But the scribe, Jeffers, was getting on in years and his hand was not as steady as it used to be, nor his eye as clear. We didn't know he had put down the wrong letters until well after the naming ceremony and well, Blat," he looked over at his son with a fond smile on his face, "blatted as a baby. Marie and I thought the old scribe had the right of it and so 'Blatolomew', or 'Blat' for short, is how we know and love him."

"There's a song in there somewhere," Sarah murmured, and her hands pantomimed motions on her pipes. "Speaking of songs," Sarah began.

Blat added a few pieces of wood to the fire and returned to his seat beside the hearth. *Now we come to it.*

Blat's father proved to be amenable to Sarah's proposal to take Blat under her minstrel's wing, especially since it was coupled with enough coin for him to hire two workers for the upcoming planting season and the promise of more coin in the future. Enough, she had said, to tide him by until his younger sons were grown and could take up the heavier chores themselves.

Blat observed these changes to his life in a kind of stupor. By the end of the evening, he was in Sarah's charge - a woman he barely knew and wasn't even sure he liked. Dazed, his thoughts all twisted around, he crawled into bed.

Even after the long day in the field, sleep was illusive. No matter how Blat looked at it, his father

12

had sold him to the first person to make a reasonable offer. He tried not to be hurt. He tried to see it the way his father had explained it to him. It would be a wonderful experience, his father said. It would broaden his horizons, his father said. Don't worry about us, we'll get along just fine, his father said. Your mother would be proud of you, his father said. This last, more than anything, convinced Blat that his father just couldn't stand to look at him anymore. As Blat had grown older, folk commented on how much he resembled his mother. Blat suspected that it pained his father to see his beloved Marie so clearly in his son's face. She had died in childbirth when the twins were born - two more boys to add to the four already in the house - a large enough family by most standards, but not so large when you tilled the soil for a living. Every hand was needed. *So if four hands replaced his two hands, that is better for everyone.* But somehow this logic didn't ease the aching in his heart.

The next morning, in a fog from a sleepless night, Blat rummaged through the cupboard for his old rucksack and stuffed it with random clothes. He was barely out of the room when his brothers began fighting over his bed and the space his clothes had taken. He looked back, sad and resigned. One day they might miss him, but it wasn't today.

His father made his favourite breakfast of porridge sweetened with raisins and honey. He ate automatically, tasting nothing.

Sarah kept up an annoying chatter while she packed her things (she had spread her bedroll by the hearth - his father had insisted). She told his father a little of what Blat would study at the Conservatory and where he would live. She promised that she would send news of his progress as well as more coin with the next minstrel to visit the area. She told him that she would look after Blat as though he were her own son.

Blat had hardly said a word the whole time Sarah had been in his home. It was as though he couldn't get his mouth to work. Her songs and stories had awakened a deep yearning inside him, a yearning that had lain quiet and peaceful until she had stirred it into this turmoil. His world was changing, but changing into what? Did he want to make his way as a singer? Was that even a real job? Everyone in the village knew that he loved to sing, but never did he suppose that it was something for which people would pay good money. *But, oh, to live the stories in the songs. To travel to exotic and dangerous places. To sing for villains and princes. To do something different*.

He had enough sense to recognise these daydreams for what they were, but it wasn't just that. Did he really want to leave the only life he had ever known? Here, he knew exactly what was expected of him: in the spring was the tilling and the planting; in the summer was the weeding and the trimming; the fall was the harvest and the pickling and the salting and the drying; and the long winter was for mending clothes and tools, and what little schooling as could be had. In another three or four summers, he would ask one of the village girls to marry him and she would come to live with them in their house, which would be enlarged to

14

accommodate her and the babies she would bear. His brothers, too, would marry and bring their wives home. More additions would be built onto the house and more babies would arrive. On and on it would go until the sound of many generations filled the ever-expanding homestead. That was his father's plan - Blat had heard it often enough to feel it was his own - and that was how his life was supposed to be. No surprises. Before Sarah.

He glanced sidelong at the woman striding next to him. Did she know what she had done to his life? Today he should be tilling the field behind the copse of alders. Would his father find reliable men? Would they know how to do the work as well as Blat had done it? No, of course not. How could they? They wouldn't get it right and the wheat would not ripen properly and his family would starve. What was he thinking? He should return home right now. He stopped and looked back. His father stood in the middle of the road, made small by the distance Blat and Sarah had already walked. Blat hesitated and looked down at his dusty boots. It was what he wanted, wasn't it? It must be. Blat raised his arm to wave, but his father had already disappeared into the bush at the side of the road.

He sighed. As much as he felt his responsibilities pulling him, his feet would not move. Guilt made its insidious way into his mind. He was expected to fulfill his duties, he was the eldest. On his shoulders lay much of the burden of the family's future. How could he even consider leaving? And why, of all the times in the world, did the thought of going home fill him with such weariness? *Gods. Guilty for leaving; unbearable to stay.* He was torn between duty and the pinprick of joy that was beginning to emerge from a remote corner of his soul. He dared not look at that joy too closely; it only made his guilt bubble more furiously.

"You can't seem to make up your mind to frown or smile." Sarah's smooth voice sliced into the morass of his mental labour. He turned to look at her and stumbled over a non-existent rut in the road. "Now if it were up to me, I'd smile," she continued, "because they say that it's easier on the face muscles. You don't have to use so many." She placed her palms lightly on her cheeks and proceeded to alternate between smiles and frowns. "Hard to tell. It feels different, that's certain. So without definitive proof, I'll go with what 'they' say." She took her hands away from her face leaving a huge smile there and resumed her loose stride.

Blat followed and stumbled again. Her smile grew even wider. "How about a walking song?" Sarah stepped onto the verge and foraged until she found a long stick about as thick as Blat's thumb, and broke it in two. She banged the two pieces together and, satisfied with the sound they made, came back onto the road and with a clatter of sticks began a lively tune. It was an old song that Blat knew well; he'd sung it many times while working in the fields. But he was determined to remain silent and distant from this woman who had forced so much change into his life without even talking to him about it first.

16

Come to think of it, no one had asked him what he wanted. Certainly not Sarah but most especially not even his own father. They had just foisted another life on him as if he were chattel to be sold. Very well. Let them think that he was the meek, pliant domestic beast that they could do with as they pleased. He would travel with Sarah and would see what there was to see. He would bide his time and make his own choices about his life.

She had a very good voice, Blat noted in spite of his dark thoughts, and the variety of sounds and beats she finessed from the two sticks was remarkable. Well she could amuse herself however she wished. Blat would have no part of it.

With a wild flourish of voice and sticks, Sarah finished the song. A small stream cut across the road and the sun was nearly overhead. She scooted down the embankment, plunged into the undergrowth, and disappeared from Blat's view. He stood on the road, uncertain. "Come on, you great dolt," Sarah's voice floated back to him. Blat shrugged his shoulders and followed.

By the time he reached her, Sarah had spread a blanket on the ground, and bread and cheese on a clean cloth. Another packet revealed cold sausage and yet another held several of last year's apples, wrinkled and sweet. Blat's stomach grumbled appreciatively at the sight. He sat on the edge of the blanket, his long legs stretched towards the stream.

"Don't talk much, do you?"

Blat shrugged and concentrated on chewing a mouthful of heavy brown bread.

"Oh, I think you have a lot to say. Just not to me." Sarah cut the sausage with her knife. As he reached for it, she moved it beyond his hand. Annoyed, he looked up and met her eyes. "You can go back if you want to. I won't even ask for the money back from your father." She placed the sausage in his hand and Blat stared at it.

"The funny thing is," he began, "I want to. Go back, that is."

Sarah sighed.

Blat glanced up at the small sound. "And then I don't want to." His stomach churned. He lurched to his feet and wandered the short distance to the stream. He kicked a few stray pebbles. "But until I decide for sure, I might as well stay with you."

The road to the Conservatory was long and the growing summer heat scorched the ground. They slept in whatever shade was to hand during the hottest part of each day and did most of their walking in the early morning and evening. The grassy edge of the road was easier on their boots and, without kicking up dust at every step, easier on their lungs. At twilight, they would stop at an inn or a tavern or a manor house where Sarah would ply her trade with an exuberance that astounded Blat. Her energy and endless repertoire of songs amazed him every single night.

When he told her of this, expecting a gracious 'thank you' for the compliment, she snarled at him. "You are easily impressed and that can sometimes mislead you into thinking that the person impressing you is better than you. Don't you believe it for a single minute. It's just that they

18

know something you don't yet. That's all. If you put your mind to it," Sarah poked her index finger into his shoulder, "you can learn most anything and do most anything. That said, there will most likely always be someone who can do a thing better than you and most likely always be someone who is much worse at it. What you lack is perspective."

Blat was puzzled and irritated at her outburst. "But you make it look so easy, Sarah, and you can sing all night long!" Blat still couldn't believe that she could do that even though he had witnessed it himself for the past seven nights in a row.

Sarah pursed her lips. "So, tell me. The first time you harnessed a horse and tilled your first row, how long did it take you?"

Blat hesitated in mid-stride at the sudden change of topic.

"Just answer the question."

He put his foot down and continued walking. *Might as well; she'll just pester me until I do.* "A while," he said. Blat remembered that day. The harness buckles were stiff and his fingers fumbled. The horse only knew him as the small human who fed him the occasional apple and did not deign to obey Blat's commands. That first row? - well it wasn't really much of a row at all. It was more like a short, crooked ditch. He had spent the better part of the morning accomplishing nothing.

"And now?"

Blat prided himself on the swift and accurate job he could do, though not so much on the day that Sarah had come into his life. He had been distracted by the song he was singing; come to think of it, that happened a lot. "When I put my mind to it, I'm nearly as good as my father." It had been days since he had thought of home. He realised at that moment that it would be very hard to return to life on the farm. The insight staggered him and he forgot what they had been discussing. "Um... thanks for bringing me along," he muttered.

She stopped and looked at him, her raised brows creating tiny furrows in her forehead. Abruptly, she pulled him to her in a fierce hug. "Now, that's real music to my ears," Sarah said into his shoulder. She pushed him away to arm's length and peered into his eyes. "Yes, you do mean it." She continued walking, a new spring in her step.

"Now what were we talking about?" Sarah pondered a moment. "Oh, yes, how one can get better at almost anything with knowledge and practice, and you gave yourself an example from your very own life. Here's another question: if you were the best plough-boy in the country but ploughed in a salt marsh, would people consider you a good farmer?"

Blat puzzled over her words. Did she mean you could be good at something but still not be any good? Maybe you could be good at some parts of something and not good at other parts. Maybe you had no control at all over how good or bad you were. But that didn't seem right. Maybe you had to look at things differently. Maybe you had to look at things as part of a bigger thing. This was exhausting; there must be an easier way. Maybe you just had to look at what other people did instead of having to guess all the answers yourself.

Excited, he caught up with her. "Are you saying that I know some parts of singing and not others? And you'll show me?"

Her smile was all the answer he needed.

Blat might not have been so quick with his enthusiasm if he had known the full significance of what Sarah meant by 'knowledge and practice.' They would be at the Conservatory in a fortnight and Sarah was determined to mould him into a fledgling singer by then - the kind of a singer that the Conservatory would accept into its novice ranks. The kind of singer that could pass the entrance audition.

Endless seemingly-nonsense drills in vocal ranges he had never used in a real song filled his mornings and evenings. Breathing became a continuous conscience effort. Little did he know that he had been doing it wrong all his life. It had kept him alive hadn't it? But once Blat had put himself in her hands, there was no arguing and no escape. After the first two days, he could barely croak his need for water. After four days, his vocal cords still slipped and slid where they would. After eight days, Blat had an epiphany: he glimpsed what his vocal cords and the breath pushed from his belly could do together. And at ten days, the control that his head must have over the art of singing was born. It was a tiny thing, to be sure, needing much care and attention, but born, nevertheless.

***

Sarah was not like some other musicians - thankfully few in number - who needed the fawning attention of hangers-on and a fancy stage in order to perform. Their songs (though such drivel barely merited the word) were invariably about whoever had most recently lavished them with gifts. If she heard about the 'limpid cerulean eyes' of some 'luminescent lissom lass' one more time, she would hurt someone. Sarah disdained the confines of such a life. She needed to be out on the road, to feel life where and when it happened, and not caged in some stultifying theatre where every note and movement was choreographed well ahead of time. There was no inspiration for new material in such an atmosphere, and neither was there room for the teaching element that every Touring Minstrel embraced.

Sometimes it seemed to her that the Touring Minstrel was the only way that any information at all was distributed to the people of Whitecap Island who lived outside the main centres. She liberally interspersed all kinds of items of interest in an evening of song. Some were general statements about the health of the rest of the country and some outlined troubles that were brewing. She did not expect her audience to take any action, but it was the responsibility of all Touring Minstrels to let the people know how their fellow citizens fared and what sorts of difficulties they encountered. And, especially, what had been done to rectify those difficulties. The villagers just might be able to use such knowledge in their own situations.

She also sang of the various philosophies that were bandied about as well as of the basic tenets of the religious orders and cults. She was not a church-going person herself, but felt that, once again, the people should know what went on. It had brought her trouble a time or two particularly from supporters of the Brothers of the Watch who wished their ideology to remain hidden. It was a risk she was willing to take.

People everywhere appreciated a good listener and Sarah was one of the best. She heard new stories and new versions of familiar tales. It seemed that every part of the country had similar legends flavoured and spiced to suit the local environs. The sea serpent of the coastal villages became the flying dragon of the desert. The wise woman of the mountains was the sorceress of the swamps. The wizard of the inland plains was the alchemist of the cities. Each version gave new texture to the narrative, new words to convey meaning, and new colour to brighten the yarn. Sarah was intrigued by this phenomenon and loved discovering clues regarding its origins and possible meanings.

As much as she loved discovering new talent. There was always a certain amount of pain, though, in separating a child from his or her family. Blat had been ready to go, even if he had not realised it, and Tomias suspected his son's as yet unvoiced yearnings. If the boy stayed he would do what was expected of him but he would never be truly happy. From what Sarah had seen of the Raike family, Tomias would never withhold that happiness from his son.

It troubled her that her garb had not identified her to the boy. It was not so long ago when all the people in all the villages, however small, showed instant recognition of one of her Guild. The deep purple of her cloak, even if it wasn't as deep a purple as it used to be, clearly declared what she was. She would let the Assembly know; they would decide what to do.

A sudden gust swirled loose debris down the middle of the road. The dust aggravated her throat even through the scarf she had secured around her mouth and nose. Had it been this dry last year? She thought not. No matter. Tomorrow, they would see Rivercrest.

The sprawling city nestled between two rivers. The waterways continued to provide the trade that was the original reason for the city's existence, but events of much greater importance now happened in Rivercrest: over the past two generations, first one and then a second of the Guildhalls had chosen it as their center for training and administration. Soon, all the major crafts and trades deemed it advantageous to be together in one place. Rivercrest was as central as any place on the island, Sarah supposed, and the weather was more temperate than in many other locations. She shuddered to think of necessarily frequent visits to, say, frigid Ozoli high up near the glacier. Or to smelly Ruapo in the heart of the swamplands. Or even Zayu, which she definitely enjoyed some of the year but not during the windy season when the sand could scour the skin from your face.

Though the requirements of her Guild insisted that she return to Rivercrest periodically, over time she had chosen to call this madhouse of a city home. *That's what happened when you returned to the same place too often.* She smiled. And then there was Jamie and her children waiting for her.

Blat, however, would be overwhelmed and she simply did not have the time to teach him about life in the city. He was so gullible. What could you expect living in a remote village in the middle of nowhere? She should know; she came from one herself. In her case, Sarah had snuck away from her latest keepers and followed behind a visiting minstrel whose life seemed ever so glamorous to the seven-year-old girl. The minstrel, of course, caught her and brought her back to the village. Sarah pleaded and begged to be taken away from the small, sad life she hated.

The previous summer, her entire family - father, mother, brothers - had disappeared one day. Dark shadows were seen at the edge of the forest and frightened voices whispered of Brothers of the Watch. She couldn't understand what had happened, and the pity in the eyes of the village folk suffocated her until she could barely breathe. She struck out with anger and tantrums at the least provocation and was passed from family to family, to share the cost of an extra mouth to feed they said, but it was more that her fits of temper disrupted the households wherever she went.

The village headman convened a town meeting and the elders struck a deal with Johane, the Touring Minstrel, to take the child with her. They convinced themselves that Sarah would have a better life away from the reminders of her tragedy. Sarah was ecstatic. She was soon to learn that Johane was a tough mistress and expected her charge to work harder than she ever had before. Sarah balked and fought and screamed her rage. Johane was unmoved by her fits and tears and, with firm but gentle resolve, the minstrel guided the budding talent that sporadically shone through Sarah's bad behaviour.

It was the music that finally soothed her soul, and if it meant that she had to learn to read and do numbers in order to sing, the young Sarah gritted her teeth, sat still, and learned. Sarah slowly healed under the minstrel's care and they grew to love each other. Her eyes stung with unshed tears. Johane had ascended to the spirit world shortly after Sarah had achieved Touring Minstrel status. That was many years ago now, but Sarah still missed her terribly.

Sarah dragged herself from her meandering thoughts and listened to Blat's scale practice. The boy was improving. At the end of his next set she would call a halt for the day. She wanted to time their arrival at the Conservatory with the afternoon mass chorus. If that didn't inspire Blat to continue his musical training, nothing would.

Blat had no idea of the kinds of situations that the world could and would throw in his path. She felt a moment of regret for the innocence that he would doubtlessly lose. No matter. She trusted her instincts. This boy was destined for greatness; she could feel it. She had done her best to prepare him in the short time she'd had; all she could do now was give him the chance. The rest was up to him.

CHAPTER 2

If paradise existed, Blat couldn't imagine it being more wonderful than this moment in his life. Graceful arches soared over his head to dissolve into the sunlight glittering through the multi-hued stained glass that garnished the summit of the Conservatory's Concert Hall.

What soared to even greater heights were the hundred voices that rose in song. Everything else that had happened in his life was dull and flat by comparison. Nothing else could ever be this good. And then the tenor sang his solo.

Blat swayed beside Sarah and she put a hand under his elbow to steady him. He barely noticed her touch. They stood that way to the end of the recital and remained in the same stance long after the singers and audience had left the building.

Sarah gently shook his arm. "Come, lad, let's get you something to eat."

Blat moved mechanically beside her, an automatic response of his body after the long miles they had walked together. His head was filled with beautiful music and he wanted to hold on to it as long as he could. When they emerged from the building, the bright daylight hurt his eyes but Sarah persisted in making him continue to one of the many vendors' stalls that surrounded the square outside the Concert Hall. She led him to a bench under an awning and shoved a warm loaf of bread into one hand and a tankard of ale into the other. Blat drank and chewed - another automatic reaction.

28

The glaze gradually left his eyes and he began to notice his surroundings.

Sarah gave him all the time he needed. When he was ready, he looked at her and his eyes shone. "Did you plan our whole walk so that we would arrive for this concert? Is that why you pushed us so hard? Well, I'm glad you did. I would have walked all day and all night to hear that choir. And the soloist!" Blat closed his eyes. "He was amazing." He looked at her. "And I swear I'm not being easily impressed."

"The soloist? If I remember correctly, he's one of the third year students. Probably his first solo."

Blat's eyes popped opened. "You're teasing me, Sarah," he accused. "That was no student." Inside, Blat struggled to hide his dismay. If that really was a student, he saw his chances of passing the entrance audition trickle away like so much refuse down a drain.

"You'll know soon enough who is a Master and who is not. Come, we should be able to catch dinner at the Guildhall, and I can tell you that the cook there is a *real* Master."

Sarah seemed unconcerned about the vast difference between his meagre voice and the one that they had just heard. Well, he had been humiliated before and even if he had to turn around and trudge back home right now, the trip had been worth it.

They gathered their packs and walked in the warm sunlight. The wide boulevard was swept clean by the merchants whose businesses opened onto the square, and the glass lanterns situated at regular intervals boded well for night-time shoppers. The range of goods that Blat glimpsed as Sarah urged him along was astounding and he promised himself that he would examine the shops more closely when he had more time. They came to the end of the merchants' district and turned down a less reputable lane that was in shadow even though the sun was still well above the horizon.

He heard it before he saw it. The Minstrels' Guildhall was much larger than the buildings to either side of it and many of its windows were open to catch the cooling breeze. It was from these windows that all manner of sound emerged. Different instruments were playing a variety of melodies and voices rose in a whole other set of songs. All of this was done at performance volume, which is to say, loudly. The cacophony was bewildering.

Sarah's brisk step quickened so that Blat had to hustle to keep up. She climbed the stairs two at a time and pushed the wooden door open onto the noisiest, most disorganised dining hall that Blat had ever seen - not that he had seen that many, but this was total mayhem. Sarah bellowed a welcome and even her powerful lungs made little more than a tiny dent in the pandemonium. She tossed her pack in a corner and gestured for Blat to do the same. By this time, several people had converged on Sarah with screams of welcome and she disappeared within their enthusiastic embraces.

A large man wearing a stained apron bulled his way through the crowd. He balanced a tray on a meaty palm and shoved people out of his way with his free arm. "Sarah!" he roared. "Love of my life!" He handed the tray to a young girl who had followed in his wake. The crowd surrounding Sarah quickly gave way. The cook, for that was what he must be, took Sarah in his huge arms, lifted her off the floor, and twirled her around and around. Sarah laughed and cried at the same time and kissed him with all her might. At last, he put her back on her feet. "Ah, you're a sight for these poor old eyes. And you've gone and lost weight again," he shook his head, his fists on his hips. He brightened. "But we can fix that. Talitha! Where's that tray?" He reached behind him without ever taking his eyes off Sarah. "Here we are, lass. Something I threw together when I heard the commotion."

He made room for her at a table by the simple expedient of looking at the people who sat there. They laughed and shuffled over. 'Never get on the cook's bad side' was one of the unwritten laws of the Guildhall. Someone had done it, of course, but not in recent memory. The tale of the horrid gruel, blackened crusts of bread, and sour wine that the kitchen provided until a proper apology was most humbly rendered was told to all newcomers. Sarah sat and the cook settled in beside her. Soon the dining hall returned to its previous state of mild chaos.

Blat looked around, wondering what he should do. The food smelled delicious. The snack that Sarah had given him earlier had barely touched the ravenous hunger of his fourteen-year old body. A hand tugged on his sleeve and he turned to see the same girl that had handed the tray back to the cook.

The tumult of the Guildhall receded to a distant muted din. He stared at her; she was the prettiest girl he had ever seen. She beckoned him to follow and Blat made his feet move. They skirted the room and entered the busy and only slightly less noisy kitchen. She led him to a long table out of the way of the dinner preparation activities, motioned him to sit, and soon brought him a platter piled high with succulent, steaming meat, mashed turnips, and warm bread slathered with butter. A mug of ale soon followed but Blat was too busy staring from her to the food and back again to do more than nod his thanks. This was more food than he had seen in forever and he was determined to eat every bit, only he couldn't stop looking at her.

"Eat it while it's hot," she said and bustled from the room.

Blat watched until the flare of her skirts disappeared around the door jamb. He would find out who she was and he would court her. The tantalising aroma of hot meat wafted to his nostrils and, dazed, he applied himself to the task at hand.

Happily replete, he smiled lazily as a different serving girl returned some time later with a selection of fruit tarts. Thinking he would have to choose one, he selected raspberry, his favourite, but she left the whole plate. He gazed around the kitchen at the bustle and suppressed a small belch. Oh, but he felt good. His belly was full and he was in love.

The cook stomped into the kitchen at that moment, bellowed a few commands, and proceeded

32

to attack an innocent mound of dough. Flour billowed in foggy white puffs. Blat closed his eyes.

Sarah found him there, sound asleep, his head on the table. "Will you look at that? Already feels at home." She beckoned to her husband, and he picked the boy up like one of the many sacks of vegetables that he hoisted throughout the day.

"Where do you want him?" Jamie-the-Cook asked.

"One of the guest rooms for tonight," Sarah replied. "The gods know that he'll need a good sleep with what's in store for him tomorrow."

Long before he was ready to open his eyes, the clamour from the kitchens dragged him awake. After a quick splash of cold water on his face, he let his nose guide him to breakfast. He couldn't believe that he was hungry after last night's amazing dinner, but there was no denying the grumbling in his belly. The dining room was set up in a 'help yourself' way and he needed no further encouragement. He would find Sarah afterwards. With his plate heaping he found his way to an empty section of bench; his fellow diners did not even glance at him. All but one of them finished before Blat and the remaining minstrel seemed content to sit and pick his teeth with a small, dull knife. When Blat had scooped up the last of the oatmeal and ate the last crumb of bread, the stranger spoke. "So. Sarah found another one," he began. "She is really very good at finding strays and bringing them to heel."

Blat felt the heat rise in his face. The dark man smirked. "Oh, don't be so twitchy. At least you look like you can take care of yourself. A farmer,

33

I'd say, by the shoulders and the, ah, unusual wardrobe." He re-sheathed his knife. "You will fit right in with the other new students. If you stay seated in your chair." He laughed, heaved himself to his feet, and sauntered out of the Guildhall.

What did he mean by that? Sarah had warned him about the different ways that people had. Was this what she meant? Was it acceptable for people to insult his friend and make what sounded suspiciously like disparaging remarks about him? He had remained calm like Sarah had cautioned him, but he would learn the rules here and he would meet this dark man again.

"Don't mind him."

The female voice behind him belonged to the girl he was going to marry. He was a little afraid to turn around. Maybe what he had felt last night was nothing more than the aftermath of that incredible concert. Music like that might just make you fall in love with the first pretty girl you saw. It would be rude to ignore her and one of the many things his father had insisted upon was good manners. So Blat turned and was smitten all over again - definitely not just the music.

"That's Murzim, and not a day goes by that he doesn't pick a fight. Mam says that he just wants to study people's reactions and that he means no harm. But I think he's just plain mean." She proceeded to gather dishes onto a tray.

Speaking of manners. "My name is Blat and I want to thank you for last night, and for…" *For what? For noticing me? For speaking to me, a stranger? For being so beautiful?*

34

"Oh, that's alright. Mam told me to keep an eye on you. One of the easier jobs she's given me." She flashed him a smile as she lifted the tray and headed for the kitchens.

Sarah entered the dining hall at that moment. She stopped the girl who nodded in Blat's direction. Sarah waved him over. "Hurry, boy, we have a busy day," she said as Blat neared. The girl looked at him sympathetically. He wondered what he was in for.

Sarah brought him to a large room hung everywhere with robes. To Blat's eyes, there seemed to be no order to the haphazard array of clothes. "First, we need the right colour for a new student. Not too flashy. Not too bold. Not yet, anyway." Sarah rummaged through the masses of material. "Ah, here's something." She picked out a muted green garment with soft gold embroidery twining around the hems of the sleeves. She held it up beneath Blat's chin. "Yes. Matches your eyes perfectly. And the gold brings out the lighter colour in your hair. Now, let's see how long it is. Damn. Too short." Sarah threw that one back on the pile and unearthed three more before she found one the right length. She stuffed it in Blat's arms and marched out the door and into the next room. This one held belts and buckles, scarves and hoods, hats and gloves, feathers and ribbons, shoes and boots and slippers - all the accessories that a well-dressed minstrel could want. Sarah searched the mountain of accessories until she found a belt and matching boots. "That's all you'll need for today." She led him back to the room where he had spent the night.

A steaming kettle of water stood by the small hearth and beside it was a pot of cleansing salt. "You know what to do. And don't forget your hair." Sarah closed the door and quickly opened it again. "You have ten minutes."

"Wait, wait," he called after her. "Who was that girl?"

"What girl? Oh. Talitha. She's my daughter."

Blat sat down hard on the pallet. *Figures.*

Blat had never worn a robe before. Breeches and tunic were far more practical for the kind of work he did. Used to do, he reminded himself. The robe felt a little too airy, but it was undeniably comfortable. He hoped he didn't look too stupid.

Sarah looked him over with a critical eye. "You'll do."

Blat somehow knew that this was high praise.

"Now we warm up."

They proceeded to one of the many rehearsal rooms in the Guildhall and went through the now-familiar vocal exercises. When Blat had a fine sheen of perspiration on his brow, Sarah declared him ready. "But first, I should tell you a little of what to expect." Sarah explained the audition process. It sounded like a mini-concert to Blat. He would simply sing a song while people listened. He had done that before, on festival days at the village hall. This couldn't be that much different.

They retraced yesterday's route. A wide border of manicured lawn separated the Conservatory grounds from the mundane world of commerce. They passed the Concert Hall and continued on to the collection of buildings behind it. There was one for harpists and one for guitarists - the favoured instruments of the minstrels. A marble statue of each instrument was positioned on the grass outside so no mistake could be made about what transpired within. In the distance, Blat could just make out the shape of a tambour; it seemed that the percussion section needed a little distance from everyone else.

A series of connected buildings housed the voice specialties and it was to these that Sarah led them. "You are quite fortunate that the committee is conducting auditions this week," she said as they approached the doors. "Otherwise, you would have to wait for mid-winter break." They entered an auditorium not quite as large as the Concert Hall and sparse in its ornamentation. This was a workplace. On a dais at one end sat nine Masters: one for each of the vocal programs. At the other end sat at least fifty hopefuls. Sarah guided Blat to an empty pair of seats. There were many auditions to be conducted today and they were held in the order of arrival. Blat sighed. He was glad that he'd had a substantial breakfast; they would be here for a while.

His turn came all too soon. These Masters did not waste time on poor singers. Some only managed a few notes before the small gong that was situated before each of the Masters was struck. Blat came to hate that sound. Some of the boys sang very well to his ears and some of the girls were positively angelic, and they were gonged just the same. But what Blat hated even more than the sound of the gong was the realisation that he was at least three years older than any other candidate.

Murzim's cryptic comment became clear: he was also at least a foot taller.

His name was called. Sarah nudged him in the ribs and he lurched to his feet. The short distance to the spot where he was to sing seemed very far away. He was sure that everyone in the room snickered at his too-tall frame and his too-old face. Everything that he and Sarah had rehearsed vanished from his mind. He stood there, trembling.

The Masters studied their papers, not even looking at him. Time slowed. Blat watched one Master stifle a yawn, his hand raised slowly to cover his mouth as though it passed through thick molasses. Another lifted a pen to make a notation. The motion was languid. Blat remembered another time at home when the same thing had happened to him. It was the first time he had sung in front of the entire village. He tried to recall how it had ended, but he couldn't remember. He guessed it hadn't killed him. He was here, wasn't he? With that immutable logic he supposed that this wouldn't kill him either so he might as well get on with it. He took a deep, silent breath and sang the same funny, charming children's song that he had sung that day in his village. It was not what he and Sarah had chosen for him to sing, but he didn't think of that until much later.

The Masters looked at him and looked at one another. "Accepted," the spokesperson announced. "Next."

Blat walked back to his seat on wobbly legs. Sarah glared at him. "What was that?" she hissed.

"No matter." Her glare transformed into a radiant smile. "Come, let's celebrate."

CHAPTER 3

From the perspective of a grown man, Blat winced at the memory of that day so long ago. *Could he have been that simple? Ever?* The first weeks of his musical training had been painful and embarrassing; he was far behind the other students in both basic musical theory and basic schooling. His determination and plain bull-headed persistence were the only things that got him through sometimes.

And Talitha's friendship, though the gods know he wished it were more. She was Sarah and Jamie-the-Cook's daughter, the one who had taken him under her wing his first days in Rivercrest. Sarah had asked her to do it (well, told her to do it) but as the days went by, Talitha did it because she wanted to. They became fast friends. Blat shuddered at what those seven long years of schooling would have been like without her. It had also been seven years since he had begun his life as a Touring Minstrel. Seven and seven. Maybe his luck was changing. *Ha.*

After all these years, he still remembered their first - and only - kiss. It was one of those good and bad situations. Good because Blat had dreamed about it since they had first met, but he had never been willing to risk their friendship by telling her how he felt. What if she didn't feel the same way? It would make things awkward and they would inevitably grow apart. He couldn't bear the thought of that. The kiss was everything Blat had dreamed it would be. Her lips were just as soft as they looked and he thought he would drown in them. She tasted sweet like summer strawberries. Talitha pulled away from him and shrugged. This was the bad part: she hadn't felt anything. Blat's minstrel training to always appear calm and in control stopped him from blurting out his love and helped him to regain his composure before she noticed that anything was amiss. If she felt no spark, he must say that he also felt nothing. It was the only way to be near her.

He had been with other girls and then, later, with other women. They were beautiful and intelligent and loving but not one had captured his heart. It was already taken.

A tremor shook the earth. With the apathy of long familiarity, Blat braced his legs to ride it out. These minor quakes had been the bane of the countryside ever since he was a young farm boy. As a Touring Minstrel, he had often heard tales about the strange goings-on of the land and the sea and even the sky. Villagers anxious to be believed would sometimes take him to the site of a particularly nasty occurrence, pointing out the trees that had toppled or the structures that had been destroyed or the land that had been violently rearranged. He would listen to all they had to say, nod his head and ask questions. These disturbing reports were more frequent of late. When he was done scouring this particular valley, he would return to Rivercrest and bring it once again to the Guild's attention.

He settled his pack more comfortably on his back and gazed at the mountain meadow that he traversed. He had timed this trip so that the spring warmth would have coaxed the delicate Lady's Slippers into bloom. They graced the protected crevices between moraine-strewn boulders and their rosy glow cast a soft light onto the purple and green lichen. The wild yellow broom grass swayed in the breeze. A minor glacier oozed its way back up the valley that it had carved for itself, leaving behind a milky lake of melt-water.

No other minstrel had travelled to this area in recent memory, but it was where he hoped to find the story that would inspire him. If nothing else, he consoled himself, it was a beautiful place.

He had been searching the land between the tongues of Whitecap Island's central glacier for six springs. During his final year of study at the Conservatory, he had happened upon an ancient chronicle. It haunted him and he determined to find the village that it said, 'nestled inside the glacier's frozen arms.' The account described beings that never saw the light of day and yet thrived. A holy purpose had been given to them a thousand years ago by fantastical creatures who promised them long life and a place in the pantheon of the gods for the work they would perform. Blat tried to imagine what type of work could merit such a grandiose reward and, even more intriguing, what type of beings could bestow such a prize. Many of the old stories of Whitecap Island were pure fantasy but some were founded on truth, although that truth might be buried beneath a bewildering landscape of imagination. He felt in his heart that this particular story was based in some part on fact. If he could find a few shreds of proof, he could write an epic song about this amazing piece of Whitecap Islander history.

The sun was low in the sky; time to find a spot to spend the night. He had discovered on his many treks into the mountains that he definitely wanted to be out of the wind, especially when the wind came off the ice. He spied a group of large glacier-dropped boulders and gathered bits of branches and twigs on the way to his chosen destination. He found a mostly level spot on the leeward side of the largest rock and cleared it of stones and brush. With some of the stones, he built a small fire pit. He arranged kindling in the centre, struck a spark to it, and fed in larger bits of wood until he was satisfied with the steady flame. He continued his nightly routine and fetched water for his pot, added dried meat and vegetables, and balanced it on the fire to cook for a while.

The stew was tasty. Blat had learned much from Jamie-the-Cook as he watched the Guildhall Master Chef create the meals for which he was justifiably famous. Jamie and Sarah would have been a hundred pounds heavier were it not for the fact that they were both the most active people that Blat had ever met, farmers included.

In between her tours of the countryside, Sarah and Jamie had had six children, just like Blat's own mother. Talitha was the eldest and had just turned twenty-eight, the same age as him. She followed in her father's footsteps and aspired to be the second renowned chef in the family. Ollila, or Lil as she preferred to be called, followed neither parent and was happy in the role of wife to her merchant husband. The two boys, Jamie Junior and Ernest, were musicians like their mother but taught at the Conservatory so that they could stay near their wives. At eighteen years old, Leonora was as yet undecided about what she would do with her life. And little Louetta who was a surprise to everyone - especially her parents - would be eight this fall. Sarah had nearly died giving birth but declared every day that it had been worth it. Louetta was a delight to her parents and brothers and sisters and she knew it. The mischief that one small girl could get into continued to astound Blat. He looked forward to hearing the latest episode in Louetta's quest to unearth every possible act of deviltry that existed in her world.

Sarah. Blat would be breaking the ground for the spring sowing and have a brood of his own if not for her serendipitous detour past his father's farm that day. He couldn't imagine himself in that life and thanked all the gods for her intervention that day. His family thrived and so did he.

Blat banked the embers of his fire and settled himself for the night. The stars shone with a brilliance impossible to see anywhere but in the mountains. He studied the familiar constellations and hummed an old children's rhyme that named them. Who would have thought that the nursery songs he had learned at his mother's knee would be considered his forté in the world of music? Ever since that audition piece, his singing Masters insisted that he perfect every one that he knew, and he knew a great many. Of course, he learned all the teaching ballads as well; no self-respecting minstrel could hold his head up and not know the great stories of Whitecap Island's past. He sometimes wondered what his destiny would have been had he sung the song that he and Sarah had prepared for the audition. *Bah, useless thought.* The past was the past and could be interpreted any way he wished. What mattered now was that he would find these illusive mountain-dwellers, learn their story, and compose something new, something that would rock the Conservatory on its tradition-bound foundations.

He was honest enough to admit that recognition and fame were also strong lures. It would make his father proud to see his eldest son excel even if many of the villagers subtly disdained the life that a farmer's boy had chosen. In their eyes, Blat would always be the son who had abandoned his duties. It went against the grain. One would think they would be grateful to have the Minstrels' Guild beholden to them. But, no, Tomias Raike had allowed something that had never been done before in the sleepy, staid village of Stokhelm Corner. When you thwarted tradition, you risked the good opinion of your neighbours.

Blat had returned to the family farm many times during his minstrel apprenticeship and then, proudly, on his own. No matter how much the villagers appreciated the news and the songs he brought them, there was the ever-present undercurrent of how he had deserted his family and how no son of theirs would ever do such a thing. They could not know of the newfound observation techniques that Blat had learned and no matter how they tried to disguise their disapproval, Blat was aware of every nuance. It didn't affect him so much; after all, in two or three days he would be on the road again and their sour talk would fade with every step he took. His father and brothers were stoic about it and denied any hard feelings but Blat knew of their discomfiture. Happily, the wives and children that filled the homestead with the wonderful smells of baking and the squeals of excited laughter quickly dissipated the brief discomfort that his visits might cause.

Of course, if he ever did find a new story, it would take nothing short of a miracle to convince the Conservatory that he had indeed discovered something heretofore unknown about Whitecap Island. He would cross that chasm when it yawned before him. Notwithstanding the low probability of finding anything at all, let alone something new, and then proving it to a horde of sceptical and cynical minds, Blat would persevere. His father would not regret that long-ago decision. And maybe Talitha would think differently of him.

With that resolution firmly in mind, Blat drifted off to sleep.

A minstrel's purple cloak generally procured him or her a warm welcome, food, and a place to sleep. He or she reciprocated with songs and tales. It was considered an honour for a minstrel to cross one's threshold and dire consequences befell the village that permitted any threat to a minstrel's livelihood. Penalties ranged from fines or imprisonment to shunning by the entire Guild. For the worst offenders, exile had been recommended and seconded by the perpetrator's own people. They knew that to be cut off from the minstrels' news would be like blinding them to the rest of the world. In some of the more isolated hamlets, a minstrel's visit was the reason for festivals and celebrations. They would never willingly risk the multi-faceted benefits of the Minstrels' Guild.

So it was with some surprise that Blat found himself surrounded by short individuals. He couldn't tell much more about them for they stood beyond his campfire's feeble light. The silhouette of their spears, however, was clear against the night sky. He felt himself prodded by the butt of one such spear in an unmistakable gesture for him to get up. They did not bind his hands, which he found surprising, but instead placed him in the middle of the group so that he had to overcome at least two of them in order to escape. *Escape to where?* It was the middle of the night in the middle of nowhere with no light to guide his steps through the rugged landscape. When Blat attempted to question his captors about what they wanted or where they were taking him, he was threatened with a gag to keep him quiet. He resigned himself to watch and listen, and learn as much as he could.

In due course, they tied a mostly clean scarf around his eyes and with firm grips on his arms just above the elbow led him closer to what he had seen in the light of day as a sheer wall of cliffs. After what Blat estimated to be about another hour of walking, the air around him seemed to compress upon itself. They had entered some sort of enclosure. One of the men who held his arms untied the scarf from around his head and nudged him forward. Blat's eyes took but a moment to adjust to the dim light and he guessed that he was in one of the many caves that lined the glacial valley. He had known that there were caves, just as there were in most of the steep-walled valleys. He had been warned time and again against using them for shelter. More than one hapless minstrel had disappeared in caves like this one - there was simply no way to know for certain if anything else lived there before you encroached upon its lair. The mountain cats and bears that Blat had glimpsed in his travels were sufficient reminder to keep well away from places such as the one in which he now found himself.

Blat examined his surroundings. The ceiling was low, at least for him, and he had to duck beneath rocky protrusions. The stone floor, however, was worn smooth; this was a well-used route. *Well used by whom? Or what?*

The rough-hewn corridor they had been navigating gradually widened but continued on its sinuous way. The path descended and it seemed to Blat that it was getting warmer, but that could be from exertion or maybe from his nerves that were beginning to frazzle somewhat.

The troupe halted before a pair of wooden doors that was unmarked in any way; here his taller height was an advantage - he could see over the heads of those in front of him. The foremost captor raised his fists and pounded a rapid series of knocks on one of the doors and they were soon admitted into the cavern beyond. Blat noted in a corner of his mind that his captors had remained silent throughout the entire march.

A flickering (and somewhat distressing and sickly) light attempted to shed illumination upon the habitat within. The central area was bustling with familiar activities. In a communal kitchen, people went through the age-old motions of cutting and cooking food and beyond that, a group of children played games under the watchful eye of an older boy perched on a jagged rock thrusting up from the floor. The immense cavern was punctuated with smaller alcoves at floor level and again further up the wall. These were linked by a series of ropes and ladders.

Something caught Blat's eye and wouldn't let it go. A colossal cylinder lay along the floor and dwarfed the farthest wall of the cavern. It entered on one side and exited on the other, so he could not see its total length. What he could see stunned him; it was the largest man-made thing he had ever seen.

"What is that... that..." He, who was never at a loss for words, stammered to a halt. His band of captors ignored him and herded him towards an enclosure. It couldn't be called a building, really, since there was no roof - there would be no need for one here inside the cliff walls. Blat hoped it wasn't their version of a prison.

The children stopped their game and stared at him as he passed closer to them. Their eyes were large and their skin pale, but otherwise they appeared healthy. Quiet, but healthy. Others stopped whatever they were doing to stare at him as well. They were garbed in coarse material cut into blocky tunics and trousers. At this closer range, Blat could discern swirling colours in blues and greens and oranges that seemed to flow on the fabric, and, even more startling, seemed to glow. Blat had seen colour and light like this before in the swamplands outside of Ruapo - the colour and light of the swamp gas. He had read somewhere that certain plants and minerals had similar properties to the gas and it would seem that these people had devised a way to capture that beauty and infuse it into cloth. It made for a striking contrast with the surrounding shades of grey rock.

There was no sound of resumed chatter as he passed them by. When he thought about it, the chatter couldn't possibly resume - it had never been there in the first place. Curious.

Blat guessed there to be about five hundred people living in this enclave within the mountains. The flickering light was giving him a headache and he wondered what it must be like to be subjected to it for hours at a time.

To his disappointment, the room inside the enclosure looked like any number of meeting rooms that Blat had had the misfortune to experience. He was gestured to sit, and food and tea was set before him by a silent serving girl. One of his captors brought in his camping gear and guitar and set them inside the door. Blat was grateful that the man was careful with his belongings, especially his instrument. The guitar itself was replaceable, of course, but the sentimental value was not. Talitha had gifted it to him when he graduated. It was a travelling instrument - practical and sturdy with a hard, waterproof case in which to carry it. She knew from her mother what a Touring Minstrel needed. Blat sighed, as he often did when he thought of her.

His stomach grumbled and he decided that these people, whatever they wanted, would likely not poison him. He chewed the dried meat and tried to soften it with sips of the insipid tea. His meal finished, he waited. He was weary from his interrupted sleep and the long walk. His strange surroundings notwithstanding, Blat's eyes began to close and he promised himself that he would rest just for a minute. He put his arms on the table and laid his head on them, grateful that he had learned Sarah's trick of sleeping anywhere, anytime.

Blat, however, had never been able to learn Sarah's trick of waking fully alert. His was a sort of wander back to wakefulness and while he wandered he flailed about, annoyed at being disturbed. The gentle shaking of his shoulder did not abate. Grumpily, he swatted at the intruder. "Let me be," he muttered. "Sleeping." The shaking continued. "All right, all right, I'm awake." He was never at his best when roused before he was ready and it took a moment for him to focus on the group seated around the table. He rubbed his eyes with the heels of his hands and shook his head. The small smile from the woman seated across the table from him reminded him of Sarah when she used to cajole him from his bed at the Guildhall. Sarah enjoyed waking him up; it was her one fault. She said that he was 'cute' when his feathers were all ruffled.

Feathers. Bah. His hair did what his hair did and that was that.

The woman continued to smile at him and with his usual surly morning attitude, he stared back at her. His glare softened as his minstrel-trained eye studied the delicate skin of her face. Fine lines followed the delicate bone structure of cheek and chin. The creamy softness of her skin would be cool to the touch. It reminded him of a fine parchment that he had admired in one of the more exclusive shops in Rivercrest. Her eyes were cloudy and her lips pale so that nothing marred the impression of endless smoothness. Her hands, which she now placed on the table, mirrored the texture of her face but were delicately traced with a network of bluish-lavender veins like an intricate map of rivers and their tributaries. This was someone whose story he wanted to know.

They sat studying each other and would have continued to do so, at least Blat would have, if not for the unsubtle clearing of a throat that intruded into the silence of the room. The elderly lady sighed and flicked a glance towards the man seated at one end of the table. "Yes, I know, you are impatient to jump to the next task." Her voice was thin and wispy, and Blat noted that he was not the only one to lean forward so as not to miss a word. She waved a hand. "Speak, then."

"It is as we have thought, and there is no time to study every moment to its fullest." As he spoke, the man stood and paced. "We must act." He stopped behind Blat's chair and placed his hands on the slat to either side of Blat's head. Blat looked at one, then the other. The hands looked very strong, gnarled and callused, used to either hard labour or hard fighting. Or both.

"What did you hope to achieve by annoying the Minstrels' Guild?" the woman asked. "Even we of the Stations know the code. Did you think they would not seek him?"

The others in the room looked from one speaker to the other. It seemed to Blat that he was a pawn in a struggle between these two people, a struggle of which he knew nothing. *Time to find out,* he thought. With a sideways glance at the hands that gripped the back of his chair with white-knuckled tension, Blat stepped into the breach. "May I speak?" He modulated his voice to his most gentle and persuasive.

All eyes in the room snapped to his face. Little insect feet crawled along the back of his head and his breath constricted in his throat. His eyes began to bulge out of their sockets and pinpricks of light burst around the periphery of his vision. A hot needle began to sear a path into the middle of his head.

The old woman raised a hand and made it into a fist. Abruptly, the pressure eased and Blat took in a great gulp of air, his eyes tearing from that final sudden flash of pain. "I guess that's a 'no'." He spoke without thinking and reared back in his chair to stave off a second attack. *An attack of what?*

A small smile flickered on the old woman's face, there and gone in an instant. "You will have your chance to speak." She looked up above Blat's head to the man who stood there. No words were spoken but an understanding seemed to come between them for he released his grip on Blat's chair and returned to the end of the table.

The people in the room were still and silent. In a moment a servant entered, touched Blat on the shoulder, and gestured for him to follow. The silence continued as he gathered his things and followed the girl out the door. No murmur of voices rose behind them as they exited and Blat turned to see if he could determine what the silence might mean. The girl tugged his sleeve. Two guards loomed to either side of him and he was hustled away.

Silent scrutiny followed him on the march through the cavern. The kitchen workers looked up from their tasks but did not whisper to each other. The children at their games grew still but did not titter and giggle after he had passed them by. In fact, the whole cavern was devoid of human voices. As Blat became more aware of this, he was certain that the only sounds were the inconsequential noises made from spoon on bowl, chisel on rock, or hands in water. There was no human voice raised anywhere.

He was led to a cave that had all the comforts he needed: bed, blanket, wash water, and chair. His young guide left and the two guards positioned themselves on either side of the entryway. Blat sighed. Well at least he could wash and change and maybe practice his guitar for a while. That always helped him relax and when he relaxed he could think more clearly.

His hair still damp from a thorough if cold wash, Blat flipped the buckles open on the battered case and gently lifted his guitar from its nest of thick padding. He loved the combination of wood and metal and gut. It was the first thing that was truly his and his possessiveness of it sometimes scared him. Growing up as he had with five brothers, nothing had been his exclusively, not even his father's regard. A weight of sadness descended upon him; he must be more tired than he thought. He eyes re-focused on the guitar. This was his alone; it even had his name engraved in the thicker wood of the neck. He could feel the slight indentations as he slid his hand up and down its silky surface. With a sigh of pleasure, he sat on the chair and tuned the strings. A little higher here, a little lower there, and, satisfied with the sound, he limbered his fingers with a few practice runs. Warmed up and in tune, he played his favourite thinking songs - songs he knew so well that he did not have to concentrate on the technicalities of the music but could instead step outside of himself and float in the ebb and flow of the melody.

As the songs blended from one into another, his mind detached itself from the predicament he was in and saw the situation from a more objective viewpoint. His captors did not wish to hurt him - not yet anyway. There was that huge cylinder he had glimpsed on his arrival. The people were unnaturally quiet, which was especially odd in the children. The group of people at the meeting was divided, but on what specific issue or issues Blat could not guess. But most unnerving, they had done something to him when he had spoken. They had done something to his head without touching him.

In his seven years on the road, the one thing Blat had learned with unequivocal certainty was that there were always more questions than there were answers, and even the answers often did little more than prompt more questions. For all that, he felt calm. The worst they could do was kill him and that didn't scare him. Much. Maybe he was just too ignorant to know what he would be missing. Maybe he had truly come to believe that worrying about something only made it worse. Maybe death was not the ending that some of the preachers claimed it to be but rather the next step on a new journey. Blat always looked forward to a new journey. He smiled.

His chording hand hurt a little and he stopped playing to massage the tendons and muscles. He glanced up at a rustle from his doorway. As many faces as could possibly fit were jammed in the opening. His guards, several children, and some older women stared at him, their eyes round and dark and unblinking. *An audience. Ah.* Blat smiled at them and strummed the opening chords to one his favourite children's songs. Until then, only the guitar had filled the little room with its sound. Blat added his voice. The eyes in the doorway opened even wider and several mouths dropped open. With a swirl of fabric, the women gathered the children and hurried them away.

Blat stopped in mid-note. "Wait," he called, a little frantic. Had he broken some law? Some

56

taboo? Gods, he hoped not. The guards glared and turned their backs to him.

A short time later Blat heard the shuffle of many feet down the rocky corridor. This might not bode well. He waited, his nerves and over-active imagination conjuring all sorts of unpleasantness. He let his breath out in an audible sigh when the elderly woman from the meeting entered his chamber and signalled for her escort to remain without. Heavy material that had been rolled and stored on a rocky shelf above the entrance was dropped down to cover the opening to the corridor. Blat jumped to his feet and offered the chair to his guest. He remained standing until she was comfortable and then sat on the edge of his bed, his long legs sticking out into the middle of the room.

She studied him for a moment. Her glance flicked to his guitar and back to his face. "It has been long since my people have heard music. They are awed and frightened. I don't think Moqor fully realises what he has done." She smiled her small smile. "He thought only to seek help with the machines; he will soon discover that he has brought far more.

"I have lived long enough to remember the songs of minstrels, oh yes. It was before my time as leader and I have been leader for more than two hundred years." Blat's eyes widened; the oldest person he had ever heard of was one hundred and six. "In three months, I will be two hundred and seventy-three years old. I am called Quirindi and I speak for all in Station, even Moqor. We are not as many as before and our sisters and brothers in other

Stations are also fewer in number. Some Stations do not have caretakers at all. We do all we can but it is not enough." She sighed and studied her hands, the translucent skin fragile and thin. "We need help and we have never needed help before." She continued to stare at her hands.

Blat had no idea what she was talking about, but it was his nature to do what he could for people in need. It sometimes got him into trouble and it sometimes got him laughed at, but that was a small price for the times when he actually did some good. "I'll do whatever I can to help you, whatever the problem is."

Quirindi looked at him then. He felt the insect-like prickling on his scalp again and reached his hands up to protect his head. The prickling immediately stopped and Quirindi flushed. "You did that," Blat accused. "You did that in the Council chamber, too!"

"You don't understand," Quirindi reached for his hand. He moved it beyond her reach. Pressing her lips together, Quirindi continued, "We must know if you will betray us."

"That, whatever you did to me, is not the way to get people to trust you!"

"I realise that now," she had the grace to look chagrined. "I hope it is not too late to make amends."

Blat shrugged. "Why don't you tell me what's wrong."

Quirindi rose from her chair. "Easier to show than to tell." She rose and the guards moved the fabric door aside for her. "Come."

Blat followed the diminutive Station leader into the corridor. Several children squatted on the floor outside his room. He grinned at them and gave them a courtly bow. A little girl giggled and immediately stuffed her hand in her mouth, her eyes squeezed shut. *What is it about human sounds?* It was just one of the many questions that swirled around inside his head.

The usual silent stares followed their tiny procession; Blat doubted that he would ever get used to it no matter how many times it happened.

Quirindi led him into the large central cavern and toward the cylinder that hulked in the shadows. As they neared the cylinder, Blat was surprised to see that it was not as smooth as it appeared from a distance but pitted and uneven with hairline fractures and deeper cracks. Quirindi trailed a hand along its rough surface as she walked along its length. The cylinder continued on through an opening in the cavern wall. To one side of the opening was a small door. They entered.

Inside was a complex array of equipment. Some of it flickered with the same unsettling light as in the outer cavern but most of it was dark and lifeless. Quirindi motioned to a worker who was rubbing an oily substance on something that looked like a large nail and he tossed his grimy rag on a pile of similarly grimy rags and slipped out the door. Blat waited for an explanation. Quirindi looked expectantly at him. If she thought he would understand the problem by showing this to him, she was badly mistaken.

Her face fell. "It means nothing to you. I should have known better than to let Moqor build our hopes." She sat on one of the many benches scattered about the room. "He insisted that if anyone knew how to fix the machines, the minstrels would or at least they would know the stories that spoke of it. It's silly now that I think about it. Minstrels are musicians, not technicians. But he can be very convincing." She gestured for Blat to take a seat. "You see, the machines must be kept working. It is our purpose as Stationers to keep them working, but much time has passed - no one really knows how much - since the task was assigned." She sighed and dropped her head. "And I am so very tired."

Blat understood none of what she said but there was no denying that Quirindi felt a desperate need. If he was to be any help at all, he needed more information. "What kind of work, exactly, is it that you do?"

She waved a hand around the room. "We keep the machines working. And, as you can see, we are no longer very good at our job. Oh, it began innocently enough. One of the lights dimmed," she gazed around the room and pointed, "on that machine over there. Then it went out. We look it apart, replaced the bulb, and put it back together just like the Readings say. But it would not light. We did it many times. A second light dimmed, then a third, and we could do nothing. At some point, the main lights in the Station began to dim as well. It was then that Moqor suggested that we look to the outside. It has never been done before, we argued.

60

And he countered that we had never been this desperate before, which was true, and so a team was dispatched. And here you are."

The team must have waited a long time for him; minstrels seldom came to these smaller glacial valleys. Could oiling bits of machinery be the holy purpose that the ancient tale spoke of? It seemed unlikely. Well, he had wanted a new tale and he had certainly found one.

"You mentioned readings. Would it be possible for me to see them?"

Quirindi's eyes opened wide in shock. "They are sacred! They are from the very first of our people!"

Blat sat beside her and took her trembling hand in his. "Perhaps an outsider's point of view is what is needed." He found himself agreeing with Moqor.

"The Council must decide," she whispered and gestured dismissal.

Back in his room, Blat found a tray of food and realised that he was ravenous. He ate, washed, and slept, too tired to wonder what would happen next.

As it turned out, Moqor himself brought the readings to him. Blat's two guards, whose names he had yet to learn, carried a table and an additional chair into his room (he was determined not to call it a cell). Moqor, as bristling and forbidding as Blat remembered him, sat with his back to the wall facing the door, his elbows out and his feet planted on either side of the table legs. He seemed to take up half of the room. *Useful posturing* Blat noted in the part of his mind that observed such behaviour.

Several frustrating hours later, Moqor gathered the ancient books and stumped from the room. Blat watched him go in a kind of stupor. He threw himself on the bed and flung an arm over his aching eyes. Strange words that had no meaning flickered across the inside of his eyelids, and sketches of machines reared themselves before his mind's eye incomprehensible in their form and function.

Moqor had been Guardian of the Readings his entire adult life; it was an honour passed from father to son and his family guarded that honour jealously. It had been part of his household since well before the Minstrels' Guild was formed and that had been more than seven hundred years ago. Moqor knew the Readings as no one else in the Station.

For all the gruelling hours they had spent together, Blat knew nothing more than what Quirindi had told him and shown him: the people called themselves Stationers and for generations their job was to maintain the machines. The trouble was that no one in living memory knew exactly what the machines did. They only knew what they had been taught by their fathers and mothers who had in turn learned the duties at their parents' knees.

The readings seemed to have always been more mystical than useful to the Stationers. Although they recognised some of the drawings as representing parts of the machines, their duties were never seen as being closely related to the readings. One thing was certain: if there were any clues in these readings, Blat was not the person to discover them. It needed a mind that worked in a different way. A mind that solved puzzles and riddles with ease. A mind that revelled in this kind of mystery. A mind like the one inside Sarah's scientist-inventor friend, Crag Bithoone. If anyone could unravel the bizarre information in the readings, he could.

It remained for Blat to convince Quirindi and her Council to bring in another outsider; he would just have to omit the part about Crag being a little crazy.

CHAPTER 4

It was decided that Moqor would accompany Blat in his search for Crag Bithoone. The Council permitted Moqor to carry a small portion of the Readings that they grudgingly allowed as essential to entice this Crag person to help them. Blat hoped it was enough to engage Crag's curiosity. The gods knew that he was difficult to pin down to a single project but when he did concentrate, the results were nothing short of miraculous. Blat had heard the stories. Like the time Crag combined those totally innocent-seeming powders together and set them to heat in the (thankfully) outdoor kitchen behind the Guildhall. The blast shook the dishes and cutlery throughout Jamie-the-Cook's domain and the ensuing verbal blast made even Crag's explosion seem like a child's tantrum. After more testing at a safer distance from civilisation, Crag produced a controlled blasting powder that found its way into road building, mining, and, of course, weapons. He called it 'Bithoone's Blasting Powder' and made a lot of money from that one invention. Not that he stopped there. Among a myriad of other innovations, large and small, Crag refined an oil to make smokeless lamps, built a system to carry water from the glacial melt to the dry desert cities, and achieved a way to heat metal to such a temperature that it could be extruded into fine strong wire that remained flexible even after several bendings. Amazing stuff. On one occasion, Blat had heard Crag Bithoone's bellow from his dormitory room but when he ran to meet Sarah's famous friend, the inventor had already left.

Moqor hiked hour after hour without the least complaint and did his share of the chores. Blat could have wished for more conversation but his days at the Station had accustomed him to expect silence.

The only odd behaviour had occurred on their first day out and made the rest of the journey more of an ordeal than it needed to be. Because of his familiarity with the immediate area, Moqor was in the lead. Every few minutes, he paused to look back. The cliff that housed the Station receded bit by bit and when they topped a rise that would be Moqor's last good view, he dropped to his knees and reached for home, his arms outstretched. Blat remained still and quiet and gazed in the direction of Moqor's supplication. Through the gentle mist rising from the land, a warm shaft of light arrowed from Moqor toward the Station and returned amplified tenfold. Moqor's face was transformed by a radiant smile that flickered on and off so quickly that Blat would have missed it had he not been staring right at him.

Moqor rose, brushed the dust off his knees, and continued onwards, without so much as a glance in Blat's direction. "What was that?" Blat had blurted. "What was that light? Why did you smile? I've never seen you smile before."

Moqor shrugged his pack higher onto his shoulders and continued walking. At the first level ground, Blat pushed up beside him and grabbed his arm. "I saw something back there."

Moqor stopped so abruptly that Blat continued on a pace or two. He turned to face a very angry Stationer. "You know nothing of our ways and so I will not kill you right now for witnessing what you did. Any civilised person would have turned away." He pushed past Blat and marched on.

Blat stared after him. *Gods*.

A silence even more profound than before fell between them. Moqor refused to look at him and Blat felt like he had wandered into the territory of a dangerous predator. He was fairly certain that Moqor would not kill him. Moqor needed him, for now at least, and when Blat arrived at the 'uncivilised' environs of Rivercrest, he would have any number of allies.

It was going to be a long, long journey.

They arrived (unscathed, Blat was relieved to note) at Rivercrest on the eve of summer. The three-day festival that celebrated the beginning of the longer, warmer days had just begun. The city was festooned with bright banners, and streamers of ribbons fluttered from balconies. Early blossoms had been woven into garlands for doorways and windows. The squares were filled with folk from both the city and the surrounding countryside. Enticing aromas drifted in the air. Staging was already in place for the acrobats and the jugglers, the puppet shows and the clowns, and the music that would continue late into the night.

Blat felt the tension in his shoulders ease for the first time in days. He usually only tolerated the city for the friends that lived there and for the supplies that he needed. But today, the throngs and the bustle, and the sound of conversation and laughter were truly welcome.

He glanced back at Moqor to gauge his reaction to the wonders of the city. As usual, he maintained a scornful expression. Throughout their journey, Blat had tried again and again to bridge the abyss between them, but the Stationer refused all apologies. Blat did not even know what he was apologising for, exactly, but he had done something that had deeply offended his travelling companion. Blat's only hope was that someone wiser and a whole lot more stubborn than Moqor would help repair the damage. He knew just the person.

Blat guided them around the festival-goers and into the quieter streets a few blocks away. Moqor's steady tread began to slow and Blat glanced back. The Stationer stared at him, the first eye contact he had made since that fateful misstep, and crumpled to the cobblestones, his head narrowly missing the step of a shop. Blat shouted for help. The shopkeeper rushed out to see what manner of trouble the festival had brought to his door. He glanced at Blat's purple cloak and rang the alarm bell that would summon the City Guard. Before long, two uniformed Guards rounded the corner. They lifted Moqor onto the makeshift sling that Blat had constructed from his sleeping blankets. It was a mercifully short distance to the Minstrels' Guildhall.

A runner was sent for the resident physician. He was out, doubtless enjoying the opening ceremonies, and Francis, the doctor's assistant, rushed into the sickroom. He gently loosened Moqor's clothing and removed his boots. He then checked for fever, pressed his ear to the Stationer's chest, and felt for any deformities around the head and neck regions. He ordered Blat to stay in the room and remain watchful while he raced for supplies.

Moqor was unresponsive. His face was grey and pinched, and his hand felt cold to the touch. Blat retrieved a woollen blanket from the chest at the foot of the bed and tucked it in around the man's cold body so that no drafts could reach him. He spied a brazier in the corner and lit the charcoal. The small room heated quickly on such a mild day and Blat found himself shedding layers of clothing.

A little colour had returned to Moqor's face by the time Francis returned and, by the uproar in the hallway, Blat knew that the doctor himself was close behind. Ilyam was a bit scary by anyone's standards. He was big and gruff and had huge hands, one of which could wrap around most people's heads in a grip that held his victim very, very still while the other hand administered whatever examination or medication he chose to inflict. He never smiled, at least Blat had never seen it - something the doctor had in common with Moqor (except for that one time). When Ilyam spoke, it was like gravel being poured from a metal barrel. Blat was thankful that the doctor was never given cause to raise his voice.

Ilyam quickly and thoroughly examined the Stationer. A rumble from the bedside sent Francis scrambling once again. He returned directly with a bizarre contraption that Ilyam set on a table next to the bed. Liquids of various colours stood in glass vials and beside them lay a tiny knife. Francis reached under the blankets for one of Moqor's hands and held it steady while Ilyam made a small puncture wound in the index finger. He then squeezed a drop of blood into each of the vials. Francis pressed a piece of linen to the wound and held it there.

Ilyam opened the window shutter and studied each of the vials in the clear sunlight. From Blat's position at the other end of room, nothing seemed to change except for what one might expect by inserting a little red blood. The doctor shook his head and turned to the Minstrel, something Blat was hoping would not happen.

Moqor had remained still and silent throughout the entire invasion of his body. His eyes, when Ilyam had peered into them, were turned up into his head so that only the red-streaked whites showed. His breathing was swift and light, and a dew of perspiration glistened on his brow and upper lip. To Blat's untrained eye, it looked like some kind of seizure. Ilyam was not prepared to voice his opinion; he never did until he was certain and he was usually certain within a few minutes of examining a patient. This delay did not bode well for Moqor.

"Who is this fellow and where is he from?" The pebbles and stones of the words cascaded across the room and into Blat's ears.

"His name is Moqor and he is from a cave society in one of the glacial valleys near Ozoli." One did not prevaricate when answering a question from Ilyam. "Do you know what ails him?"

A black scowl lowered the doctor's brow and Blat wished with all his heart that he could turn back time for just a few seconds and stifle himself.

"You will tell me everything you know about this man and you will do it now."

This was an imperial command if Blat had ever heard one.

With the gift of words that every minstrel possessed and spurred to loquacious heights by an overwhelming desire to satisfy Ilyam's request, Blat recounted everything he had seen and heard at the Station. Francis's deep brown eyes grew wider and wider as the tale unfolded. Ilyam stood with his back to the Minstrel gazing out the still-unshuttered window. When Blat was done, Ilyam shook himself as though he was settling this new information into his body.

Without a word, Ilyam ensured that his patient was as comfortable as he could be and set a novice apprentice to sit watch in the room. "You come running to find me in the medical library if there is a change, any change at all." The young girl nodded vigorously, never taking her eyes from Moqor's face.

Blat was released and made his way to the kitchens. He was exhausted and hungry. A little of Jamie's food would go a long way to set him straight. He had forgotten that everyone would be at the festival and was left to forage for himself - not that he minded. In his days at the Conservatory, he had had occasion to scavenge late night snacks. He knew where Jamie secreted the desserts and the cheeses that required aging. If he took just a little from each tray, the theft would go unnoticed. His plate satisfactorily piled with delectable goodies, Blat hooked a chair out from one of the dining tables and proceeded to devour everything in front of him. It felt good to be alone, even if only temporarily; these moments recharged him for the next foray into the mass of bustling humanity.

He managed to sneak to his room without being seen by the decidedly few Guildhall warders and he was pulling off his boots when the babble of excited conversation made its inexorable way toward his end of the residence. As the bubble of noise approached he could distinguish individual voices. One boot on and one boot off, he hobbled to the door and flung it open just as Talitha, Sarah, and the irrepressible Louetta invaded his domain. Hugs and squeals of delight engulfed him. Louetta had jumped on his bed and leapt to his back, her little arms wrapped tightly around his throat.

"Here, dear, you'll strangle poor Blat, and him just back." Sarah gently loosened her daughter's ferocious grip and Blat's colour returned to normal.

Louetta raced to the door and looked back over her shoulder. "Well. Are you coming? The puppet show is starting!" With an apologetic glance Talitha hurried after her sister.

"I'll tell you all about it later," Blat called after her. She waved at him, her other arm reaching to grab a handful of Louetta's bright orange tunic, the colour no doubt chosen so that her minders might have some small chance of finding her when the little firebrand escaped them.

"Whew." Sarah slumped in Blat's only chair. "I don't mind taking a break from that one. And this is only the first day of festival! Do you suppose she'll wear herself out?" They looked at each other and burst out laughing. As far as they could tell, Louetta had an inexhaustible supply of energy.

"So, what's this? Back so early. We didn't expect you until the snow. Not that I'm complaining, mind you. We could use another dozen pairs of hands to keep that diminutive demon out of trouble. Gods, I miss the road at times." Her brush with death at Louetta's birth coupled with the arthritis that flared in her hip had forced Sarah to rethink her priorities. She stayed close to home now and travelled vicariously through Blat's stories.

Blat rummaged in the top shelf of a cabinet and removed a dusty bottle of Ruapan brandy and two small glasses. He poured for them and handed Sarah a glass. "To a successful journey," he toasted. Sarah's gaze sharpened.

"You found it?"

"Better." He raised his glass and Sarah automatically touched hers to his. They drank the fiery liquid.

Blat repeated his story, this time with the detail that a minstrel would appreciate. Sarah kept their glasses full and dusk was falling before both story and brandy were done.

"There's something familiar about this. Something keeps tickling the back of my brain," Sarah said. She swung her head back and forth as though the motion would force the thought out into the open. "I hate it when that happens."

"Just let it come, Sarah. When you try to force it, just like love, it runs and hides." These were the very words that she had offered him one day when he had complained of the same difficulty.

Sarah cuffed him on the shoulder. "Insolent pup." She heaved a sigh. "Well, at least I can take a look at this Station man, see if the sight of him brings anything to mind."

Blat followed her to Moqor's room. The young novice of earlier that day had been replaced by a different young novice. He did not even glance at them when they entered the room. "No change," he reported in a whisper.

They approached the stricken Stationer and studied his face. Blat could discern no change in Moqor, except perhaps that he was a little paler.

They retreated from the room and Sarah shook her head. "Nothing. Well, festival or not, we have to convene a meeting of the Masters and quickly. You look dead on your feet, lad. Get some rest and I'll set the wheels in motion." She strode in the direction of the main doors to put her words into action.

Moqor died during the night; he simply stopped breathing. Ilyam examined him closely once again to determine if there could possibly have been some injury that he had missed. He found nothing. Moqor's illness and death remained a mystery.

Blat had no idea how a Stationer's remains should be handled and so it was easy to convince the Assembly of Masters that Moqor must be returned to his people. The Masters also feared that relations so newly begun may already have deteriorated beyond repair with his death. They assigned a senior Touring Minstrel with exemplary diplomatic skills and a small contingent of Conservatory security guards to accompany the body. Blat drew a detailed map to guide them to the Station. A second group copied the readings that Moqor had guarded and, with it, searched the archives for anything related. The original readings would be returned with Moqor's body. Blat would lead a third party to find Crag Bithoone; he had been last seen in a village north of Rivercrest.

The summer festival swirled around Blat and the two men chosen to accompany him. Laden with various odd bits of fragile equipment, trail food, and camping gear, the expedition required the services of a pair of mules. This would slow them down but the scholars insisted that if they were to do anything at all, they must have their instruments. The pair of them poured over a copy of the readings as they rode, trusting that Blat would not lead them over the edge of a precipice. More likely, they didn't think of Blat at all. Their fascination with the information that Moqor had brought with him was simply too engrossing. It opened a new world, they said. And they wanted to be the first to make any breakthrough discoveries.

They stayed at inns and taverns along the way. Blat sang and played in the evenings, earning them their suppers and lodging. No sense in spending the Assembly's money when he didn't have to; no telling when they might need a little extra.

The village where they hoped to find Crag Bithoone was near the River Salix and north east of

Rivercrest. They chose the least disreputable of the inns for their lodgings. The two scholars, Ugi Nyall and Hamal Bisk, kept to their room arguing and waving their arms about. As far as Blat could tell, they had not agreed on anything except that they disagreed on everything. Blat left them to it and inquired as to the whereabouts of Crag Bithoone.

"Oh, that one," the *Mighty Duck's* innkeeper snorted. "He'll be along in about a hundred years. He owes me money, so ye'll not see his face around here and no mistake."

Blat had the same bad luck when he queried the patrons. It would seem that a lot of people were looking for Crag Bithoone and for much the same reason. No money? Only Crag could have spent all his money in so short a time. How could someone so brilliant be so irresponsible?

The search continued.

The second to last outpost along the river was a dismal place. The rushes on the floor were barely recognisable beneath the filth, and the tables were crusty and sticky with unknown substances. Blat decided to ask his question and leave, and the sooner the better.

"No, I ain't seen him." The barkeep picked his teeth with a sliver of kindling and spit a nasty gob onto the long-suffering rushes. He turned his back and Blat got a whiff of his unwashed body. Slightly green, Blat staggered to the door and out into the fresh air.

***

In a dark corner of the tavern, an eye gleamed from beneath a shabby hat. He left a copper on the table, sauntered to the door, and watched as the trio led their animals from the yard and turned north towards the final way station on the river path. Beyond that lay the foothills with only game trails that meandered through the wilderness.

Crag Bithoone was a solitary man. He didn't like people looking for him. Sure, he had done some amazing things in his day. The sorry fact was that people expected him to do amazing things all the time as if it was easy, as if it didn't tear the soul out of a man. To make it worse, he had let his creations fall into the hands of some high and mighty government types. Oh, he had tried to get them back, but there was something about the money they had given him to get whatever he needed. But they didn't mean only that, oh no. They also meant that they could take everything he made because they claimed they had paid for it, and they had made a fortune by exploiting just a few of his pieces. He resented the fact that they placed more importance on mere money than what his blood and sweat and genius had conceived. He had earned every penny and what was his, was his. They just didn't understand.

But what they did, or should he say didn't do, with most of his inventions staggered him: they hid them somewhere. They might even have destroyed them. He shuddered at the thought. He had heard a rumour that he had blasphemed. Blasphemed! It smelled of the Brothers, but what did those zealots have to do with anything? He couldn't steal his things back and he couldn't rebuild anything without money to buy the tools and other paraphernalia that he needed. It was impossible.

He let the three men gain some distance before he gathered his things and took a different, more direct path to the sorry excuse of an inn at the other end. He could talk Sammy into letting him use one of the outbuildings to do some work in return for a modification or two to the still that he kept out back. The innkeeper was always looking for ways to get more liquor from less grain.

Maybe these three had a better offer for him. He would listen and learn.

***

This last inn was, if possible, worse than the previous one. Aptly named *End O' The Road*, stale ale, sweat, and other best-not-mentioned smells assaulted Blat's nostrils. He received the same gruff answer when he asked the innkeeper about Crag Bithoone.

Sighing, Blat secured food and lodgings for the night; it was either here or outside in the intermittent drizzle that had soaked them all day. The innkeeper was happy to shave a few coins off the price if Blat would perform for his customers.

"It's been a while since one of you wandering minstrels took the time to drop by. So much for keeping the folk apprised of the goings-on." He harrumphed and turned to wipe the bar top with a corner of his apron. "April here will look after you."

77

A young girl about twelve years old scurried out from behind the bar. She gave Blat a shy glance and raced out the door. Blat followed, curious to see how she would extract Ugi and Hamal from the backs of their beasts.

As usual, the two scholars were deep in discussion. They had been oblivious of their surroundings the entire journey. Such focused attention was admirable and, at first, Blat humoured them by leading their horses and the pack mules, preparing camp when they had to sleep out of doors, and cleaning up. But early on he had had enough and forced them to help. You would have thought he was assigning some insurmountable task instead of the simple chores necessary for eating and sleeping. They did the work so grudgingly and so badly that Blat almost gave in and did it himself. Almost.

"Sirs," the young girl called up to them. They didn't even pause in their discussion, which had become heated. April tugged on the end of Ugi's dangling cloak. "Sirs?" she repeated, "I'm to look after your horses." They continued to ignore her.

Blat strolled over and winked at her. These two had had their rude and selfish way long enough. It was time to begin their training for the return journey to Rivercrest. He reached under Ugi's horse and loosened the girth. With a sharp tug, the saddle swung precariously sideways. Ugi continued to argue his point as he clutched the pommel and scrabbled to right himself. His efforts caused the weight of the saddle to slip further down the horse's side and, with a satisfactory splat, he sprawled in the mud of the inn's courtyard. Hamal spoke on, unaware that his adversary no longer listened and that Blat repeated the girth-loosening trick under his nose. With arms flailing quite dramatically, Hamal was silenced at last by his own messy landing. Blat then handed the reins to little April who had watched wide-eyed, a hiccupping giggle in her throat.

Blat left the two men struggling to their feet and looking bewildered. He knew he should feel remorseful, but, well, he didn't. He helped April tend the horses and unload the mules (she really was too small for such a task - he would say as much to the innkeeper). Blat retrieved the saddlebags from the mountain of equipment and supplies, and gave her an extra penny to keep an eye on their things.

Ugi and Hamal confronted him outside the inn doors. "How dare you do such a thing, you insolent... musician!" Ugi puffed with indignation. Hamal stood with his hands clenched and noticeably favoured his right leg.

Blat was at first inclined to ignore them until they had calmed down. He went with his second inclination. "You were rude to this young lady." He pointed to April. They hadn't even noticed her yet. At this comment, she gasped and opened her mouth to protest. Blat continued smoothly. "She asked you politely to dismount not once but twice. But you were so full of your own selves that you had no thought for anyone else, and I am heartily sick of it. This was just a little demonstration of the many ways that I will get your attention and your full assistance on our return journey. Do you understand me?"

Blat looked meaningfully at the saddlebags dragging down April's arms. They were not stupid, these two, and, after only momentary hesitation, grasped that they were to unburden the girl. This they did and quietly followed Blat into the inn. He was sure to hear about this later but for a few blissful moments they were speechless.

Blat played for the woodsmen and trappers who lingered for a short time in the common room and retired early to his chambers. This far in the wilderness did not make for many patrons or for late nights.

It was sometime in the hour before dawn that the bellowing oaths awakened him. It seemed to be coming from the stables. Blat threw a cloak around his shoulders, stuffed his feet into his boots, and stumbled into the courtyard. The innkeeper, dishevelled and in a night robe, stood with his fists on his hips and glared through the open stable doors.

Blat peered around his shoulder and tried to understand what he was seeing. Slime seemed to have exploded from the centre of the stable and inundate every available surface both horizontal and vertical. It was as if a huge vat of one of Jamie's more colourful stews had taken on a life of its own and decided to blast itself from its confinement.

Spattered and still in full-throated bellow, Crag Bithoone gave vent to his ire. Even covered in muck, Crag was easily recognisable - the timbre of his voice was unmistakable to a musician's ear. The chaotic circumstances were not surprising now that Blat knew the source.

He put a reassuring hand on the innkeeper's shoulder. "Crag Bithoone," he pitched his voice to penetrate the thundering from the other man. Crag stopped as though felled by a tree. The silence was profound.

"Eh? Who's there?" He scraped a hand across his eyes removing some of the goo and peered into the darkness. He shuffled towards the stable doors, kicking detritus out of his way. He studied Blat in the flickering torchlight and turned back to the stable. "Don't know you." Crag bent to pick up a jagged piece of metal and wiped it on his trousers. "Couldn't take the pressure. Just look at that break. Bah!" He dropped the shard back on the floor.

Blat noticed April cowering in the corner. He went to her and touched her on the sleeve. "Please calm the animals and take them out of this mess." The young girl dug deep into a mound of hay for clean straw with which to clean the befouled bridles. Fortunately, the stall doors had protected the beasts from the worst of the mess and soon she led the skittish animals into the outdoor enclosure.

"You'll pay for this, Bithoone." The innkeeper was not a happy man. "And you'll clean every bit of this mess. I don't know for the life of me how I let you talk me into this, but mark my words, it won't happen again." With a final glare, he stomped back to the inn for what was left of the night.

Blat could not imagine what Crag was up to, but it was bound to be either brilliant or crazy.

81

Most importantly, they had found him at last. Ugi and Hamal were going to love this.

"You are... incompetent!" Ugi had difficulty expressing how much he loathed this interloper and 'incompetent' was about as foul a description as he could imagine for a so-called man of science. There was no denying that this Bithoone fellow had been lucky in the past; some of his inventions were quite ingenious. But that was in the past. No one had seen or heard from him in some time and by the looks of him, he had spent that time drinking the swill in hovels such as this one.

Crag Bithoone ignored the bumbling idiot and continued to pore over the readings and sketch images on the parchment that Blat had provided.

Hamal, however, was of a different opinion. In fact, he always disagreed with Ugi - it was a given. He leaned over the scruffy inventor to study the diagrams that were becoming more and more intriguing and, well, inventive.

Crag rolled his head on his shoulders and stretched his arms out to each side, flexing his fingers as he did so. "I need a drink," he stated. He stood and headed to the common room and the dark ale that the innkeeper served.

His name was Sammy Toule and he had inherited *End O' The Road* from an uncle on his mother's side. He and Crag went back a long way, but it was the silver that Blat generously placed in Sammy's hand that allowed them to stay on at the inn. They had taken over most of the second floor of the building with its private dining room serving as the scientists' workroom. They shared the two

82

larger bedrooms and had access to the innkeeper's privy. Silver did amazing things.

After five days, Blat patience was nearing its end. He had listened to the scientific debate for a while hoping that the words would eventually make sense. That had been a waste of time. He practised his guitar until his fingers and forearms ached. He sang every song in his repertoire. He entertained the inn's few guests each evening and he explored the immediate environs during the day. He wondered how far the other team had travelled toward the Station with Moqor's body and how the Stationers would react to what had happened. Now *that* would be interesting. This, on the other hand, was slowly driving him mad.

He stomped up the stairs and strode to the workroom door. He lifted his fist to knock and stopped. It was quiet. It was never quiet. He eased the door open and saw something he never thought to see: all three of these noisy, bickering, annoying men were nodding and smiling.

When they spotted him, they all started speaking at once and Blat let them carry on for a few moments. It was pleasant to hear excitement in their voices for a change. At last, he motioned for them to stop and looked at Crag for what he hoped would be an understandable explanation for what had inspired this camaraderie.

"The readings, as the Stationers at one time must have known, are indeed instructions for maintaining their machines. But what do the machines do, that is the big question. And we," he paused to include Ugi and Hamal - a very generous gesture, "have pieced together from these few fragments of information just what they do." He beamed at Blat. "They control some kind of magnet!"

Blat looked from one to the other. "But why?"

"Oh, we don't know that yet," Ugi chimed in.

"But we will," Hamal added. "It turns out that our esteemed colleague," he nodded his head in Crag's direction, "has seen something very similar to this cylindrical object before and it might, therefore, have machines nearby as well. Perhaps functioning machines. And it is much closer than the one you have described."

"If we can study them with our own eyes and perform a few tests," Crag said, "we may be able to determine if the cylinders and machines are related and why these Stations -uninteresting name that - exist in the first place. I can't imagine why I never wondered about it before now."

Blat considered. "You mean you've seen a cylinder before?"

"Oh, yes. In fact, I've seen two. Sort of." Crag began rolling his notes and stuffing them into a travelling case. "The one I saw most recently was in a Station stripped of most everything and not a soul around. I poked around for a day or two but was unable to figure out what the cylinder was or what it had been used for. I didn't see any machines but I also didn't find a room adjacent to the cylinder. Maybe I missed it; I was in a bit of a hurry." He reached under the table to extract a second carrying case and packed an assortment of writing materials and small boxes into it. "The other Station was

84

occupied by Brothers of the Watch so I didn't actually see a cylinder but the rest of the place looked the same so I assume it has one as well." He reached around Ugi for the rest of his writing supplies and placed them inside a separate pocket of his case.

Blat, Ugi, and Hamal stared at him. Blat was the first to regain his power of speech. "Brothers of the Watch! Are you crazy? They kill anyone who doesn't know their mumbo jumbo passwords and their secret handshakes. They train practically from birth. It's impossible to even find one of their hideouts let alone go into one!"

Crag smirked and left the workroom to finish packing. His voice drifted back to them. "I suggest you get packing. We'll try the empty Station first."

Ugi and Hamal were adamant. They must return to Rivercrest with the breakthrough they had discovered. Perhaps the combined minds at the Conservatory would be able to determine the purpose of the machines without having to venture into a Station at all. Perhaps the dangerous journey was not necessary. They feared what their superiors would say if they damaged any of the valuable equipment. They delivered all this without once looking into Blat's eyes. Blat didn't need his years of training to see that they were afraid, but not of what any superior would say - they were afraid of the Brothers. They would be crazy *not* to be afraid. It didn't even matter that they would go to the defunct Station and not the guarded Station. As far as Ugi and Hamal were concerned, anything that interested the Brothers was to be avoided.

Nothing would sway them. They gladly (too gladly?) left some of the equipment that Crag would need for various tests and departed for Rivercrest with remarkable speed.

"Cowards. Superstitious cowards." Crag sneered at the rapidly retreating backs of the two scholars. He looked at Blat. "I guess you'll have to do."

With that less than flattering comment, they turned their horses towards the forest trail that led to the glacier.

CHAPTER 5

Blat considered his luck in travelling companions. The best had been Sarah. That first eye-opening journey with her remained bright and clear in his memory. It had transformed him from a farmer tied to the land to a songbird flying free. The several apprentice tours with senior minstrels from the Conservatory varied from gruelling to unbearable to hilarious depending on the teacher. More recently, Moqor had been taciturn and dangerous, and the two scholars ranged from annoying to downright rude.

Crag Bithoone managed to have all of these traits. Not all at once or for great lengths of time, but have them he did. One moment he was telling amusing stories from his childhood and the next he was belligerent and ornery. Stony silence usually followed. There didn't seem to be any particular trigger for Crag's mercurial mood swings. Blat wondered if the inventor hadn't experimented once too often on himself. When confronted with his odd behaviour, Crag denied any such thing and refused to discuss it further. Because Sarah spoke so highly of Crag, Blat was inclined to trust him but this erratic behaviour could get them both killed. Who knew when their wits would be challenged by attack from the vagaries of nature as easily as from bandits? On the evening of the third day, Crag broached the subject himself.

The higher they climbed, the scarcer the vegetation had become. They camped that night within one of the last copses they would likely see for a while. This would be a good place to leave the animals; there would be nothing for them to eat along the icy trail to Station Two as they referred to their destination. Perhaps it was the thought of leaving so many comforts behind - they could carry only so much equipment on their backs, or maybe Crag was having one of his ever-rarer moments of lucidity. Whatever the cause, Blat was grateful.

"It's like this, boy," Crag began. "When I was a lad, younger than you, I began to have what you might call extremes. One day I would be happy and normal," he glanced across their small campfire at Blat, "well, mostly normal, and the next day I would be depressed and angry and shout at everybody. It got so that my friends - the few I had left - avoided me on my dark days. But would I leave well enough alone? Of course not. I sought them out and verbally abused them until the first punch was thrown. I loved that part. Pain seemed to bleed away my rage. Figuratively and literally." He absently rubbed his left shoulder.

"I tried various concoctions from doctors and such, and sometimes they helped. But lately... it's getting worse. Age, probably. Whatever holds the darkness back is breaking down and you're getting the brunt of it."

"Sarah misses you, you know. She wants to see you." Sarah had made Blat promise to extend the invitation to her old friend; he would fall out of her good graces if he returned to Rivercrest without Crag in tow.

Crag closed his eyes and smiled. "I miss her too. More than you can know. She was my first lover, did she tell you?" At Blat's open mouth, he continued, "I guess not. Gods, I loved that woman. But when Jamie arrived in Rivercrest, I didn't stand a chance. Oh, we parted amicably enough, but I will always wonder what would have happened if that cook hadn't shown up.

"At any rate, I'm glad she can't see me now. With her stubborn streak, she would have me run ragged going to this doctor and that specialist. I'm all one for tests and experiments. Just not on me. Not anymore. So you see, you will have to put up with my mood swings and acid tongue, but don't fret, when we get to the Stations, I'll be all scientist. I thank the gods that my mind still works when it has something interesting to anchor it."

In the morning, Crag took one taste of the tea that Blat had prepared and threw it, cup and all, into the ashes of their campfire. He glared at Blat and stomped off to collect the things he would need for the remainder of the trek.

Blat silently retrieved the cup and rinsed it in one of the many rivulets nearby. He loaded his own pack quickly and efficiently, released the animals from their tethers, hid the gear that they had to leave behind, and waited for Crag to join him.

The sullen glower in Crag's eyes warned Blat to keep his mouth shut. He followed the inventor out of the copse that had sheltered them for the night and into the crisp breeze wafting off the glacier. Cold and uncomfortable though the ice crossing would be, it would lead them swiftly to their goal.

Some of the terrain upon which they travelled was quite familiar to Blat; it was much like his journey to Quirindi's Station, or Station One as Crag had dubbed it. By the end of the day, an overcast sky threatened rain and possibly snow. They had to move quickly and, indeed, travelled until dusk made the footing dangerous. After a cold meal, they huddled together for warmth and were on the move again before dawn.

"We'll be there today." They were the first words Crag had spoken since his revelation of two nights ago.

They scrambled over a pile of stony rubble and gazed into a valley; they had reached their destination. It was so similar to the Station One valley that Blat pointed to where he guessed the entrance to the caverns would be.

Crag grunted by way of reply and trudged on with scowling glances at the darkening sky.

Between the two of them, they found the entrance before it was fully dark. Exhausted from the long day, they went in only far enough to be out of the biting wind, ate cold rations, and wrapped themselves in their blankets. Tomorrow would be soon enough to explore.

Station Two was dimly lit by chimney holes cut high into the rock ceiling. Crag and Blat assembled crude torches to allow them to peer into the shadowy corners. They walked the length of the cylinder and Blat noted that it was deeply pitted and scarred, much worse than the first one he had seen.

Hidden behind an outcrop of stone they found the room that should have held the machines, but it was dark and mostly empty. Crag examined wires that extruded at irregular intervals from the walls.

"These were cut. And not so very long ago. See?" He held up an end for Blat's scrutiny; there was a metallic glint where the wire had been severed. "These ends would show signs of corrosion within a very short time, say, a few weeks. But it's hard to be sure in this dry air. A bit unusual, that, for a cave system near so much ice.

"If it was the Brothers that took the equipment," Crag muttered, "they must think it's valuable in some way. Or they discovered the purpose of the Stations. Whatever. Ugi and Hamal were right about one thing, though: if the Brothers are interested, it bodes ill for the rest of us." Crag surged to his feet and stormed out of the machine room.

Blat watched him go. It looked like a good time to leave Crag alone to battle his demons.

He had not been permitted to examine Station One to his satisfaction but there was no one to stop him now. The similarities between the two Stations were uncanny and Blat felt certain that he could find his 'room' if it would have been any help. He wandered through meeting rooms, workrooms, living quarters, and other enclosed areas whose purposes were unclear. He examined the kitchen facilities and took a quick look at the waste disposal system. There were a number of corridors off the main cavern and Blat chose the largest one - perhaps it led somewhere important. The walls were carved with geometric designs that had no meaning to Blat. He would have to point them out to Crag.

An arched doorway opened on to a small grotto. The light from a chimney hole shone directly onto a design that covered a low, round table. Blat circled it, trying to make sense of the lines and the swirls. He stood with his index finger and thumb cupping his chin and studied a familiar shape. What was it? It nagged at him; he was certain he had seen this before. Lost as he was in dredging up the slippery memory, he waved a negligent hand as Crag joined him.

"By the gods!" Crag whispered. "How could I have missed this?" He rummaged through the small pack that he carried with him, took out writing materials, and busied himself with numbers and equations, muttering and cursing under his breath. Blat peered over his shoulder looking from Crag's work to the table design, but if there was any connection between the two, it eluded him.

At last Crag looked up from his work and gave Blat one of his rare smiles. It changed his face completely. This must have been the person Sarah had befriended.

Blat waited patiently while Crag enjoyed his moment of revelation. He understood the luminous feeling that came with true inspiration. He quashed a flicker of envy - what he would give for that kind of moment to transform his life once again. It had happened to him during his third year of study and like every aspiring musician, he constantly experimented with new tunes and new lyrics. With all of the thousands of songs already written, it was hard, if not impossible, to compose something fresh, especially something that would cause the old

Masters to pause and listen. But he had done it. Once. Sarah took him aside one day after the accolades had died down. The trouble with it happening, she had said, is that now it is expected. Anything he wrote had to be equally spectacular or people would think he was not trying. Anything he wrote would have to be as good as or better than that one song. Anything he wrote would be compared and contrasted to it.

Gods! How could he have known that he had put himself into such a position? If he had known, why he would have… What would he have done? Not written the song? No. That was unthinkable. Perhaps when enough time had passed, his not-quite-as-good-as-that-other-song songs would become accepted for the fine work that they were. And they were fine songs, Sarah said so. He held on tight to that belief.

Crag had been talking for some minutes, oblivious to the fact that Blat was not paying attention. The minstrel gathered himself and interrupted the scientific exposition. "Wait, wait. I can't understand anything you're saying. Pretend I'm a child. Make it simple."

The inventor was startled into silence at this intrusion and his obvious annoyance did not bode well for acquiescing to Blat's request. Blat considered slowly backing towards the archway and making his escape.

Crag rubbed his hands vigorously over his face. "Very well. Here is the simpleton's version." Blat chose not to interrupt again, but would discuss the drawbacks of name-calling at a more appropriate

93

time. "The table is a representation - a picture if you will - of the nearby planets and stars. See this blob?" He pointed to a round object about a third of the way across and a third of the way down from where they stood looking at the table. "That's the planet where Whitecap Island is. If you look closely you can see the outline of the island."

So that's what Blat had found familiar. He knew the shape of the island very well; he had walked it many times.

"These other landmasses on our world," Crag used the feathered tip of his quill to indicate them, "must be islands like ours. Incredible, isn't it? And here we thought Whitecap Island was all there was. But even more incredible are the indications of more worlds within our very own star system. Ha. They'll have to listen to me now. I knew there had to be other forces to keep things in line."

Blat decided to focus on the part that he could understand. "You mean to say that there could be other people on our world we know nothing about?"

Crag had begun to scribble notes once again, but looked up at the question. "But of course, my boy. Lots of them." He peered at the circle that represented their world. "Awfully far away though, and through the-gods-know-what kinds of perils. Look at all that water. And what are these markings? Get my glass, boy. You know the one I mean."

The contents of the inventor's pack lay strewn about the floor from Crag's earlier forage for parchment and quill. It took Blat some minutes to find the lacquered box that held the curved glass in its velvet nest.

Crag took it from its protection, gave it a cursory polish with his sleeve, and placed it over the miniature likeness of Whitecap Island. Details abruptly sprang into view. The central glacier was a pearly star with its arms draped demurely down its sides. Darker fissures and rugged valleys separated the arms. To the west, the land transformed from green to brown to tan as the desert gained control. In the east, the swampland was a morass of streams and bogs, and too many shades of green to count. The north seemed dull by comparison with its forests creating an undisturbed carpet. The Rivers Nykan and Salix dominated the south, their striking blue slashes forming a giant 'X.' There was no sign of Rivercrest or of any civilisation.

"Back off, boy, you're steaming the glass."

Blat jerked back. "Sorry," he mumbled. He wandered around the room and considered. As far as he knew, there had been people on Whitecap Island for a very long time. So why, with all the other details so clear, would there be no depiction of the marks that man has made? It could be that whoever made this table simply chose to ignore them. It could also be that the design was solely for artistic purposes with no intention of being accurate. Or it could be that whoever made this did it so long ago that no one had been born yet.

"Take a look at this, Blat." Crag waved him over. "What do you make of these?" He pointed to a red dot that Blat had missed on his first

95

examination. "And here, and here." Two more red dots were visible.

The two men looked at each other for several seconds. "Stations," they said in unison.

The inventor would not eat or rest if Blat didn't make him do both. In the two days since the discovery, Crag had painstakingly reproduced the design on the table giving it the practical but boring name of 'The Map.' The area where Rivercrest was located had three tiny blue dots whose significance remained to be discovered.

In between feeding them and forcing Crag to rest periodically, Blat explored the rest of Station Two. The Stationers or the Brothers or whoever it was that had emptied the place had not left much behind. He was certain people had been living here though; otherwise, he would not have found the usual debris that humans inevitably left in their wake. The huge cylinder was the only interesting artefact aside from The Map. He climbed on top of it to get a look at its curved surface closest to the cavern wall. He peered under it see if it rested on any kind of supporting structure. It did not; it lay directly on the stone floor. He followed it as far as he could into both cavern walls until the space around it grew too tight for him to squeeze through. He went into all the rooms that might form a border along its length, but there was no access to either the beginning or the end of the cylinder. It could be miles long or it could end a few yards beyond what his torch showed him.

Maybe Crag would have some thoughts on it.

He trudged back to The Map room mulling over how he could squeeze a decent meal from their dwindling supplies. A puff of air where there should be no air circulation stopped him in his tracks. He slowly turned his head to peer into the darkened room beside him. The slight rustle of fabric sent him into a crouch with his dagger in his hand. He scuttled to the side of the entranceway. "Come out where I can see you," he commanded, threat clear in his voice. "And put your hands behind your head."

A tired whimper preceded the pair of scruffy heads emerging into the torchlight, small hands linked white-knuckled behind their heads as he had instructed them. The rest of their bodies followed and Blat wrinkled his nose at the pungent odour. These two had not seen soap and water in many days.

"Turn and face me. Slowly."

They shuffled around in a slow circle. Blat felt a pang of pity for these two bedraggled youngsters - a boy and a girl about twelve years old. They had the pale skin and large eyes of Stationers and based on his cursory survey of them, were most definitely no threat to him and Crag.

Blat slipped his dagger back into his belt and angled the torch so that they could get a look at him, to see that he, in turn, was no danger to them. It was then that the young boy rammed headfirst into his midriff. The torch flew from his hand and Blat landed painfully on the rock floor, the breath knocked out of him and his head ringing from its bounce on the unyielding surface. As he struggled for air, the boy wrested Blat's knife from its sheath and pressed it to Blat's throat. The girl grabbed the guttering torch and demanded in a hoarse voice, "Where have you taken them?" The boy pushed a little harder drawing a thin line of blood. "Where have you taken them?" she repeated.

"Who?" Blat managed to croak.

"You know who," the boy hissed in his face. "Now tell us."

With the weight of the boy on his stomach and the knife at his throat, Blat truly wished he could answer the question. He hadn't managed a breath yet and tiny pinpricks of light hovered around his vision. "Need to breathe," he mouthed. The boy either did not understand or chose not to understand, and the pressure continued. Blat slipped down into the dark.

A not-so-light tap on his cheek roused Blat to the agony of a splitting headache. He pushed at the hands that shook him. "Good. You're awake." Crag brought a cup to his lips. "I put pain medicine in that; I imagine you need some."

Blat nodded and had to wait a moment while the nausea passed. Crag helped him to take a few sips. "Better? Good." Crag moved away and tended a small fire and the pot that bubbled above it.

Footsteps sounded in the corridor and Blat surged up. "There are others in the Station," he said. He had managed to get to his knees before Crag spoke.

"Oh. You mean the twins. Yes, we've met. They came running to find me when you passed out.

They thought they had killed you." He chuckled. "You should have seen their faces."

"You can laugh?"

"Well, not at the time, of course. I followed them to where you lay. They told me the story on the way and I knew even before I saw you that you had likely just fainted. But they didn't know that. We carried you here and I sent them to clean up before dinner."

The twins stood in the archway of The Map room. "Come in, come in," Crag motioned for them to enter. "As you can see, Blat is perfectly fine. Or will be soon enough. Let's eat this while it's hot."

Crag Bithoone, the eccentric, moody scientist-inventor, spooned out portions of the stew he had concocted and made them sit in a circle around the cook fire. He insisted that the dinner conversation be restricted to comments about the food and would permit no questions or explanations while they ate. It was bad for the digestion, he told them.

Bemused, Blat dutifully ate and studied his erstwhile attackers. They were younger that he had first thought. With the grime removed from their faces, he placed their age at closer to nine or ten. Young to be on their own in the wilds. The girl kept her eyes on her bowl and ate neatly. Her brother stared at Crag and then at Blat and back again, all the while gulping huge mouthfuls of food as fast as he could shovel them him.

Crag didn't bother to ask if the two youngsters wanted seconds. He merely reached for their bowls and refilled them. He scrounged in his pack and produced half a dozen wrinkly apples, soft but sweet. The girl's eyes widened and nibbled the treat with a slight smile on her face. Even the boy slowed his frantic devouring to savour the taste.

"Take the dishes to the spring and give them a good wash, there's a good pair." Crag sent them off and set the kettle to boil for after-dinner tea. "I love having extra hands to give work to, hands that don't balk or talk back." He leaned against his pack and pulled a pipe from his pocket.

"Have you found out anything about them yet?" Blat asked. "What about their names?"

Crag took a moment to light his pipe before looking at the minstrel through the fragrant smoke. "Didn't need to. They are Station children that were not taken with the others. Their clothes, their manner, their quietness, all point to this. I don't know how they were missed, but they will tell us. As for their names, why I'm sure they know their own names." He took a long draw on his pipe and blew smoke rings at the ceiling.

The twins returned and placed the clean dishes where Crag indicated. The tea wafted its fragrant aroma into the air as Crag poured it into mugs.

The twins took cautious sips and glanced at each other. "Thank you very much for the food. My name is Tangshi and this is my sister Tintina. Please call us Tang and Tina; it's what we're used to."

"I am Crag Bithoone, inventor and scientist. And your fearsome opponent over there is Blat Raike, Touring Minstrel of the Rivercrest Conservatory."

Tina's hand flew to her mouth.

"Oh, don't worry, Tina, he's not half bad," Crag's eyes crinkled in amusement, "though he does tend to get long-winded at times. But that's a minstrel for you. More words than brains. Now, take scientists. Well maybe not just any scientist, but me for example. Do I ponder out loud, muttering every little thought that passes through my head? Do I ask endless questions?" Crag stuttered to a stop. "Alright, I do ask a few questions. But do I fabricate answers out of thin air? Do I turn every blessed thing into some kind of metaphor for life? No, no, no. A true scientist searches for the truth. He doesn't dress things up to sound pretty, and he doesn't pretend things are there when they're not, and he doesn't let his imagination fill in those pesky blanks."

Blat wondered where this was leading to and fervently hoped that Crag was not spiralling down into another of his bleak moods.

"So what I see here, my young friends, is a Station that has been stripped of its equipment and people. But to what purpose? And speaking of purpose, what is the purpose of the Stations to begin with? Ah," he raised his index finger, "that is the most important question. And I believe that this incredible Map," he waved his finger at the table, "may give us some of the answers."

Tang looked up, a fierce gleam in his eyes. "I understand a little of what you're saying, sir. But what is important to us, what is very important to us, sir, is to find our parents." Tina reached over to grip her brother's hand.

Crag surged to his feet and paced to the far wall. "Yes, yes. I'm sure we'll find your parents. But you must understand, I can't be sure what the Brothers need them for. Brute work, most likely. Ha. They probably missed the significance of The Map. Stupid, arrogant fanatics. Too blinded by their misplaced zeal. They didn't even spot me following them to the Station that time." Crag rubbed his hands together in remembered glee, then turned and stared at the twins. "It was the Brothers of the Watch, was it not, that took your people? Long black robes? Surly tempers?"

Tang and Tina nodded in unison.

Blat thought it high time for some of that 'dressing up' that Crag accused him of doing. "They would not have been taken," he said in a soothing voice, "if they were not of some importance to the Brothers. They will be treated well." Everything Blat had ever heard of the Brothers made what he had just said a blatant lie, but it was what would get Tang and Tina through the undoubtedly difficult days ahead. "Can you tell us what happened? It might help."

Their hands still linked, Tang began their story. "It would be twenty or so days ago, I'm not too sure, about mid-dayshift. Tina and I were helping Dorie in the kitchens, peeling tubers. When the alarm sounded, we didn't even know what it was and just stood there with our hands over our ears. It hurt. Dorie, who is as old as anything, was worse than us. She curled up on the floor and didn't move. That was when we heard the other sound," he shuddered. "It was like a needle in the back of your head and it sort of turned off the feeling in your body. Tina dropped the peeler in her hand and I watched it fall but my arm couldn't reach for it. It was like I was frozen. Then men in black robes came. I felt a tug on my sleeve and there was Tina pulling me. I tried to shake her off; but she made me move. We moved so slowly that I was sure we would be caught. But we made it to our secret place and waited and waited."

The sack of Station Two had taken five days. As the numbness wore off, Tang and Tina took turns watching the raid from a peephole in their refuge. They could see a very small portion of the activity and could not understand the shouted commands of the Brothers. Their people were used as the muscle to ferry out pallets of equipment and supplies. There was no need for restraints because the first thing that the Brothers had done was gather all the young children into a makeshift corral in the middle of the communal cavern. Six armed Brothers stood guard around the enclosure. The obvious threat to their children kept the adult Stationers in line.

When Tina saw their mother bent under the weight of a pack much too large for her to carry, she pushed past Tang and scuttled to the entryway of their hiding place. Her brother tackled her to stop her from racing out into the midst of the Brothers. She would only be captured too, he said. Wait, he said. They would think of something. They would save their parents. They would save everyone.

They managed to steal food during their vigil and when they finally deemed it safe to emerge, they scrounged through their home for anything that could be of use to them in their rescue mission. But they didn't know where their people had been taken or how to get there or how to free them if they did find them, and as the days passed, their resolve eroded.

"When you were here before, sir, we didn't know what to do. You could have been with the Brothers. But before we could think what to do, you left." Tang straightened his shoulders. "We planned an ambush for the next time anyone came here.

"We heard your voices in the main cavern, but we were too far from our secret place to get there in time. In didn't matter, though, you didn't even notice we were here."

Tina cleared her throat. "I told him that you weren't like the others and that we should just ask you for help but he wouldn't listen. He made us do the ambush to force you to help us." Her tone carried only the slightest hint of disdain. She would defend her brother to the death, but she didn't have to agree with him all the time.

The two men sat in silence digesting what they had heard. Blat could not imagine what the Brothers' purpose was; he only knew that what they had done was against Whitecap Island's laws. Even though the Stationers had only recently revealed themselves, it did not exclude them from the protection of their fellow Whitecap Islanders from their fellow Whitecap Islanders. Interesting that both abductors and abductees should be shrouded in such mystery.

Crag emptied his pipe in the coals of the fire. "You mentioned that you found some items that had been left behind. Any chance of having a look at them?"

Tang shrugged. "It's not much; just some pieces of metal. I'll bring them to you." He rose and trotted out into the corridor. Tina watched her brother leave and gazed in his direction until the sound of his footfalls receded to a faint tap-tapping and then faded altogether.

She turned to the two men. "We are very grateful for the food but you haven't yet said if you would help us." She focused her gaze on Blat and he felt the odd and familiar tingle at the back of his head.

"Oh, no you don't!" Blat put a hand to his head. "Stop that right now!" Abruptly the tingling stopped.

"What? What?" Crag looked from one to the other.

"You mean you didn't feel her little trick? The one where they have a look inside your head while they shove a hot poker in it?"

Tina looked stricken. "I'm sorry. I didn't know it would hurt you. It's something that all Stationers can do once they reach a certain age. But with girls, it sometimes happens sooner." She lowered her head, a blush tinting her neck and cheeks. "Tang doesn't know. Please don't tell him; he would feel bad that I can do it before he can."

"If one of you doesn't tell me what you're talking about, I swear…". Crag clenched his hands to stop himself from swearing.

"It would seem that Stationers are weirdly quiet for a very good reason, Crag. They can speak mind-to-mind." Blat's understanding of the Stationers soared with that one insight. "Am I right?" Tina nodded, still looking at her lap.

Tang returned at that moment and, at Tina's swift shake of her head, Blat and Crag nodded their agreement to keep her coming-of-age skill to themselves.

The twins had discovered a veritable treasure-trove of items that the Brothers had missed. "They didn't find all the secret places. And we're lucky because our father is Guardian of the Readings. He knows about nearly every place to hide things. 'You can't be too careful with your valuables,' he would say." Tang and Tina shared a long watery stare.

So their father was Moqor's counterpart. He might be valuable to the Brothers regardless of their ultimate purpose in taking everybody and nearly everything from Station Two. It was a matter of much speculation as to how the Brothers extracted information from their recruits - the term they used for their prisoners - and Blat did not want to give the twins anything more to worry about. Instead, Blat opened his guitar case, immediately diverting the twins with this strange new curiosity.

When he began tuning the strings, they shuffled a little farther away from him. Blat pretended not to notice. He gently eased the first few notes of a simple, soothing melody from his beloved instrument and was soon lost in the moment. The first song flowed into a second and then a third and, without thinking, Blat added his voice telling the story of a bright morning far out on the water and how the waves glinted in the sunshine and how it reminded the songwriter of the sparkle in his lover's eyes. When he finished the last note, he sighed contentedly and rested his fingers for a moment.

Blat looked up at a delicate touch on his sleeve. Tina stared first at the guitar and then at him with round eyes. Blat read the clear sign of a budding music lover and smiled gently at her.

"Do you want to hold it?" He extended his guitar toward her.

She drew back from him, shaking her head. In less than five seconds, she moved forward again and touched the warm golden wood with tentative fingers. "How does it work?" she whispered.

Blat needed no further encouragement and regaled her with the minute details of how a guitar is constructed.

A short while into Blat's explanation, Tang stifled a yawn, curled up on his blankets, and was asleep in seconds.

Tina, however, paid avid attention to Blat's every word, but even her enthusiasm began to wane after a time. She slouched against the cave wall, her chin lowering in little jerks toward her chest. With a gentle touch, Blat eased her onto blankets and covered her. She mumbled something unintelligible and did not wake. It never ceased to amaze him how deep a child's sleep can be. He remembered when he cared for Sarah's children - or even his own brothers for that matter - that he could pick them up, sling them over his shoulder, climb the stairs, and drop them into their beds all without a break in the light snore coming from his charges. That must be what complete trust is like. What a shame we lose it.

He left Crag puzzling over the weird assortment of items that the twins had recovered and rolled himself in his cloak. His head still throbbed where he had banged it on the cavern floor and his eyes were sore from the continuous flicker of torchlight and firelight. He hoped that they could leave the cavern soon. Regardless, he vowed that he would take a walk in the fresh air first thing in the morning, if it was in fact morning when he woke up. He had lost track of day and night.

The aroma of freshly steeped tea woke Blat from an unpleasant dream. He had been wandering around endlessly in corridors that never opened onto anything new, only each other. It was unsettling. Tina brought him a hot cup and he banished the last vestiges of the dream luxuriating in tea in bed. He could not remember the last time that he had felt so pampered.

"You'll spoil him, lass," Crag shot over his shoulder. He and Tang had spread out the assortment of items and were attempting to categorise them. "He's lazy enough as it is, sleeping in to all hours." Tang grinned at the scientist then bent his head to examine a curious object much like a corkscrew. He placed it with a similar but smaller one.

Blat ignored him and winked at Tina. She blushed and turned to gather the breakfast dishes. "There's porridge," she mumbled as she hastened from the cave.

108

Cup in hand, Blat wandered over to look at the array that Crag and Tang were studying. The weird pieces formed a curious pattern to Blat's eye. He had always loved puzzles and this looked to be a particular interesting one. "Do you mind if I rearrange a few?"

Crag waved his permission and stood to stretch.

Blat moved one piece beside another. The third choice was obvious and a fourth fit snugly inside it. The next six were trickier and took some time. It was like a piece of music where one phrase might easily segue into another and then suddenly there was the bridge that took the melody in a completely different yet harmonious direction. He began to hum as he worked, fitting the notes together to complement the various pieces of the object that was emerging under his hands.

Crag rejoined them and, with Tang's help, used the various corkscrews to stabilise the growing collage. Sometime later, the trio stood back to get a look at what they had constructed. Blat mopped the sweat from his brow with his sleeve. His throat was dry and he felt tired and exhilarated at the same time. The thing - whatever it was - looked right; it looked complete.

The song that had been born at the same time as the device continued to play inside Blat's head and he could picture the chording that would accompany it. He closed his eyes and concentrated to be sure he would remember it.

"If I ever insult your intelligence again, minstrel, remind me of this moment." Crag circled the contrivance, his hands clasped behind his back.

"Unless, of course, you saw something like it at Quirindi's Station?" Blat shook his head. "And you found the pieces of this whatever-it-is cached all over the Station, did you?" Tang and Tina nodded.

Blat opened his eyes and pointed. "If you look here, this could be a reservoir for something, probably some type of liquid. And see here," he directed Crag's attention to a funnel-like shape, "something should go in here too. Any ideas?"

Oh, Crag had ideas, alright. "I think the important question is, what is it for? When we know that, we will have a clue what to put or what not to put inside of it. No, make that two questions. What substances must be inserted to make it activate? No, no. Three questions. Why was it scattered all over the Station? Had it ever been assembled before? When? Why?"

"That's six questions, Mr. Bithoone, sir. I been counting." Tang proudly held up his fingers.

Crag glowered at the boy and Blat moved to put a hand on the inventor's arm. Crag surprised them all with his bellow of laughter. "Right you are, my boy, and plenty more questions where they came from. That's how you find out about things and how they work: keep asking questions until you have the answers you need. You see, you must ask a lot of questions because you don't always ask the right ones and you have to keep on trying out new ones."

Tang nodded his head. "It's like when I ask my father to explain things to me. I have to keep asking and asking and asking."

"He sometimes asks until he gets the answer at the end of our father's temper." Tina rolled her eyes.

"At least I want to learn stuff. All you do is huddle with your friends and sneak looks at Rodger." He added a helpful sneer to his voice on the last word.

"Do not!"

"Do too!"

"Do not!"

Blat had a brief déjà vu of his own brothers having a similar disagreement. Siblings, it seems, are much the same everywhere.

Crag, unexpectedly tolerant at this outburst, continued to study the construct. He touched it here and there, and depressed one of its levers. "It must have something to do with the cylinder out there and the machines that the Stationers maintain. But why was it disassembled and scattered? What purpose could that possibly serve?" He muttered to himself a while longer.

Blat, suddenly aware of his sweaty and dishevelled state, was also just as suddenly aware of how hungry he was. He decided that a wash could wait and, with Tina's help, concocted a meagre meal from the remainder of their supplies. "Whatever else we do," he interrupted Crag's monologue, "we need more food. I'll take Tina with me to forage beyond the cave entrance."

"Yes, yes. Go ahead." Crag waved a hand in Blat's general direction. "We must move this thing to the main cavern where there's more natural light. Whatever its purpose, we shall start there. Tang and

I shall devise a way to safely relocate it without having to take it entirely apart." He absently put an arm around the boy's shoulders.

Whatever bonding was happening between them, Blat was happy to see it - for both their sakes.

After a brisk wash, Blat gathered what they would need and led the way to the cave entrance.

As they neared the entrance, Tina fell farther and farther behind. Blat turned and could barely discern her pale face in the torch's light. He didn't really need to see her face; the anxiety fairly radiated from her. He retraced his steps and crouched down before her. He offered her his hand and she took it in a desperate grip. Blat rose and walked slowly towards the growing light ahead of them.

"You might want to squint your eyes," he said, "like this." Whereupon he scrunched up his face as hard as he could and a little of the fear left her face. "I won't let go of your hand, Tina. I promise." She whimpered a little.

They stood at the lip of the cave entrance for several minutes. Blat took deep breaths of the fresh morning air, for morning it was, the sun only just rising above the eastern cliffs. The light was soft and diffuse and the meadow stretching out in front of them was bathed in pastels.

Tina used her free hand to shade her eyes and her breathing calmed. "Why, it isn't ugly at all."

"No. That it isn't." Blat glanced down at her. "Have you never been out at all?"

She scuffed her sandals on the rocky floor. "Well we do it on a dare now and then, but

112

everyone is scared and excited and running so fast that you don't have much of a chance to look. And sometimes it's so dark that you can't see much anyway. But even the adults don't go out for long, and I don't think it's because they're scared or anything. It's not good for them or something. Stek Framer's father stayed out longer that he should have once and he got so sick that they had to make a bed for him right by the cylinder. The worst part was that no one could speak to him, you know, the way we speak. He got better after a while but it was pretty scary." She stopped abruptly. "Sorry. I talk too much when I'm nervous."

When one of Sarah's children became loquacious, Blat normally slunk away after the first few minutes. Their chatter, however charming, concerned dolls and games and friends. This child made him regret every time he had 'disappeared' during one their talkative streaks. How many times had he missed something as crucial as what Tina had just intimated?

The Stationers not only maintained the cylinders; it would appear that the cylinders maintained them in return. That could be why Moqor had died. That could be why, with the failure of the machines that were linked to the cylinder, their entire population was dwindling - Quirindi had mentioned that their numbers were not what they used to be.

The Brothers of the Watch had doubtless taken the captives to the Station they had commandeered. But why? From what little Blat knew, the Brothers worked towards fulfilling several prophetic visions that their founder had proclaimed to be their destiny. They thought in terms of generations. So if the people of this Station were doomed to die out anyway because of their failing cylinder, how could they be a threat? Were the people of Quirindi's Station also being rounded up by the Brothers? He wished he knew. Wait. Maybe Tina could mind-speak them. But first they needed supplies.

Once her vision adjusted to the increased level of light, Tina proved to have a good eye for finding the edible greens that Blat showed to her, and a deft hand at plucking berries from the bushes. In short order, they had gathered enough food for the day and returned to the cavern's entrance. Tina looked over her shoulder before entering the tunnel and Blat detected a certain amount of regret. She had come a long way in a short time.

Meanwhile, Crag and his apprentice - as Blat had come to think of Tang in his head - had built a platform upon which they had manoeuvred the device. Then, using the rounded legs of a table affixed to the underside of the platform in a way that Blat couldn't quite fathom, they were in the process of rolling the contraption down the corridor. Crag's commands and curses reverberated off the rock walls and seemed to slide off Tang. Good thing the boy had a tough hide for he certainly had a tough task master. With Blat's additional muscle, they continued to the main cavern where Crag called a halt equidistant between the cylinder and the machine room's door, wiped his sweating brow with a grimy handkerchief, and absently handed it to Tang who in turn mopped his face.

114

The meal of fresh greens and berries was consumed with gusto. Blat took Crag aside and told him of Tina's outpouring of information. It was more critical than ever to learn why the cylinders were failing; they could be intrinsically tied to the very lives of the Stationers. It was far more critical than knowing why they existed in the first place, although the answers were likely related.

Blat watched Crag and Tang ponder their next step. Crag had decided that the two artefacts - the device and the cylinder - must somehow be joined and that activating liquids must be poured into the funnel-type holes in the device. Blat knew the bends and turns of the device as well as anyone. He took the time to study the cylinder's surface again as well as the bare walls of the adjacent machine room. There were no protrusions or indents of any kind - no hook, no handle, nothing - that suggested a way to connect them.

Tang and Tina, for all their knowledge of the Station, had never discovered or heard of any such orifice on the cylinder or the machines. The cylinder itself was treated with awe and respect, and only touched by those in charge of its maintenance.

"What, exactly, do they do to maintain it?" Blat asked.

Tang explained the tedious task of removing fallen ceiling particles and dust from the top of the cylinder. It had to be done in such a way so as to cause minimal disturbance to the cylinder. Elaborate scaffolding was erected and moistened cloths were delicately patted over the surface. Dust and other small particles were trapped in the fibre of the cloths.

Tina knew the cloths well; she had often been part of the work team assigned to rinse the cloths. The liquid used to moisten the material chafed her hands and sometimes they bled and then it would really sting. It smelled bad too.

Crag stopped pacing. "What kind of smell was it, Tina? Was it sour or sweet? Did it sting your nose as well as your hands?"

Tina nodded vigorously at the last question. "It was kind of like, well, the waste disposal system just before it needs to be cleaned."

"Ha. Ammonia. That would explain the pitting on the surface of the cylinder."

The thud of many boots reverberated down the tunnel from the cavern's entrance.

Blat gripped Tina by the waist and Tang by the collar and propelled them into the machine room. He crouched by the doorway, dagger in hand.

Crag threw a blanket over the device and disappeared into the shadows at the far end of the cylinder.

The torches that the intruders carried threw tendrils of smoky light ahead of them. The cavern grew brighter.

Nervous sweat trickled down Blat's forehead and stung his eyes; his palm grew slick where it gripped the handle of the dagger. He put the knife down and wiped his hand on his tunic. If he had to die in this rocky tomb, he would die fighting with his weapon firmly in his hand.

Tina leapt to her feet and rushed into the main cavern. Stunned, Blat's reaction time was too slow to stop her. She ran towards the intruders who had reached the entranceway of the main cavern. The tableau of that small girl facing what looked like a dozen swarthy men would remain forever etched in Blat's mind as both the bravest and the stupidest thing he had ever seen.

It was neither.

The leader of the invading troupe knelt before Tina, their foreheads practically touching. Tina stepped back and raised her voice. "It's okay; they're friends. This is Pivka from Station One."

Tang had already sneaked by Blat and was on his way to his sister. "I was going to tell you," Tina said to him in a small voice.

Her brother looked at her for a moment and shrugged. "Girls always get the skill earlier."

Blat rose from his crouch and approached the group, glad to note that Crag remained under cover. He stopped as he recognised some of the faces; these were indeed people from Quirindi's Station.

Pivka nodded at Blat. "Minstrel," he said. Pivka was one of the guards who had been posted outside his cell.

The newcomers set down packs and supplies and made themselves more comfortable. Crag emerged from hiding and joined them. Pivka nodded approval at the new arrival and the small show of protective preparedness towards the children. A fire was laid in the kitchen's hearth and, with a fragrant broth beginning to simmer, they gathered to learn each other's news.

The contingent from Rivercrest bearing Moqor's body had indeed reached Station One. His death had come as no great surprise. Moqor had been well aware of the risks of a journey so far from the Station. He had taken on the task himself because it was he who had convinced the Council that outsiders might be able to help. The beam of light that Blat had seen return tenfold to Moqor was a gift from the people of the Station to help sustain him; it should have lasted longer than it did. This was another consequence of the machinery failing to support the cylinder.

Blat heard the beginnings of a song in gruff Moqor's story; the minstrel in him would remember every detail to retrieve later when he had the leisure to compose.

The senior members of Station One had long known that their lives as well as their livelihood were ending and had chosen to accept this fate. It was, ironically, Moqor's sacrifice that spurred them to further action and convinced them that some - especially the children - might be saved. It was hoped that young Stationers could be weaned from dependence on the cylinders.

Quirindi and her Council sent a contingent to Station Two and another to Station Three; they needed to discuss these things as a people. They hoped to gather all the Stations' Readings together and study them; they believed that by putting all their minds to work on the problem that a solution would be found.

"Wait," Blat interrupted. "Did you say Station Three? When did they leave? When will they get

118

there? Can you communicate with them? Can you communicate with Quirindi?" It seemed that naming the Stations 'One', 'Two', and 'Three' had not just been a convenience that Crag and Blat used for themselves. Sometimes the easiest solution was the right solution.

A grimace flashed across the Pivka's face. Blat immediately lowered and smoothed his voice. "I'm sorry for causing you pain," he murmured. "I will try to remember that we communicate in different ways."

The Stationer bowed his head. "I thank you. Yes, Station Three. They left when we did, four days past, but the way is more difficult and longer. Not all will arrive." Pivka glanced up at Blat. "And, no, I cannot communicate with them or with our own Station. They are both at too great a distance."

Crag rose and strode down the tunnel to The Map room. Puzzled, the rest followed.

"Pivka, have you been to Station Three?" Crag asked without looking up from his study of The Map.

The Stationer nodded. "Once. When I was much younger."

He looked about twenty-five to Blat, then he remembered the longer life spans of the Stationers. Pivka might easily be eighty years old.

"When, exactly, did you go, and what did you find there?" Crag asked.

Pivka considered. "It was forty-eight turns of the seasons past and the Station was much like my home."

"Have you been here, to this Station, before?" Blat interjected.

"No. It was another team that made the journey. It was at the same time and there were Stationers here then. We shared much, but did not visit again. The journey is too perilous to us."

"This Map shows a more direct route to Station Three than the one that I travelled before," Crag said. He pointed with the tip of his stylus at a path that twisted and turned over the top of the glacier. A sane person descended to the valleys that radiated out from the glacier and made his circuitous way along this far less dangerous path. It took three or four times as long, but the odds of arriving alive increased dramatically.

Blat patiently pointed this out to Crag who paid him no attention. He was busy drawing the details of the path onto a scrap piece of parchment. Blat's ever-louder insistence that The Map must be thousands of years old, wildly inaccurate, and totally useless did nothing to penetrate the scientist's concentration.

Tang had been watching his mentor work and laughed. This brought Blat's tirade to an abrupt halt. "But look, Blat," the young Stationer said, "it changes."

By this time Pivka and the eight members of his team, and Tang and Tina were crowded as close as they could to Crag and his glass.

Crag lifted his head to smirk at Blat. "You don't think I would risk my precious hide, do you? This thing is showing current conditions. Here, Pivka," Crag handed the glass to the Stationer, "have a look at the route you took to get here. Tell me if it is the same as when you walked it over the past few days."

The Stationer peered where Crag indicated. After intense scrutiny, he smiled. "It is as he says, the path is the same."

Stationers, mind-to-mind speech, and now maps that update themselves, Blat thought. He really should be getting used to having his world turned upside down, but it still made him a little dizzy.

Crag rushed out of the room. Seconds later, he rushed back in. "Well, come on, Tang. We have to prepare and I need your help."

The boy raced after him.

Blat followed at a more decorous pace leaving Quirindi's Stationers and Tina pouring over The Map.

In short order, Crag and Tang had constructed a sturdy conveyance from assorted pieces of discarded wood and held together with strips of cloth. It was decidedly odd-looking, though. It had both wheels and skis, and the skis were on top and upside down.

"Wheels for the forest trails and skis for the snow," Crag explained to a puzzled Blat. "You just flip it over." The inventor bustled away to gather his things which were strewn about the Station.

They had no time to waste. The other team that Quirindi had dispatched should be about halfway to Station Three by now. If Crag and Blat were to find them before the Brothers did, they must leave now.

***

Tang had been withdrawn and isolated ever since Crag insisted that he and his sister accompany Pivka. *I should never have befriended him*, Crag thought. *No, that would have been just as wrong. For both of us.*

It was time to go and Crag sought him out to say goodbye. "It's a very dangerous place where we're going and I can't take you with me. You understand that, don't you?" Tang shrugged and kept his eyes on the ground.

What could he say to make the boy understand that he wasn't leaving him because he wanted to, but because he had to? What could he say that would show Tang how much he valued him? "Tang. Look at me." The boy raised defiant, hurt eyes which threatened to undo Crag's resolve but instead gave him an idea. "You have a very important job to do." Crag paused for effect. "You must take the device apart, yes take it apart, load it onto to our ski-wagon, and go with Pivka to Station One. When you get there, you must reassemble it." The boy's eyes grew wider and wider as Crag spoke. Crag put his hands on Tang's shoulders. "I know you can do it."

Tang nodded, the hurt in his eyes transforming to fierce determination. "You can count on me, sir."

The exchange was quick and quiet, but had profoundly changed them both.

***

Tina was not as easily dissuaded. "I'm young. I can be away from a Station for many weeks. Ask Pivka, he'll tell you. You need me," she lowered her voice, "you need my mind skills."

It could be an advantage, Blat thought. But it was too risky; he just didn't know enough of what the Brothers could do. On impulse, he offered her his guitar. She had been eyeing it from the very first and Blat had taken a few minutes to show her some of the basic chords. "I was hoping you would look after *Gertrude* for me."

"*Gertrude*?" She lifted a hand to her mouth to hide her smile; her eyes sparkled.

Blat mock-glared at her. "Every musician of high calibre names his instrument. *Gertie*," he sniffed at her snort of laughter, "is very special. You can practice and amaze me with your skill when I come to collect her."

She gathered the case carefully in her arms, hugging it to her chest. "I will, Blat."

Tina turned to tell her brother, but Tang had gone back to the main cavern. Clangs and bangs reverberated down the tunnel signalling that he was hard at work.

CHAPTER 6

Blat was cold and miserable.

The journey over the top of the world, for that was what it had seemed like, had taken three gruelling days of trudging through ice and snow. The glare from the sun on all that whiteness had forced them to cover their eyes with strips of thin cloth. The Map proved accurate, though, and they had had to make only slight adjustments. They were very lucky; the weather had remained calm.

They had seen no sign of the Brothers of the Watch - not surprising since it was unlikely that they would look for intruders coming from the direction of the glacier. To Blat's knowledge, travel across that forbidding and dangerous landscape was only rarely done, and then by those well-versed in ice-lore. The crevasses alone could take weeks to circumvent if, of course, you didn't fall through the thin layer of crusted snow that often hid them from view.

"The advantage that The Map has given us could make all the difference." Crag studied the land surrounding the entrance to Station Three through another of his inventions. The polished glass made distant objects appear nearer and clearer. Brothers could be seen guarding the mouth of the valley that eventually opened onto the western desert. The entrance to the Station itself was patrolled by four Brothers weighed down by an arsenal of weapons. But no attention whatsoever was wasted on the approach from the glacier.

Before darkness fell, Blat and Crag concealed the gear they would not need inside the Station and positioned themselves near the largest chimney vent. If this Station resembled the other two - and Crag's memory of it was fairly certain that it did - the chimney would be enormous by the time it reached the cavern floor, and the fire, especially during the summer, would be small. When supper was finished, the fire would be either banked or, better yet, extinguished and they could climb down using ropes and a breather mask that Crag had invented. Blat wondered how many more of these useful items were crammed into the scientist's baggage. He was a handy fellow to have on a quest.

The sun had slipped behind the glacier and the first stars materialised as if by magic, the clear air polishing them to crystal brilliance. They waited until full dark and then waited a while longer.

"They'll be sleeping by now." Crag rose and stretched the kinks from his stiffened muscles. "Early birds, these Brothers, and creatures of habit. Made it easy for me to wander about when I was here before. Though I didn't stay long; I'm not entirely crazy. They did the same things every day: pray, work, pray, eat, pray, sleep. Very boring."

Crag descended first. He insisted. This was, after all, the first real test of the breathing mask. Crag would make any necessary adjustments and, at two sharp tugs of the rope, Blat would pull up the presumably fully functional mask attached to it.

There were rocky outcroppings nearby to which Blat secured one end of the rope. He then gripped it with his left hand, guided it around his shoulders, and coiled it twice around his right arm. He gave thanks that he had built upon the strength begun in his farming days. The life of a Touring Minstrel kept him fit; he walked everywhere and carried what he needed. With a nod to Crag that he was ready, Blat spread his legs and tensed his muscles, ready to take the scientist's weight as he scrambled over the lip of the vent.

After a few seconds, the strain eased. Crag must have found the hand and footholds that were undoubtedly carved into the stone so that the chimney could be periodically cleaned of soot and of any birds or animals who made their nests in the warm updraft or who were unfortunate enough to have fallen in and snagged themselves on something and been unable to escape.

Blat felt two brief tugs on the rope. He hauled it up, careful not to bang the breathing mask against the side of the chimney. The mask was damp from Crag's breath and he grimaced as he pulled it on over his head. He dropped the rope over the edge and lowered himself after it. His climbing skills were more than sufficient for this easy descent. In a few minutes, he huddled beside Crag and tore the mask from his head. He gasped as quietly as he could.

"I don't much like your so-called breathing mask." Blat hissed in annoyance when he had enough breath to speak. "It didn't filter the air. It didn't let in any air at all!"

Crag looked at him and shrugged. "Needs some work." He dropped the mask into his pack and stepped into the cavern proper.

126

Blat shook his head and hid the rope in a corner of the fireplace. He hoped that the weather would continue mild because a large fire in the hearth would not only block their path of escape but also warn the Brothers of the presence of intruders – burning hemp had a distinctive odour. With those unpleasant thoughts, he followed Crag.

Blat strained his sensitive ears for a repeat of the slight sound he thought he had heard. Yes, there it was again. A sort of hum in the air. It was impossible to tell the direction from which it came; it seemed to be all-pervasive. Crag could not identify it either. It would have to wait. Their mission was to find out if the captives from Station Two were here and, if so, free them. It did not matter for what purpose the Brothers wanted them - it was bound to be bad.

They split up to cover as much ground as possible before morning. Blat chose the immediate vicinity and the numerous private quarters for his scrutiny and left the other communal areas to Crag. The kitchen space had long shelves with fresh and dried food stores as well as dozens of pots and pans and utensils of every description. Other areas were cordoned off by rock-and-wood walls and within these were the various accoutrements of an austere lifestyle: hard benches facing a lectern, hard benches facing a raised dais, and hard benches facing long tables scrubbed clean. The Brothers did not pamper themselves with cushions to sit upon or with decorations of any kind to brighten the harsh stone environment.

He continued to the corridors where at Quirindi's Station the families made their homes in caves chiselled from the mountains' bones. Torches were set into sconces about every fifty feet and illuminated small sections with a flickering, smoky light. Blat held his breath and peered around the edge of the first entryway. It was deserted. After a quick scan, he determined that there was no other way into or out of the tiny living area. The second and third entryways also opened onto empty living spaces. He went more boldly through subsequent openings and when he continued to find nothing, began to check the caves at random. Cave after cave was deserted and cleared of furnishings. By the time Blat reached the end of the fourth corridor, he had found absolutely nothing to tell him the whereabouts of the people of Station Two or what had happened to the people of this Station before the Brothers had taken it over. Or of the Brothers' interest in the Stations in the first place. He hoped Crag had better luck.

Blat trudged back towards the main cavern. The hum he had heard earlier grew louder as he passed a small irregular opening in an otherwise smooth wall. This Station was so similarly laid out to Station Two that he had passed it a couple of times already without noticing. What he did not expect to see, he didn't see. He cursed himself for the lapse. In this, of all places, he needed to stay alert and remain totally aware of his surroundings. Falling into a blasé attitude would send him straight into the path of a Brother.

He squeezed through this aberration in the floor plan and entered a narrow crevice that turned abruptly, cutting off the torchlight that guided Blat's steps. He put a hand on the wall and continued to move forward. The fissure twisted again and narrowed even more. The top of his head grazed rock and Blat had to hunch as well as scuttle sideways. The closeness and the darkness were beginning to unnerve him. He would go a few more yards, he told himself, and, if he found nothing, would backtrack to the corridor.

The crevice doubled back on itself and Blat discerned a dim reddish light simultaneously with a tenfold increase in the volume of the humming sound. He forced his body forward, ignoring the abrasions that the rough wall inflicted on him. The space, mercifully, enlarged and he could stretch his arms and stand to his full height.

The light came through a hole about six inches in diameter that afforded a funnel-like view into a vast cavern, far larger than any other Station cavern he had seen. Rounded humps disappeared into the distance. As his eyes adjusted to the fitful light, the humps became recognisable. Cylinders lay row upon row as far as Blat could see. Something wasn't quite right about them, though: insect-like movement squirmed on the surfaces. The longer he stared, the more unsettling the vision became for the movement seemed to take on an oily iridescence. A small round object bobbed up, then descended again. There was another one. He strained his eyes, wishing for one of Crag's glasses.

A round object bobbed up again and remained raised above the surface of the cylinder and it was facing him. He knew this because it was a person's head, and, with that ominous knowledge, the familiar shapes of arms and legs, hands and feet snapped into clarity. The cylinders were covered with people.

A different kind of motion on the edge of his narrow view channel drew Blat's attention from the nightmare vision of the prisoners. He shuddered at his first close-up look at a Brother of the Watch. The floor-length robe blended with the rock-wall background so that the pasty, hairless head seemed to float above the cylinders. The Brother occasionally touched one of them and made a notation on a tablet that he carried. It reminded Blat of Jamie-the-Cook's attention to his feast breads when he checked and double-checked the temperature and humidity of his masterpieces. His stomach rebelled a little.

A low moan came from one of the prisoners. The Brother hurried to the cylinder and placed his hands on it. A soft glow emanated from the column and seemed to disappear into the Brother. The Brother dropped his hands and swayed, a look of ecstasy on his face. After a time, he wandered along the cylinder, stopped, and removed an object tied to the rope at his waist with which he dug at the cylinder. He then proceeded further along the column and out of Blat's line of sight. There was the clank of a chain being pulled through metal, followed by a thud, and then the sound of something being dragged along the floor. As the

130

Brother emerged into the aisle separating the cylinder from the cavern wall, Blat had a clear view of the Brother's burden: a body. Blat could not tell if the person was alive or dead but from the colours in the clothing, it was definitely the body of a Stationer.

His vigil at the peephole had left his muscles stiff and his mind sickened. He must find Crag. Blat had gone no more than a few yards down the tortuous crevice when he heard angry shouts coming from the big cavern. He squeezed and scraped his way back to the peephole.

The Stationers throughout the huge space were agitated; the silhouettes of their twitching arms and legs looked like some overturned bug struggling to right itself. Blat strained to see what had caused the commotion. Two burly Brothers dragged a prisoner past where Blat could see. There was no mistaking the rangy body and definitely no mistaking the muffled curses that defied the gag in Crag's mouth. One of the Brothers backhanded him and the scientist slumped. The captive Stationers ceased their thrashing about and became eerily still. Blat could hear Crag being dragged further along the cavern wall. The sound of wood scraping along the rock floor was followed by the shuffle of sandaled feet, briefly muffled, and then the wood scraping sound was repeated. Crag was unconscious and incarcerated.

Blat was on his own.

Blat retraced the path to one of the more remote living quarters and sat on the hard sleeping shelf. He drew his knees up to his chest and wrapped his

131

arms around them. He had to think and he had to think more clearly than he ever had in his life. He wished Sarah was with him; she had often helped him sort out a problem. Blat, she would say, think it through logically. First, figure out exactly what you want to accomplish. Make a list of what you know and what you have, and of what you don't know and what you don't have. The gaps between the two are what you work on.

Sarah's reasonable step-by-step process returned a sense of calm and purpose to Blat. Almost anything seemed easier when you had a plan.

What did he want to accomplish? That was easy: free Crag, free the Stationers, fix the Stations so the Stationers can thrive, and don't get killed.

What did he know? He knew where Crag was imprisoned; that was a good start. He also knew where the Stationers were held. They were chained to the cylinders – a simple physical restraint – but they were also likely controlled by some kind of mental power similar to what Tang and Tina had described when their Station was taken. The mental control can be disrupted, as demonstrated by the restlessness of the Stationers in reaction to Crag's agitation. The light that the Brother had drawn from the cylinder looked like the light that Moqor had hoped would sustain him. It seemed to Blat that the Stationers were being forced to provide it for some doubtless nefarious purpose. Crag and Tang could fix the Stations' machines. Probably. Blat chose to ignore the part that much of what he knew was speculation.

What did he have? To start with, he had his wits and determination, for all the good that would do. He moved closer to the entrance where a torch some way down the corridor shed a little light. He rummaged around in his pockets and pack. When everything was displayed on the floor around him, the answer was dismal: a knife, some rope, the stub of a candle, a skin of water, parchment and quill, and some squashed journey bread. *Great,* he thought, *everything a minstrel needs for a major rescue. Ha.*

What did he not know? He didn't know how he would free anyone with Brothers everywhere. He didn't know anything about mind control except that it hurt. He didn't know what the Brothers were up to, why the Stations were important, what the cylinders did, or why the machines had failed. He certainly didn't know how not to get killed.

What didn't he have? He didn't have any mental powers that could be used against the Brothers or help the Stationers escape. He didn't have a hundred strong, well-armed men. He didn't have a secret passageway map. Blat sighed. He didn't even have his guitar.

He considered his 'have' and his 'need' columns. The chasm between the two was wide and deep. He would have to tell Sarah that her logical thinking might be useful for repairing an instrument, but sometimes it only made things worse.

He wondered how much time had passed since he and Crag had stood on top of the chimney. It was one of the many things that Blat hated about caves: you could never tell the time of day. Well, he wasn't tired. He would implement phase one of his rescue strategy. It was simple, really. He would put his right foot in front of his left, then his left foot in front of his right, and repeat the process until something better came to mind. That, he concluded, was the sum total of his deep thinking. There were just too many unknowns and too many variables for him to plan anything. He needed more information, and then he would do what seemed right at the time.

The basic layout of Station Three was familiar but it was Tang and Tina's impromptu guided tours at Station Two that proved really useful. They knew the back ways of a Station like no adult ever could. These passageways were cramped and dark and, for exactly those reasons, mostly unused. The same principal seemed to apply at Station Three.

He sent a word of thanks to his third-year memory teacher. Old Professor Jasden had drilled his students mercilessly. Some of the parents had even expressed concern when their children could not help but recite everything they had seen every minute of the day. For some, it had become an obsession to be able to recall even the tiniest detail. This skill was, of course, essential to the Touring Minstrel since it was a requirement of the job to report anything unusual or noteworthy about a journey. Roads and bridges were repaired, village squares rejuvenated, penal codes changed, and holdings taxed all based on the detailed reports of Touring Minstrels. So once Blat had traversed a tunnel or corridor or had seen a unique rock face, he could recall it.

The main corridors were wide and well lit - places to be avoided. Radiating from these like the arms of the glacier were secondary tunnels which in turn gave access to narrow alleys leading every which way. Even the ever-resourceful twins had admitted to not knowing all of them. Some of the entryways were ingeniously disguised with illusion, while others were too small for a normal-sized adult to squeeze through. No one knew why the smaller ones had been created, but the children of the Station were grateful and made regular use of them. Given Blat's six-foot height and broad shoulders, he could not manage all of them but that still left miles of tunnels to explore in his search for information.

Whoever had shaped the Stations were masters. The floors were smooth and, in the communal caverns, the walls had been chiselled with geometric designs that meant nothing to Blat but were nevertheless pleasing to the eye. The more utilitarian areas had rough bare walls with jagged outcroppings of rock serving as shelves and supports from which the Stationers hung all manner of useful and decorative objects. At least that was the case at Quirindi's Station. Here, in all the tunnels and alcoves that he had examined, all was bare and austere. It was becoming more and more difficult to keep straight in his head where he had already been and where he still needed to check.

Fatigue washed over him. He knew better than to continue his scout of the Station feeling like this. He would rest for a few hours and start fresh. He retraced his steps to the quarters he had chosen and sprawled on the rocky ledge that served as a sleeping pallet.

He woke aching all over from his exertions. The last of the journey bread satisfied his hunger and a mouthful of tepid water finished what remained in his skin. Sustenance would soon become a problem. Blat added it to his mental list of things he did not have.

He kept as parallel to the main corridors as he could manage, winding closer and farther away in turns. The secondary passageways twisted around workrooms and storage rooms, sleeping quarters and larger barracks.

The low murmur of voices wafted from one of these barracks. Blat lowered himself to the floor and crawled from the protection of the alley. He inched toward the edge of the archway that served as the door to the barracks. His back twitched to be so exposed. A leather curtain kept most of the corridor light from disturbing the occupants within. Blat lowered his head to the floor and peered under the curtain.

The murmur of voices came from the direction of a pair of bunks about midway down the room. The remaining twenty or so pallets were empty. The two Brothers must be recuperating from a sickness, or perhaps they were night guards and this was in fact daytime. Regardless, Blat could make out nothing of their conversation and began his retreat to the relative safety of the alley.

"Well, well. What have we here?" The voice was a nearly inaudible whisper. "Keep moving exactly as you were. Don't want to disturb the Brothers, now do we?"

Blat obeyed. Whoever had found him moved soundlessly; he had not heard a thing. If his captor wanted to remain quiet, Blat was all for that. He retreated into the alley until it rounded a corner and hid him from sight.

A boot prodded him to turn over. Blat stared at the worn and grizzled face a few inches from his own. Deep lines etched the dusky skin where the scruffy beard did not cover it and bright blue eyes studied him in turn.

"You got a death wish, boy? Spying on them Brothers'll get you killed for sure. Don't you got no sense? And what're you doing here anyway? This is my stake."

Blat propped himself on an elbow to better study the man. His clothes were made of tough, sturdy material as were his boots. There was no sign of the long robe that a Brother would wear and the fellow had hair on his head - lots of hair. Blat released the tight knot of fear that was strangling him and swallowed.

"Sorry."

The man shrugged. Booted feet sounded in the main corridor and Blat silently followed him further into the depths of the caves. After many minutes of walking, they turned into a side tunnel and abruptly turned again, this time into a slightly more open space.

"Wait here."

Blat stood where he was as the man shuffled around in the dark. Spark hit wick and a cosy living space was revealed in the light of the candle.

"That's better. Come in, come in. Make yourself at home, such as it is." He bustled about a small stove and put water on to boil. "Can't have a story without a bit of tea, eh?"

When the preparations were completed to his satisfaction, the man settled himself on the pile of blankets that served as his bedding and motioned for Blat to do the same.

"So then, first things first. I'm Angus Willoughby, prospector extraordinaire. And I been here since long before them black robes. This is my stake and I mean to get it back."

Blat extended his hand. "Blat Raike, Touring Minstrel, though I seem to have toured myself into the wrong place this time."

Willoughby guffawed and slapped his knee, spilling hot tea on himself. "Blast!" He wiped at his wet trousers. "No matter; was worth it. Haven't had a laugh in a while." He grinned at Blat; his yellow-stained teeth matched the yellowing V-shaped streak that outlined his chin in the otherwise black beard.

The smile vanished from his face. "But that's not all you're here for, eh? I seen 'em catch that other poor fellow. He with you, boy? Thought so. Him I seen before. Looks like he got no sense neither, coming back here. And them other fellas, about six of them I'd say."

Six, Blat thought. *They must be the survivors from the team that Quirindi sent.* "Have you ever

138

seen anyone else, besides the Brothers and the recent captives?"

"Nope, and there ain't no one but me can stay clear of them Brothers. You are just lucky I found you when I did or you'd be trussed up like your friend." He sipped his cooling tea. "Now just so happens I'm heading out for a bit and I'll let you tag along. It does me no good, no good at all, to have the Brothers all stirred up. They're crazy enough as it is with their moaning and chanting and carrying on. Drive a man to drink. So we'll finish our tea and leave them to it."

Blat was thinking furiously. He must somehow convince Angus Willoughby to help. He would not, could not leave Crag to the machinations of the Brothers of the Watch. "Mr. Willoughby, sir," he began, but the old man cut him off.

"I ain't helping no one, you hear, no one but myself. I got my boys to think of and Effie won't never forgive me if I'm late getting back."

Had the prospector turned a little strange living so close to the Brothers?

"And, no, I ain't strange," Angus interjected.

Blat sat there with his cup halfway to his lips. "How long have you had this stake, Mr. Willoughby?"

"Call me Angus; that mister stuff makes me feel old. Now let me think," he rubbed his bearded chin. "I got it from my father and he got it from his father, so I'd have to say somewhere around ninety, a hundred years it's been in the family."

That's a long time, Blat thought to himself.

"Aye, that it is," Angus replied.

"So. Can the rest of your family speak mind-to-mind? Or just the ones who spend a lot of time at the stake?"

Angus squinted at Blat. "It don't work nowhere but here. And you keep that to yourself, you hear? You go telling anybody something like that and they'll just think you've lost what little sense you have." He sighed. "It's them damn big pipes of ore they got stashed in the lower level. It ain't so bad here, but when I get closer, I can here every dumb, stupid thought goes through their heads. It's downright annoying, that's what it is." Angus got to his feet and paced the length of the room. "They're always up to something, especially that one fella - what's his name? Krodan, or some such - he's the craziest of them all. Thinks he's got to save the world from all us sinners. With the things he gets up to, he'll be a damn sight lucky if he can save his own sorry self."

"What's he up to, Mr. Willoughby? I mean Angus? Can you just tell me that?"

The prospector turned to face Blat. "Why the same thing as any greedy, self-serving, power-hungry man I've ever known. He's up to no good. And he wants everybody and everything on dear Whitecap Island to do his bidding." He picked up a travelling pack and stuffed a few items into it. He grabbed a shapeless hat hanging from a rocky outcrop and jammed it on his head, blew out the candle, and left Blat in the dark staring after him. A moment later, he popped his head back through the doorway. "You comin'?"

Blat scrambled to his feet and followed. He realised that he would not get much more information from Angus, but he could at least learn an easier way out of the Brothers' stronghold than up the chimney.

The rough tunnels and short ascents up hand-hewn steps were not part of Blat's memory of Station Two. They must have been hewn by the generations of Willoughbys, which meant that they would not be on any map that the Brothers might have of the Station. They walked and crawled and climbed long enough for Blat's leg muscles to cramp a little. When at last he sensed fresh air, he was more than ready to stop, but the draw of open sky above his head drove him on.

Angus told him that the Willoughby entrance was hidden behind massive boulders and was perhaps a twenty-minute walk from the Station entrance. A narrow pathway meandered around the big rocks and Blat trusted that his memory would not fail him now. He must be able to return.

When they emerged into the open, a hillock hid them from any Brothers on watch. Angus had gone twenty feet before he realised that Blat no longer followed him.

"So. A hero, are you?"

Blat shrugged.

The old prospector studied him for a moment in the clear light of dawn. "Be mindful of the Brothers with a red band around their arms. They're Krodan's henchmen. You can't hardly tell the rest of them apart. Well maybe the Servers or should I say the slaves. They'll be the ones on their knees cleaning up after the rest of them. I wonder how some of them keep on. You don't have the mind-to-mind talk so you won't be much interest to Krodan. That's what he's looking for; it makes him stronger. That's what he's doing to those poor devils in the lower level. Bastard. That was my best site. Found the prettiest opals there." He adjusted the pack straps on his shoulders. "Must be off." He disappeared behind a rocky outcrop, then reappeared further on near a flat patch of scrub grass. Blat kept him in sight until Angus strode into a stand of poplars at the far end of the glacial valley.

With a final look at the brightening sky and a deep breath of the sweet air, Blat retraced his steps through the rocky maze and into the black opening of the Willoughby stake.

CHAPTER 7

Krodan knelt on the rocky floor with his arms stretched out before him in the position of supplication. He had been suffused with the life force of five sacrifices - the most he had dared take at one time - and believed in his heart that the Eldest would smile on him this day. His body vibrated with energy and he could see tendrils of power oozing from him in every direction. It must be enough.

He squeezed his hands into fists and concentrated all his gloriously enhanced power into them. When he felt his fingers sizzle and his palms begin to scorch, when he could stand it no longer, he released the power into the Woman. She began to glow, dimly at first, barely discernible, then brighter and brighter. Her eyelids flickered and it seemed that She took a breath. One of the Brothers chosen to bear witness crumpled in a swoon; this display of weakness briefly distracted Krodan from his mission. That Brother would suffer for his sin.

The Woman raised Her index finger from where it rested on the arm of the throne. Krodan stared with such intensity that his eyes burned. Her finger pointed at him! He was indeed the chosen one! The certainty of it pulsed through him in a wave of carnal pleasure.

As suddenly as it had begun, it was over. The light faded from Her face and Her features solidified back into stone.

Krodan slumped in defeat. His hands felt as if the flesh had been flayed from them in thin strips.

But that was as nothing compared to the anguish that clutched his heart. He would have fallen onto his face if the stalwart Brother at his side did not steady him. Krodan cradled his abused hands close to his aching chest and breathed as deeply as he could.

He had been so sure it would work this time. The Stationers had all been healthy young women and had all borne at least one child. The moon was at its fullest and the tides at their highest. With Her precious finger She had given him the final proof that he was indeed Her consort. Today should have been his triumph: the Woman made living flesh and all the power of all the Stations his to wield. She would have made it so. Krodan raised his eyes to the Woman above all women. The prophecy was clear. She was the key. She had the might to scour the land clean of pestilence and sin. She would prepare the way for the Brothers to bring their life of prayer and sacrifice to the people, to place the people in the hands of those who would care for them and who would not allow the sins of the past to return. All would be under his control. All would be as it should be.

As he gazed at Her, his eye was drawn to Her hand where the index finger remained poised in the act of singling him out among all others. It was surely a sign.

The Eldest, however, would not be happy with today's working and Krodan cringed slightly at the many ways in which the Eldest's displeasure could manifest itself. Upelo would listen and nod in sympathy as Krodan described all that had transpired. Sometimes the Eldest would frown and Krodan was quick to withdraw whatever statement he had just uttered.

Krodan rose from his position of supplication, knees aching, and, unsupported, shuffled toward the archway. Brothers on either side separated the leather hangings allowing him to pass through to the outer corridor. He continued along it at a slow pace, appropriate for one of his rank, even though the Eldest awaited him. This was far from the first time that he had appeared before the august leader of the Brothers of the Watch, but in the perverse way that memory had, the first experience flashed before him now...

The night was full of darkness and screams and he was very afraid.

The silent man held him in a painful grip and the gag in his mouth made it hard to breathe. He tried not to cry because he knew that if he did his nose would plug up and then he would suffocate - suffocate on his own snot. Even at five years old, he knew that was no way to die.

They travelled a long way; farther than he had ever gone. He was tired and hungry and if they didn't stop soon he really would cry and that would be the end of him. Where was his mother? Why hadn't she come for him yet? He should not have thought of his mother. He sobbed against the disgusting rag in his mouth and as he had predicted, his nose began to fill. The man continued to pull him along, an iron grip firmly in the front of his tunic. He struggled against his captor, desperate to rip the gag from his mouth so he could take even a small breath. He was shaken like a dog and bright pinpricks of light danced in his eyes before the world spun around and went black.

When he woke, his head hurt and he felt sick to his stomach. A smelly blanket covered him and he needed for the swaying movement to stop. He pushed the blanket away and sucked in the night air. The man lowered him to the ground and thrust a bladder of water at him. He drank greedily and promptly spewed the whole thing back up. The man huffed in disgust, grabbed the bladder, stomped out of sight towards what sounded like a small creek, and returned with more water. He drank more slowly this time.

"Where's my mum? I feel sick." He hated the whine in his voice but couldn't help it, he was too miserable. "Who are you and where's my mum?"

The man said nothing, just pulled a rag from his pocket and motioned how he would stuff it back in his captive's mouth.

For the rest of that long journey, he remained silent. Tears would suddenly well in his eyes but he was quick to swallow them and even quicker to stifle the sob that burned in his throat.

They arrived at a rock wall and the man scared him badly when he approached with the rag, but this time it was to cover his eyes. He stumbled along a rocky floor for a time and was shoved to his knees. The blindfold was removed as were his clothes. A pair of old men slopped tepid water over him and he was scrubbed with harsh brushes and coarse soap. He was given a black cassock to wear and a bowl of thin soup to eat. His boots had disappeared and the cold in the floor seeped up his legs and made him shiver. Too exhausted to care anymore, he was driven with a dozen other boys into a large cavern lit with pots of fire. They stood before a fancy table. An old man sat there. His robes were pure white; he had never seen clothes so white. One at a time, each boy was brought closer to the table.

The first boy fainted and the second one sicked up on the floor. The third boy also fainted. They were dragged from the room by one of the men who stood in the shadows around the edges of the room. The next boy seemed to glow for an instant. A man came forward and placed his hands on the boy's head. There was a second, fainter glow just before the boy collapsed. The man picked the boy up in his arms and carried him from the room.

It was his turn. He didn't know what to wish for except to go home. The old man raised his head and looked at him. A searing shaft of light pierced his brain. He thought his head would explode. Just as quickly, the light became more bearable and he felt warm and good all over. It was like when his mother came in to sing him to sleep, only better. There was a bit of pain behind his eyes, but he could ignore that. With a sickening lurch, the light was gone. His knees wobbled and he forced them to straighten - whatever else was to happen, he didn't want to be dragged from the room. He felt hands on his head. A little of the light returned and he felt strong again. Just as quickly, all the strength was drained out of him and he toppled into the arms of the man behind him.

Though he wasn't to understand it for a long time, he was now and forevermore a Brother of the Watch.

As the days and weeks passed, he craved the light-in-his-mind contact. It was the only time he felt good. Everything else was pain and learning and hunger, but he was much better than those who had been dragged from the Eldest's chamber. They were the ones who did all the mundane chores. They were nearly invisible and always silent and, when he happened upon one of them cleaning his room, he looked into the other boy's eyes for a moment. There was nothing there - no spark of resentment, no spark of interest, no spark of anything.

He shuddered at the memory and understood the Brothers' wisdom in keeping the servants properly cowled and with their heads bowed. Their minds were inferior and they were fortunate to be allowed to serve the Brothers. Years later as part of his advanced training, Krodan had learned how the testing was done. If the mind was worthy, it withstood the Eldest's scrutiny and the recruit was welcomed into the ranks of the Acolyte Brothers; if it was not worthy, it was purged and the recruit joined the Order of Servers. It was a fair and just system. The strong always ruled the weak.

Krodan could not remember what his name had been before the Brother had brought him before the Eldest or if he had a family. All of that had not mattered in a very long time.

He disciplined his thoughts and entered into the presence of the Eldest.

The founder of the Brothers of the Watch had no need to ask; Krodan gladly opened his mind for examination. He had done everything as it should have been done and Krodan's only wish was for enlightenment. During the meticulous and painful probing, the Eldest shredded Krodan's mind for every nuance of the ceremony, savouring some parts and discarding others. He pondered the significance of the raised index finger for some time.

When Krodan was at last released from the Eldest's grip, he embraced the oblivion of unconsciousness.

Shortly into his convalescence a stranger was found lurking in the tunnels. He hurriedly dressed. As the Priest Elder of this Station - an appointment which Krodan relished - he would question this outsider himself.

***

Blat retraced the route to Angus's room without difficulty and continued on to the peephole where he had last seen Crag. From what he could tell in the decidedly narrow view, the cavern was darkened and the only sound came from the occasional movements of the Stationers lashed to the cylinders. He must try to help his friend regardless of how terrified he was.

A number of corridors curved in the direction of the cavern and then veered elsewhere. Between getting no closer to his goal and being constantly vigilant for Brothers, Blat's nerves were frayed.

The Station remained still and he refused to let the opportunity escape him. He took a small sip of the water that Angus had generously left him and tried a totally new strategy - he moved in a direction away from the cavern. Almost immediately, the tunnel doubled-back on itself and opened onto a smaller corridor that curved in an arc. At the end of the arc, the corridor widened into a circular space with a choice of three entranceways. Through the first was a stone statue of a woman. She seemed to beckon to Blat and he stepped into the room. He shook his head to clear it; he did not have time to linger. Beyond the second entranceway was this Station's map room, and through the third was what he was looking for.

The cavern seemed larger at floor level. The walls to each side of the archway disappeared into the shadows beyond the rows of cylinders. There was no sign of Brothers guarding the prisoners. Blat found this strange until he remembered that no sane person would enter an enclave of the Brothers.

He edged along the wall in the direction that Crag had been dragged. A number of alcoves were carved out of the rock. Most were open and bare, but a thick wooden door had been wedged into place in front of one of them where, normally, a leather curtain sufficed to keep out wayward drafts and ensured privacy. Blat dug his fingers into a crack between two of the boards and gently pulled. No movement. He pulled harder, fearful of any noise the wood would make scraping the floor. It did not budge. He examined the door more closely, feeling every square inch. There must be a way to open it, perhaps a trick of some kind, but he couldn't find anything. *What would Crag do?* he wondered. *Ha. Probably blow it up.*

He sat with his back to the door and closed his eyes. He needed to clear his mind. He breathed in slowly through his nose and let it out even more slowly through his mouth. His hands roamed the wood that he could reach from his seated position. It was then, when he was quiet, that he felt the knot in the wood. His sensitive fingers determined its size and texture and noted that it protruded from the wood around it. He depressed the knot. With a silent puff, the door popped open a scant inch. Blat jerked out of the way and came to a crouch. Nothing assaulted him except for the stench. It would seem that the Brothers of the Watch had shoved Crag into this tiny, airless cell and had just left him.

"Don't talk," Blat whispered, unsure if Crag was even conscious.

After a cursory glance to ascertain that no one had entered the cavern, Blat shoved the door fully open and winced at the scraping noise; it couldn't be helped. Their time undiscovered could be over in an instant. The small space had forced Crag into a foetal-like position and the scientist could not, at first, straighten his long legs. Ignoring the feeble protests, Blat hauled Crag up and over his shoulder. He closed the door with his other shoulder, pushing it snugly into the archway.

The sound of many feet in one of the side corridors injected Blat with the strength to break into a quick shuffle. He cleared the archway exiting the cavern, traversed the antechamber, and reached the refuge of one of the dark, unused tunnels. His burden had remained completely silent throughout the journey for which Blat was grateful. Belatedly, he hoped that Crag was not injured.

He had worried for nothing. After some water and a brief rest, the scientist resumed his belligerent, though somewhat subdued, nature.

"Took you long enough. I could have been crippled in there, not to mention dead from thirst." Crag sipped a little more of their diminishing supply of water. "My story's a short one: they caught me, tied me up, and threw me in that closet. Period. I couldn't hear a damn thing through the door and they didn't even ask me any questions. Left me to rot. Cocky bastards. What about you?"

Blat gave him a brief summary of what he had discovered so far: an alternative exit from the Station thanks to Willoughby, the peephole into the cavern, The Map room, and the room with the statue of a woman in it. And he had freed Crag. He had not done too badly, even if he had to say so himself. Maybe they really could find a way to free the Stationers. First they must rest, especially Crag, before the next foray into the Brothers' tunnels. A careless mistake could get them both stuffed into the closet-sized cell.

The Station was once again inordinately silent when they crept closer to the main corridors. Blat didn't much care what the Brothers were up to as long as they stayed away. They made their slow, careful way to the circular space from which the cavern, The Map room, and the room with the statue were accessed. He left Crag in The Map room and went to have a closer look at the statue of the woman. Perhaps they would find clues to help with their rescue mission.

He was not prepared for the lifelike beauty of the lady in the chair. Her skin looked soft and warm and Blat expected her eyes to open at any moment. He shoved his hands into his trouser pockets to keep himself from caressing the gentle indentation just below her cheekbone. The indigo of her robe flashed with brilliant gems set in intricate patterns around her bodice and drew his eyes to the swell of her breasts. What was he thinking? The woman was chiselled from stone. But this was unlike any other statue he had seen - this was the work of a master of his craft and a gifted artist.

Blat tore his eyes from the woman and studied the scrollwork on the ornate chair upon which she was seated. He had seen many forms of writing in his studies and in his travels but did not recognise these symbols. The rest of the grotto, though it felt more like a shrine, was bare except for a few urns of various shapes and sizes, and the ever-present torches in their sconces. He looked inside the urns and studied the drawings on them; he was no further enlightened about the woman. Or about why the Brothers had shackled the Stationers to the cylinders. Guilt twisted his guts. Here he was mooning over some statue when people were suffering and perhaps even dying a few yards away! He went to find Crag.

The Map at this Station also had a reproduction of the local stars and planets and details of Whitecap Island. It explained why the Brothers had left such a useful tool at Station Two; they didn't need it with an exact replica already in place.

In addition, there were smaller map tables scattered about the room. After a cursory glance, Blat determined that these contained not geographical images but rather technical ones and Crag was fully absorbed in his study of them. Blat doubted that Crag had even heard him enter. Exclamations of discovery and mutters of frustration were expressed in roughly equal measure as the scientist slowly moved around the room. Crag was particularly annoyed that he did not have his writing materials or any of his equipment; the Brothers had confiscated his pack when they had captured him.

Blat knew better than to interrupt him just yet and perhaps the new tables would yield something useful. He decided that the most useful thing he could do would be to stand guard.

The slap of sandaled feet snapped Blat out of a pleasant reverie about the woman. He hissed a warning to Crag but it was already too late. The sound of the approaching Brothers must have been dissipated by the convoluted tunnels and it was only when they were nearly upon them that Blat had heard them. The Map room offered few places to hide. Crag crouched behind the legs of the largest map table and Blat flattened himself to the wall beside the archway. At least they would have surprise on their side for what little time it bought them.

The Brothers, and there were many of them, strode past the entrance of The Map room and entered the main cavern with the cylinders. And the Stationers.

There was no time to scramble to the hidden peephole. After a few seconds of whispered discussion, they decided to risk exposure to find out what the Brothers were up to. Blat figured that if they could make it unseen to the cavern archway and if the Brothers were far enough away, they could creep along the base of the cavern wall to one of the alcoves. If he remembered correctly, there was one a few yards beyond the entrance.

Blat brought his mouth close to Crag's ear and whispered his plan. Crag nodded for Blat to lead the way.

The Brothers had gathered around a cylinder that stood apart from the others. Blat had not been able to see it from the peephole's limited range and had no time to look around when he had freed Crag. It was about one third again as big as the others and had a much smoother finish. A not-so-gentle nudge from Crag propelled him the last few feet into the alcove's protective shadows. They crouched on either side of the opening and peered at the ritual unfolding before them.

A low chant, barely audible at first, began to swell from the normally mute throats of the Brothers. As the volume rose, it echoed through the cavern, bouncing and reverberating from the walls and roof. "Quaaw-drick! Quaaw-drick!" It sounded like the hoarse squawk of a crow. Blat had no idea what it meant.

The Brothers moved in a slow shuffling gait around the cylinder with their arms stretched out before them and their heads thrown back. In the torchlight Blat had an unobstructed view of their faces. He wasn't sure what he expected but the normal-looking features were a little disappointing. The only thing of note was that not one of them had a single hair on his head. Their naked pates glistened dully in stark contrast with their black robes.

Distorted shadows of the Brothers rippled across the surface of the cylinder and seemed to give it a sluggish life of its own. It was then that Blat noticed how still the Stationers had become. Their constant small movements had ceased and they lay like the dead. Alarmed, he rose from his crouch and took a step beyond the alcove. Crag gripped his wrist and pulled him back.

The Brothers' chanting reached a crescendo and as one they pivoted and placed their hands on the cylinder. The very air seemed charged with power. A blinding light burst from the cylinder. Blat squeezed his eyes shut.

The glare quickly receded and Blat squinted through tearing eyes. The Brothers were strewn every which way on the stone floor. He blinked rapidly and used the sleeves of his tunic to brush the water from his face. As his eyesight recovered, he saw that all the cylinders in the cavern shone with diminishing levels of brightness the farther away they were from the large cylinder. The Stationers remained motionless.

A rustle of cloth brought his attention back to the Brothers. Those that could were crawling to others who still lay prone and administered a firm slap to first one cheek then the other. Soon, they were all on their feet, hoods up, and retreating through the archway, but in somewhat less than the crisp order in which they had entered. The cavern was once more quiet and unguarded.

Blat and Crag emerged from their hiding place. "Did you learn anything?" Blat asked. "And thanks for holding me back," he added.

The scientist waved a hand in acknowledgement and was soon engrossed in studying the big cylinder.

Blat cautiously approached the nearest Stationer. She was an older woman, about forty or so, pale and very thin, but her expression exuded bliss. He examined the shackles that bound her limbs and was surprised to see that the Brothers had pounded metal staples directly into the cylinder. In addition, a long chain was threaded through rings in the shackle around her neck and lay across her throat. He would have to pry underneath the rings to reach the staples and, in the process, tighten the chain which would strangle the Stationer. Very clever. The ends of the chain were embedded into either end of the cylinder with no visible way of extracting it. Maybe Crag had something sharp enough to cut through its links. With the chain out of the equation it would be a matter of popping the staples to release the shackles.

"Help us."

He would never have heard her feeble murmur if he had been even a few inches farther away. Blat brushed the hair from her face. Her eyes were open and weary. He reached for his water bladder and let a trickle wet her dry, cracked lips.

"More. Please."

She took two or three sips of water. Her eyes closed. Blat gently touched her shoulder but she did not reawaken. He went to the next person but all the water in the world would not help this Stationer - he was clearly dead. Blat gritted his teeth in anger and moved on. The next person struggled for consciousness, Blat could see it, but he just did not have the strength. He checked cylinder after cylinder. Many were alive but all too many were dead. The Stationers were treated as nothing more than a power source to be drained until it killed them.

He had not learned the fate of the Station children as yet and, he had to admit, was a little afraid to find out. Likely, the suitable boys were indoctrinated into the Brotherhood and the girls put to work. What kind of work that was, Blat refused to think about.

His heart felt like it was being pried open and forced to accept what could and did happen on his world. The atrocity of it all staggered him. Blat no longer cared about finding a great story for a song. He no longer cared about the dreaded repercussions of angering the Brotherhood. He no longer cared about what would happen to him. He only cared about ending this.

He ran to the far end of the cavern. His guess was right: this was where the Brothers kept supplies to bind their captives. He found a short length of chain and raced back to where Crag scraped at the base of the main cylinder.

"I don't care what you're about to discover." Blat shoved the chain into Crag's hand. "We have to find a way to break through this. I'll try to find out how the Brothers cut it."

Crag glanced at the length of chain in his hands and looked more closely at Blat. He recognised fanatical resolve when he saw it – he had seen it many times in his own shaving mirror. It would be best to humour the minstrel.

Without waiting for a reply, Blat returned to the far end of the cavern, snagging a torch from a wall sconce on his way. He found bent staples, a selection of mallets in various states of disrepair, and more short lengths of chain, but nothing that resembled a cutting tool. He scrutinised the entire circumference of the cavern, illuminating cracks and crevices with the torchlight. He examined the alcoves. Except for the clutter at the back, there was nothing useful. It made sense, Blat knew, to keep anything beneficial as far away as possible from your prisoners in the unlikely event that one of them broke free.

Crag had had no luck either. "If I had my pack," he muttered.

"Then that's our next task. Come on."

They took a long, circuitous route to the main eating area, scouting out the whereabouts and numbers of Brothers on their way. The plan was to remain hidden until the common room was empty, and then to see if anything was left of the equipment they had hidden in the chimney, at their best guess, about three days ago.

Time slowed to a crawl. Silent Brothers went about the mundane tasks of preparing and serving food to equally silent Brothers. They had likely acquired some telepathic ability from being in the vicinity of so many cylinders. Whatever the reason for their silence, it was eerie.

One of the servitors wrapped leftover food and stored it in a locked cupboard. If the lock was not too difficult, he and Crag would have fresh provisions. A smart Touring Minstrel learned to use every opportunity that presented itself.

When the last of the cleanup was done, the Brothers filed down the corridor that led to their sleeping quarters. Blat and Crag waited another full hour to make certain no one returned.

Blat crept out from behind the barrels that had hidden them and, keeping low to the ground, made his way along the wall to the hearth. It was still warm from the supper cook fire but there was sufficient leeway for him to skirt around the embers. He grabbed the rope from the far corner and their sooty but sound packs and rejoined Crag. He had a moment of self-congratulation before Crag clutched his arm and pointed. Blat's blackened boot prints were clearly visible on the lighter grey of the rock floor.

The broom Crag swished around did nothing more than spread the soot into grimy blotches, but at least the imprint of a boot was eradicated.

160

Perhaps the Brothers would think it was one of their own who had stomped around inside the fireplace. *Not likely*, Blat thought. In his turn, Blat applied a wet rag to the blotches which only served to add a muddy texture to the mess.

With a sigh, Blat turned his attention to acquiring food. The cupboard's lock was easily sprung and he chose random packages so as not to leave it too obviously ransacked. In a flash of inspiration, he filled a sifter with flour and sprinkled it over the sooty mud on the floor. It didn't fix it, exactly, but it was no longer immediately noticeable. It might buy them a little time.

They returned to the captives' cavern and, from his recovered pack, Crag cobbled together what he believed would break the Stationers' chains. It would be a bit noisy but there was no help for it.

The problem that Blat struggled with was how to sneak that many people out of the Station. Would they even be able to walk? He may have overestimated their odds of success, but the alternative was unacceptable. He would not leave them to be butchered by the Brothers.

They had counted forty Brothers in their skulking about the Station. Blat found it hard to believe that so few Brothers had captured and contained so many Stationers. With sixty cylinders and eight Stationers per cylinder, that was nearly five hundred people, although not all were still alive. The Brothers must have more than chains and the threat to the Stationers' children keeping them in line. He remembered the mind pain that Tang had told them about, and Blat had seen

161

firsthand the euphoric effects of the glow that emanated from the cylinders - it acted like a drug. And, with no food or water, the Stationers were weaker with each day that passed.

Crag was ready to try the paste that he hoped would blast the chain apart.

"Shouldn't we try it on a piece of loose chain first in case it's more powerful than you think?"

"That would be the smart thing to do." Crag shook his head, his brow furrowed in worry. "But I just don't know if I have any to spare."

They chose the cylinder located furthest from the cavern entrance. The scientist used his dagger to place a small amount of the gooey substance on a piece of chain as far away from a Stationer as possible. He covered it with a bit of rag and beckoned to Blat for one of the torches.

With his arm outstretched as far as it would go, Crag touched the fire to the rag. The pop was loud but not as bad as Blat had feared; some of Crag's earlier explosions had been, in a word, thunderous. This one simply did the job. Crag was definitely a good man to have on a quest.

Blat ran the chain out through the neck rings, pried the staples up with a shard of metal pipe he had found, and helped the first Stationer down from the cylinder and to a seat on the cave floor. At this rate, it would take far too long to free them all. Blat put that thought out of his mind and shoved the pipe under the next staple.

Some of the survivors were in better shape than others - stiff and dehydrated, but desperate to escape and willing to help their neighbours. Relief flooded through Blat. This was the one thing he had been secretly counting on. With extra help, they stood a much better chance.

Pop after pop, Blat heard Crag continue down the line of cylinders. The finite amount of the explosive paste was not yet depleted. As more and more Stationers were freed, the rumble of voices grew louder. Blat hurried from group to group begging them to be quiet and to follow him.

The Stationers trailed in his wake. Some carried the unconscious and others provided stronger arms for the weaker to lean on. They had to leave the dead behind; nearly one third of the Stationers had been murdered by the Brothers. He wondered if Tang and Tina's parents were among them. He guided them to Willoughby's exit. Blat had briefly considered taking separate paths to the same destination but there was no time to be clever about it. His gut told him to hurry.

He smelled fresh air and led the Stationers into the blush of pre-dawn light. Blat assigned the hardier survivors the task of getting everyone clear of the entrance and hidden among the tumble of boulders and the nearby hillocks. There, they could rest and forage for food. The glacier above provided hundreds of rivulets of icy meltwater that would quench even their great thirst.

Blat felt an urgent need to help Crag but the passageway was clogged with Stationers blocking the path. He muscled his way through apologising as he went and veered into a secondary tunnel. He would risk the more public, and dangerous, corridors to reach the scientist as quickly as possible. The Brothers seemed to visit the cavern at random intervals and Blat had no way of knowing when they would discover the escape.

Crag was nearing the end of the cylinders when Blat rushed to his side. There were three more to go.

Another pop was followed by a sharp tug from two burly Stationers. The chain clattered to the floor. Two to go. They had a good system going, so Blat concerned himself with helping the newly freed Stationers down from the cylinders.

It was then that he heard the sound he was dreading - sandaled feet slapping along the corridor. They were out of time.

A glance confirmed that the final cylinder's chain was broken and that the last of the Stationers shuffled toward the tunnel.

He grabbed Crag's sleeve. "Any stuff left? I'll distract them."

Crag shoved the remainder into Blat's hands. There was an ounce or two.

"If you light it all at once, get as far away as you can." He held Blat's eyes for a few precious seconds. "I'll get them out of here and to safety. Do your best, boy." Crag hurried into the tunnel.

There was no time to think. Blat slapped the goo on top of the nearest cylinder, jammed a length of rag into it, and touched the torch's flame to the end of the cloth. He ran as fast as his tired legs could carry him and dove in between two rows of cylinders.

Even with his hands over his ears and his head tucked into his chest, the roar was deafening. Bits of cylinder rained down.   Screams from the direction of the Brothers warmed Blat's heart. Intermingled with the screams of pain were screams of outrage.   Blat realised that he must have destroyed, or at least badly damaged, the large cylinder. He grinned through the dust that settled on his face.

He rose to a crouch and scuttled to a little-used tunnel; he would lead the Brothers in the opposite direction of the escape route. At the entrance of the tunnel, he cleared his throat and took a deep breath.

"Hey!   Over here!   Brothers of the Watch!" Several heads turned his way.   "Watch this!" Whereupon Blat made a very rude gesture and ducked into the tunnel.

CHAPTER 8

Krodan shook with fury. The Acolytes on either side of him made futile attempts to brush the dust from his ceremonial robes. Irritated, he impaled their minds with a shaft of pain and took grim satisfaction when they fell to their knees. But he should not squander his power on grovelling servants; he would need all his formidable strength when the Eldest learned of this latest sacrilege.

As the dust settled in the cavern, he saw the true extent of the debacle: not only was the holy Quadric in shards, but the Stationers were gone.

He lurched forward, stumbling on an obstacle in his path. A Stationer lay at his feet - a dead Stationer. Many more were strewn about, left to rot on the stone floor. He sent a command for Servers to get rid of the corpses and cleanse the cavern.

Rage bubbled to the surface. His Protectors would find the violator; Krodan would have at least that much satisfaction. The wretch, whoever he was, would suffer a great deal before leading the Brothers to the escaped Stationers. And then he would suffer more for destroying the Quadric. Krodan hoped he was young and strong so that he would last a long, long time.

Perhaps the Woman would like to watch. Perhaps She would open Her eyes and show him Their beauty. A stab of lust clenched his groin. She would welcome his seed and together they would create a god; he would be the father of a god. Sometimes, the thought astounded even his considerable ego.

With an effort, he disciplined his mind to focus on the present. First, he would interrogate the transgressor.

***

Blat raced along the passageway and skidded into a dark offshoot. He kept his arms stretched out in front of him to guide the way; he could not risk a torch. Shortly, he very much regretted this necessity. The bangs and bruises on his knuckles would delay his next session on the guitar, if he ever had a next session on the guitar. He was not at all surprised by how much that particular thought pained him.

He could not see the visual cues he counted on and Blat was no longer completely certain where he was. This was a dangerous situation: he could stumble into a main corridor or, worse, a main living area. He slowed his pace and strained to hear the least sound. He cursed the Brothers for their annoying silence. It was not, therefore, as much of a shock as it should have been when the soft shush of a robe came an instant before he was grabbed from behind and his arms pinned to his sides. A second Brother breathed the stench of old onions into Blat's face as he bound Blat's wrists together and gagged him, all in inky blackness and complete silence. He was shoved along the narrow passageway and into a larger tunnel.

A sturdy rope was secured to the bindings on his wrists and the Brothers took turns tugging on it, pulling him off balance and banging him into the rock walls. When the way became wide enough, a Brother walked on either side and gripped him painfully just above the elbows.

They emerged into the nexus leading to the cylinders' cavern, the statue of the woman, and The Map room. Familiar territory, for what it was worth. The Brothers brought him before the statue, shoved him to his knees, and forced him to bow his head.

He heard a third Brother enter the room behind him. Blat's captors moved back to stand guard at the entranceway. He felt the strange prickling in his scalp. It quickly transformed into dull nails pressing into his brain. Blat tried to block it and he was heartened when the pain lessened. But the new Brother merely toyed with him. The nails sharpened and seemed to pierce his eyes, his ears, his tongue. He toppled to the floor. He screamed through the gag in his mouth and tears ran down his face. He could not get enough air. Purple circles swam before his eyes and he fainted.

He was in the same position when he awoke although the gag had been removed allowing him to breathe more freely. The familiar prickle touched his scalp again and a Brother knelt beside him to stuff the revolting gag back into his mouth. The pain began again.

When he came to the second time, he was given a little water. He swallowed before he cared whether it was poisoned or not. His throat was raw from the muffled screams that tore it and he was exhausted.

"Where are they?" The voice was soft and rough at the same time. "You might want to tell me before I do permanent damage to your brain."

Blat gritted his teeth. "If you do that, I won't be able to tell you anything at all, now will I?" He manoeuvred a little to the left and peered through the torchlight at his tormentor. He was young and had the first facial hair that Blat had seen on a Brother. It was styled into a goatee and was as black as the eyes that glittered beneath the edge of his cowl. Blat had described many evildoers in his day - they were the necessary antagonists for many a story. But he would be hard pressed to convey the malice and loathing that oozed from this Brother. And that wasn't all of it. Blat sensed a cold calculation that kept a bubbling cauldron in tenuous check. This was a man balanced on the razor-sharp edge of barely controlled sanity. His tormentor snarled softly; it was the most ominous sound Blat had ever heard.

"Now you will feel the power I wield."

Blat was gagged for a third time. His head was held still while strong fingers forced his eyes open. He tried to look anywhere else but at the black stare of this Brother. It was no use; he fell into the abyss.

Between eternities of pain, Blat drifted in and out of dreams. One of them began as a pleasant vision of working on the family farm, surrounded by his brothers and father. Another was of a favourite inn where he liked to perform. A third was of Sarah and Jamie-the-Cook and Talitha sitting around a table and laughing at one of his stories. And, oddly, there was one of a woman whose name

169

he didn't know or couldn't remember, but she was beautiful even with her eyes closed. She could be the one to help him forget about his futile desire for Talitha.

His pleasant reveries faded as if a dark cloud passed overhead, and he found himself wandering aimlessly in the ancient ruins of a castle. No matter which way he turned, the way led ever downwards. Rock walls closed in on him and grew damp and slimy, the steps more treacherous. Feeble light showed nothing of where he was going and there was no turning back. He slipped and fell, banging his head on the worn steps.

He lay still, remembering and clutching the fleeting dreams of his life, certain that they were important. Phrases from childhood rhymes danced in the distance. If he could only catch one of them he could dance too. He reached, felt himself become thinner and thinner, and brushed a word in a friendly refrain. He coaxed it towards him, ever so gently, so as not to frighten it away. It settled in his hand and he rejoiced at the brief warmth that flooded through him. From that tiny fragment and after a lifetime of pain, he was able to reconstruct the entire song. He rested, content for a while. As if song called to song, he sought another. It was a roundelay and he had to concentrate to hear the overlapping parts. After that, it seemed that all the songs he had ever known paraded themselves before his eyes. With each new piece of music, he became more solidly Blatolomew Raike. The music wove around him and cocooned that vital part of his mind that made Blat who he was and he gripped it hard.

***

"You must not." One of his Priests whispered. "The Eldest would not be pleased if you kill him."

Krodan sent a blinding-fast strike into the mind of the Priest; he would not tolerate such insolence. The man crumpled and was dragged from the chamber, whimpering like a child. Krodan sneered.

He turned to the Woman and stiffened. A single, perfect tear glistened on Her cheek. He rushed forward and gently touched Her hand but it had not become the warm flesh that he yearned for. She remained encased in stone; only the tear was real.

At first, he was at a loss. Why would She weep for him when he was in complete control, when he was at the pinnacle of his strength and virility? Then he understood: She was his and if any tears were shed, they were tears of pride for him, for his bold strategies to extract the whereabouts of the Stationers from the interloper. Even as he watched, enchanted by the beauty of it, certain that She had at last chosen to grace him with Her presence, the tear solidified into a drop of glittering crystal rock, returned to stone like the rest of Her. Krodan's chest constricted.

He must explain this to the Eldest as well as his lack of success in gleaning information from the prisoner. He savagely kicked the minstrel with his booted foot. At least the Stationers had some worth, but this one? He did not even have the gift; it was

171

like scouring the mind of an insect. He was a useless singer.

The escaped Stationers had been tracked onto the glacier but signs of their passage were obliterated by a fierce storm that continued to rage even now. The Stationers must be dead given their weakened state and such weather conditions. The Eldest would reprimand him for that too. Krodan's lip curled in a snarl. He kicked the prisoner again, hearing the satisfying crack of a rib.

The sound of quick footsteps entering the Woman's sanctuary was yet another affront to Krodan. She must be approached slowly and with reverence. He turned and dealt decisively with the offending Brother who, in his cowardice, stepped back, but not quickly enough to escape the biting lash of Krodan's fury.

Krodan smoothed his hand over the sudden dampness on his head. "Well, what is it?" He resented speaking out loud, but the Brother would never again be able to use his mind that way. Krodan sighed. The Eldest would not like that very much either.

"The Eldest awaits," the Brother hissed through his pain.

"Re-tie this one's hands behind his back and make certain his ankles are secure. Leave him here," he commanded. The Woman would see how he dominated other men and how he would soon dominate Her. It was what She would want.

The mind-burned Brother bent to do his bidding.

"And take that gag out. We don't want him suffocating on his own mucus." Krodan wanted Blat very much alive.

***

Blat lay on the stone floor. His side throbbed where Krodan had kicked him and his head felt as though dull blades had scraped his brain pan raw. The flickering torchlight made his eyes ache and the taste in his mouth… it was better not to think about his mouth. The bindings around his wrists and ankles were tightened beyond his feeble attempts to loosen them. At least the Brother hadn't wrenched his shoulders too far and Blat was able to manoeuvre himself into a sitting position with his back against a wall and his legs stretched out in front of him. He needed to rest and gather what meagre strength he had left. Krodan would return and if Blat had not escaped by then, he would at least prepare himself as best he could for the next onslaught.

He breathed in as deeply as his cracked rib allowed and exhaled slowly. He felt a minuscule loosening of the tension in his body. Breathe in, breathe out. Simple. He willed his muscles to relax - not an easy thing to do trussed up as he was. Gods, he would pay a year's earnings for a sip of water. He opened his eyes to study his surroundings.

The woman was looking at him. Blat did not think to question how this could be; he did not think

173

of anything at all but that she was looking at him and that it was the most important thing in his life.

She had eyes of the clearest green and of the deepest pain. Blat shoved himself to his feet, scraping his back along the rough wall, but ignored this new pain. It was insignificant in her presence. She glanced down at his feet and Blat remembered the ropes in time to avoid embarrassing himself with a fall. He hopped closer to her, hating the inelegance of it.

"My lady," he bowed his head, "how can I help you?" His throat was raw and his voice rough from the screams that he hadn't been able to hold back.

He detected a flicker of laughter in her eyes and Blat realised how ill-suited he was at the moment to help himself, let alone a woman trapped in stone. He smiled through his humiliation and searched the room. The edge of the pedestal which held her chair looked sharp. He turned and squatted so that the rope that held his wrists together could be rubbed against it. He ignored his protesting shoulders and rubbed faster. A strand gave way, then another. In minutes his hands were free and he spent a moment in breathless agony while the blood rushed back into his fingers. He undid the bindings around his ankles and shoved the rope into a pocket. He smoothed his ragged tunic, pushed his fingers through his hair, and turned to face the woman.

"It would seem that I just needed a little incentive," he rasped.

Her eyes smiled at him then took on a look of such despair and longing that Blat felt the tears sting

174

his eyes. "What must I do, my lady? I know nothing of magic."

The muscles in her jaw moved ever so slightly; she was trying to speak. Blat clambered onto the pedestal and brought his hand to her face, gently touching her cheek. The tiniest of frown lines appeared on her forehead. Then her lips parted.

At first, only a slight hiss was audible. Blat leaned forward so that his ear was next to her mouth. "Destroy cylinders."

Incredulous, Blat stepped back, nearly falling from his perch. "You want me to destroy the cylinders?" She blinked once, slowly. He took that for a yes.

His mind raced. The cylinders were somehow linked to the Stationers' wellbeing. If he destroyed them, would he be destroying any chance the Stationers might have for survival? Were the cylinders in the next room even the same kind of cylinders that the Stationers needed? He couldn't think, his head hurt too much. Gods, where was Crag when he needed him?

The woman's eyes pleaded with him before a great weariness seemed to come over her. The beautiful green eyes dulled, her lips paled and froze. Blat reached a trembling hand to her - she had returned to stone.

His chest was tight with the sob that struggled to escape. It couldn't be possible that he had lost her just minutes after he had found her. He was in love. There was nothing that the logical part of his mind could say that would change his heart. He studied her face so that every curve, every exquisite

175

line, every feature was etched in his mind. With a final caress, he turned and stepped down from the pedestal. He must remain free until he could come up with a plan.

The corridor outside her shrine was empty. Krodan had the arrogance to believe that Blat would remain incapacitated until his return. *Too bad for Krodan*, Blat thought.

He crept along the wall and entered the main cavern. There was no sign of the chaos that he and Crag had wrought except for a slightly lighter strip of stone floor where the main cylinder had been. It was as if the Stationers had never been brutally shackled and chained to the cylinders, their life being slowly drained out of them. Blat made for a tunnel on one side of the cavern.

One thing was certain: if Blat didn't get a drink of water and soon, the greatest plan in the world would remain just another untried idea. He wound his way towards Willoughby's hideout and stumbled into the humble refuge. The water in the skin was tepid and carried the taste of its carrying sack, but to Blat it was sheer ambrosia. He was careful to sip when what he really wanted to do was upend it and pour the entire contents down his throat. Blat knew it would be some time before his singing voice regained its flexibility and mellow tone. Further foraging produced a soft, wrinkled apple and some desiccated meat. He chewed methodically, sipped water, and chewed some more. Exhaustion crept up on him like a warm tide and he slept, curled on Angus's hard pallet.

When Blat opened his eyes he wasn't sure, at first, if he was awake or asleep. He rubbed his eyes. The total darkness was exactly the same whether his eyes were open or closed. After a few minutes of groping, Blat found what he needed and lit the stub of a candle. Everything in the small cave was exactly as it had been before he slept. Somehow Blat thought things would have changed, that there would be answers waiting for him. *Ha.*

He felt an urgency to do something, anything. It would be a waste of time and energy to gallivant off into the tunnels like some kind of brainless hero. Without a plan Blat would just tire himself out for nothing or, worse, get himself captured again. Krodan would not be as gentle the next time.

Blat forced himself to sit and consider. Crag and the Stationers were free - two things accomplished from his list. Even though Blat had lost track of the number of days since the Stationers were rescued, it was likely that they had already reached their empty home. It wouldn't be long before Crag found another shortcut using The Map and brought them to Station One. Quirindi would welcome them and her Station had provisions.

He hadn't gotten himself killed. Yet.

That left one task unfinished: fix the Stations. This was where Crag was supposed to come in; he was the genius scientist-inventor.

But all that was before Blat fell in love. Everything was different now, everything had changed. Her desperate plea filled his mind, repeating itself over and over: destroy cylinders, destroy cylinders, destroy cylinders. It would free

177

her and he needed this more than anything, regardless of the price.

Love was surely blind. It made a man do a thing that he would otherwise never consider - something that would bring him unending shame and self-loathing, something that would take his life and break it into a thousand pieces. It would make him destroy the cylinders - all the cylinders everywhere. It would make him destroy what gave life to an entire struggling culture.

He would do it without hesitation. Blat would sacrifice everything and everyone for just one kiss.

***

That maniac Krodan had finally made the tiniest crack in the black wall suffocating her and, at long last, she could begin chipping away at her prison.

Mir d'Luka seethed. How long had it been? The darkness permitted no tracking of the passage of time; it had relentlessly persisted until she was doubtless quite mad, only how would she know? A bubble of laughter clogged in her throat.

It had begun so easily. Her kind had always had the ability to mind-speak. But when space travel became practical, disaster struck. They discovered that time away from the home planet seriously debilitated their ability for telepathy and in the breakdown of communication many lives were lost. Without the instant mind-to-mind orders, the crews of the complex spacecraft made mistakes, and mistakes in space were lethal.

178

One of the teams assigned to resolve the problem, the d'Arrolu team, discovered unusual properties in an ore found only in the molten rock beneath the surface of the southern landmass. They returned to space confident that the cylinders created from the magma would sustain their telepathy. It wasn't until much later that the requirement to renew the ore periodically was understood. Side effects such as sterility and brain anomalies became more frequent. Even with the demands of a burgeoning population, the leaders decreed that use of the ore in space travel would be strictly limited to gathering raw resources and never, under any circumstances, would it be used to exploit an inhabited world. The risk of contaminating or damaging a susceptible species was too great.

Mir was second officer on the exploration ship *d'Capi* when the primitive planet was discovered on a routine sweep. Its natural resources were astounding and it wasn't until after the retrieval Stations had been established that sentient life was found. There were only a handful of primitive creatures and Captain d'Iklomed was blinded by the possibilities that this rich world offered. It meant prestige and wealth. It meant a political position, and d'Iklomed was nothing if not ambitious. Mir tried to talk sense into him: the law stated that they could not touch a planet with intelligent life on it no matter how simple that intelligence was. Captain d'Iklomed knew this.

She had no choice but to circumvent d'Iklomed and bring her concerns to the rest of the crew. She was ignored and outvoted. They wanted to return with the hold filled to bursting. They wanted the bonuses and the promotions that would come their way. The homeworld would be very grateful.

Her sense of honour would let her do no less: she sent a message.

It was intercepted before it left the ship, and, in an attack she could never have imagined, the ship's medical officer trapped her in this stony nightmare. A procedure designed to preserve life had, with a perverted twist of thought, become this unending hell.

In a flash of what she assumed must have been guilt, they left her mind intact. It was against their most ingrained code to damage that precious organ. She snorted - a strange experience without the use of a throat or a nose. It would have been a far, far kinder act to have killed her outright. She had no doubt at all that a misshapen, evil thing dwelled inside her grown large feasting on thoughts of vengeance.

The Brothers came. At first, she thought the babbling inside her head was an aberration of her fractured mind, talking to itself. It went on for some time and, eventually, a pattern emerged. She perceived that it came from elsewhere, from outside herself. If she could have, she would have wept.

Although she came to know their language, she did not understand, and did not want to understand, their strange ways. What mattered was that they treated her like a goddess. It was child's play to manipulate them, and she had the beginnings of a ready-made army at her command.

Krodan's infusions of energy were pitifully insufficient and only increased Mir's frustration. And when the control cylinder was shattered, her body began the slow process of reanimation. But it was still not enough. Krodan would keep trying to free her; that was a given. He had the ego and the warped desire to pursue his goals no matter what the cost. His little bits of power did help, though, and Mir used him ruthlessly.

And now there was that ragged fellow Krodan tortured; he might also prove to be useful. She slipped into his weak mind and compelled him to do her bidding.

***

The light was barely discernible at first but was getting brighter. It could be Willoughby returning. *Better to be safe,* Blat thought. He slipped down the corridor to a cubbyhole with a convenient escape tunnel.

From his hiding place, Blat heard the intruder enter Willoughby's cave. He strained his ears to hear a familiar voice. Instead, he heard water tinkling into a pot and the rustle of pouches being opened. He waited, ignoring the rocky protrusion trying to make a permanent dent in his shoulder.

The aroma of stew wafted into his nostrils and saliva immediately pooled in his mouth. Still wary, he crept along the passageway to the dimly lit entrance of Willoughby's refuge.

"Ah, there you are. Took you long enough," Crag said, turning with a bowl of stew in his hand.

181

"Here, have some of this." He peered at the minstrel. "You look like you could use it."

Blat grinned and reached for the food.

They ate in companionable silence until every morsel was gone and the fragrance of hot tea wafted from their mugs.

"Some of them didn't make it," Crag said, not looking up from his mug, "including Tang and Tina's parents; probably wouldn't have made it anyway. The life was gone out of them, and no amount of food and water and rest was going to give it back. I don't know what would have. It was that blast of light from the big cylinder - you remember, when the Brothers did their fancy dance around it - that finished them." Crag stood to pace, saw as if for the first time the close confines of the cave, and sat down again. "Poor kids. They're in Quirindi's care now and she'll look after them. But she can't risk any more of her people to help us and I can't say as I blame her."

Blat pictured Tina with *Gertrude* in her lap and was very glad that he had given the guitar to her for safekeeping. Music would provide some small consolation. And Tang. The young Stationer would throw himself into the mystery of the device. It would help, but only time could heal certain wounds. Time... "Wait, wait. How long has it been since we were separated?"

Crag pulled at his lower lip and considered. "Let's see. A few of the stronger ones went up to lay a false trail for the Brothers and then that storm blew in. We rested for two days at Willoughby's spread. Nice place. One of the Willoughby clan,

Lorren I think, snuck back in here to get an update from The Map. He didn't lay eyes on you though. I told him you could take care of yourself and I was right. The new snow made the trek across the ice a mite slower, a little over six days, and we lost a few more along the way." Crag rubbed a hand across his forehead. "I brought them directly to Quirindi's Station. Made no sense to take them to their empty home."

Blat could only nod. He must have been under Krodan's mind torture for days.

"I came back as soon as I re-supplied and checked on young Tang's work. Remarkable boy. Quirindi's people were working on the riddle of the device when I left, but I figured you'd been wandering around on your own long enough, getting into who knows what kind of trouble. So I'd say, all in all, I've been gone nearly two weeks. Now, what have you been up to?"

The tale was quickly told since Blat had spent most of the time in a state of pain or unconsciousness. When he came to the part about the stone woman, it was as though he was seeing her for the first time again. The rush of emotion and sense of urgency was overpowering.

Crag grabbed his shoulders as Blat tried to lunge passed him and out of the cave. He shook him until the glazed look left the minstrel's eyes, and made him sit and have a drink of water. "What's the matter with you? Have you lost your mind? You can't go harrying off like that." Crag studied Blat's face. "What have they done to you, boy?"

The surge of mindless reaction faded and Blat trembled. He put his head in his hands and winced at the tenderness of his scalp, just behind his ears. He sipped more water to cool his burning throat. "He was inside my head for days. As far as I can remember, I didn't tell him anything important. But I probably did." Blat looked at Crag, eyes full of misery and pain. "He wanted to know where the Stationers had gone. It won't take him long to send his henchmen to Quirindi's Station."

"Oh, buck up, boy. Any moron can read The Map. He must have been rooting around for something else and we could spend the rest of our doubtless short-lived lives trying to guess what it was. No. We will do what must be done."

Blat swallowed. "And what would that be?"

"Simple. We round up the Brothers and convince them of their wicked ways. They'll be ever so contrite and we'll all live together happily ever after." While he spoke, Crag rearranged the cloth-wrapped bundles inside his pack. He glanced at the minstrel and chuckled at the dumbfounded expression on his face.

"Idiot." He continued to chuckle as he finished with the bundles. He turned his attention to a spool of twine, examined it, and stowed it on top of the bundles. He drew the pack straps tightly together, securing his cargo.

"Those are explosives, aren't they? You mean to kill them." Blat was on his feet and gripped Crag's arm with angry strength. "You can count me out. I've never killed anyone in my life and I don't plan on starting now."

The two men glared at each other. Crag wrenched his arm from Blat's hold. "Just a minute. Who said anything about killing? You've got it all wrong. I'm going to trap them is all. What kind of a man do you think I am? Kill them. Though I admit it's tempting. No, no. I'll just make it so they can't do any more harm." He swung his pack onto his back. "Coming?"

He strode through the archway and down the corridor. Blat stared after him for a moment, then shoved the remaining food packets and water skins into a second pack and hurried out of Willoughby's haven.

A little breathless, Blat caught up with the scientist at the next cross-corridor. "What's the plan?" he whispered. "Did you bring enough explosive to destroy the rest of the cylinders?"

"Damn it all, boy. Use your head. Even if I wanted to blow up all those cylinders, the entire cave system might collapse on our heads. Can't do it. Don't want to do it. The Stationers might need them."

Blat looked away. Crag stared at him in the brighter light of the opening where they had stopped. The minstrel had changed; not just his ragged, thin appearance - that was easily explained by his incarceration. It was his eyes. There was a fever there, a burning.

Crag knew quite a bit about problems of the mind, given the swirling mess inside his own head. The gods knew he fought every moment of every day for control. Damn it all again. He could barely fix himself let alone try to fix someone else. They

185

would have to wait for a healer to help Blat. He thought briefly about leaving Blat behind and discarded it. He needed help to set the trap. There were so many things that could go wrong: they might be caught, or the simultaneous charges might not be quite so simultaneous, or the Brothers might never again all be in the place at the same time. As a reluctant afterthought, he added that Blat might sabotage the mission or sneak off on his own mission. He would just have to be extra vigilant.

The scientist's words were playing over and over in Blat's head. He didn't care if the entire island fell on his head as long as she was freed from her torment. He would see it done.

These caves and tunnels had become his entire life. Blat knew them better than anyone. She had seen to that. In their all-too-brief encounter, she had given him a gift: a gift of knowledge. It was overpowering in its enormity and detail, and much of it was incomprehensible. Tantalising bits and pieces swam before his mind's eye only to recede into the depths again. If the glint from a mineral shard in the rock brought the briefest memory of sunlight to him, it quickly passed. If the tinkle of water reminded him of an old melody, it vanished with his next step. He would free her. That was all that mattered.

She had told him her name - Mir - beautiful, like she was.

Blat watched as the scientist moved cautiously from one corridor to the next. He followed, not particularly concerned about the route they were taking; he knew that Crag must wend his way to the

186

cylinders' cavern - it was the only place where the majority of the Brothers convened. Crag thought he could end the Brothers' stranglehold by capturing the ones at this Station, but he was wrong. The Brothers had not been idle these past years, and they had not been stupid. Their bid for power was built on more than the terror and fear of village peasants: it infiltrated all the great merchant houses, the political parties, and the other religions. Even the Conservatory. A slight flutter of alarm discomfited Blat. He shrugged it off like so much rock dust and it evaporated from his mind.

He did not wonder any longer how he knew these things. Information was of interest only if it was useful in freeing Mir. Blat scanned through what he needed from his newly acquired storehouse of facts. If his calculation of the date was correct, a new moon would rise in the next day or two. This was a holy day for the Brothers, and one that they celebrated in a frenzy of flagellation and penance of both mind and body. It would begin privately in individual cells, and continue in the big cavern where they eyed each other to see who had inflicted the most damage on himself. They would fling themselves onto the cylinders and rub blood and tattered skin into the surface, draining themselves of energy. At the pinnacle of the ceremony, the Priest Elder - Krodan, who had watched the entire spectacle from the sidelines, would feed on the power that the Priests had so painfully and generously infused into the cylinders. It was a vile exhibition of masochism and gluttony.

That moment of the Brothers' total depletion and Krodan's ecstatic gorging would be the perfect time to destroy the cylinders.

It should be easy to convince Crag that the Brothers would assemble in the cavern; after all, they had already witnessed one ceremony take place there. Crag would want to seal all the exits except for one that could be easily controlled. What was his plan after that? To confine the Brothers until they died? How would he provide food and water for them? How would he remain continually vigilant? Was he expecting reinforcements to help carry out his plan?

Blat shrugged these questions aside. What he should be concentrating on was getting the explosives away from Crag and placing them where they would do the most damage to the cylinders. If the Brothers were destroyed at the same time, it couldn't be helped. There was nothing he could do about it. He brightened. If they were destroyed, they would be out of the way when he escorted Mir to the outside world. With that thought, he felt completely justified in his actions and pushed the bothersome twinges of panic and guilt from his mind.

The circuitous route that Crag chose had Blat fuming at the delay. He grabbed Crag's arm. "We should go directly to the spy hole that I found, wait until the main cavern is empty, and set the charges. We already know all the entranceways and we already know that the Brothers convene there. Sure, they might gather in another place but we can't wait for some other gathering in some other place and hope we stumble upon it. Trust me on this. There will be a ceremony of some kind and soon."

Crag looked at him in disbelief and shrugged off Blat's hand. "And you know this how?"

"Krodan spoke of it, gloated about it really," Blat explained, lying with ease. "We have work to do and not much time to do it. And the longer we wander around, the sooner one or both of us will be caught again." Blat shivered. Though the memory was wispy and vague, he felt certain that he did not want to be caught again.

"If you don't stop nagging at me...," Crag snarled. He needed to check the offshoots of the main cavern to be sure that his blasts did not destroy more than they were meant to, and the only way to do that was by the long, convoluted route that meandered around its perimeter. He didn't have to explain himself to this upstart minstrel controlled by who knew what compulsion, although Crag was beginning to have his suspicions. Blat hadn't mentioned the stone woman in some time. Did he think that Crag would forget Blat's inexplicable reaction when the minstrel spoke about her, insisting that he must free her? She was a statue, for the gods' sake! Crag was deeply worried about what was going on inside the minstrel's head, but there was no time to do anything about it even if he knew what to do.

Satisfied at last, Crag acquiesced to Blat's continued and ever more insistent demand that they sequester themselves at the location of the peephole. When they arrived, they ate a quick meal while Crag described what was to be done next.

It was the middle of what the Brothers called their quiet time, though that was a misnomer if ever there was one since they barely spoke or made much noise of any kind in their not-quiet time. However much Blat was confused at the moment, the minstrel was right about one thing: they did not want to be caught again. The Brothers' quiet time reduced the risk. They entered the main cavern.

While Crag unwrapped and placed the explosives, he had Blat run wire as thin and flexible as sewing thread around the base of the walls. He watched the minstrel for a moment admiring the near invisibility of the Stationers' invention. The wire was a thing of beauty. It was extruded from the same phosphorescent minerals used in their clothing on top of which was painted a light coating of paste made from an ore dust that Crag had never seen before. The result was a fuse wire that didn't sputter and flare down its length, but rather contained its fire until released wherever the minuscule layer of ore paste was scraped away. The Stationers used it in mining and, Crag was delighted to learn, in their creation of light displays for festivals. He hoped that he would see this with his own eyes one day.

When all was in place, they gathered grit from the more remote edges of the cavern and scattered it onto the length of the wire as well as onto the small bundles of explosives placed to either side of the tunnel openings. At the main entrance that led to the antechamber, Crag used even smaller bundles of explosive. He only wanted to barricade this entrance, not completely block it. He then cut a separate length of wire and tied either end around fist-sized rocks. He gave this to Blat with instructions to return with it to the spy-hole and lower one end of the wire down to him.

Crag surveyed the work as he waited for Blat to make the journey. Unless you looked closely, the uneven mounds on either side of the entranceways appeared to be nothing more than a build-up of grit accumulated over time. He trusted that he had understood what Willoughby had told him about how the rock would react and had calculated the size of the charges correctly. No time for misgivings now.

Once he tied off the wire that Blat dropped down to him, he would join the minstrel in their hiding place and the wait would begin. When as many of the Brothers as they dared wait for were in the cavern, Crag would light the wire and the timed charges should completely seal all but the one entrance. This was when he would have to trust Blat if the plan was to work. One of them had to be near that entrance and be ready to light more charges in case the smaller bundles did not provide a sufficient barricade. It was crucial to block the Brothers' exit, but have enough of an opening for negotiations with the trapped men. So far, Blat was co-operating. Crag prayed it would continue.

Blat hurried from the cavern with the wire and rocks, keen to have Crag's scheme in place. But there was no possible way that he could pass Mir's prison and not step in to gaze upon her. His breath left him in a gasp. She was more beautiful than he remembered and needed his help so badly. "Soon, my lady, soon," he whispered, and forced himself to turn his back on her and continue with his task.

It served his purpose to destroy the tunnel entrances and, as he assisted Crag, he had counted the extra charges in the bottom of the scientist's backpack. There should be enough to damage many of the cylinders. The timing was the only outstanding issue and, being a musician, his timing was very good.

All was in readiness. Crag and Blat took turns at the peephole, alert for any activity. They tried to sleep but the cramped space allowed for no real rest.

Late on the second day of their vigil, the Brothers began to shuffle in. Crag, whose watch it was, roused the minstrel with a soft-spoken word.

The Brothers were stripped to their loincloths and covered in bloody gashes made by the short whips with which they continued to mutilate themselves. It was terrible to see, but more terrible was the look of rapture on their faces. They murmured nonsense and wove among the cylinders in a stumbling, disjointed shamble. One of the Brothers trailed his hand along the cylinder below the spy-hole and Crag saw the dark smear he left behind.

It was time to light the charges. As Crag turned to tell Blat, a rock struck him a glancing blow on the temple. His last thought was that he should have known the minstrel would wait until now. It was, of course, the optimum time to sabotage Crag's plans.

Blat was not fooled by the scientist's seeming faint. He chose a larger rock and raised it to strike a

192

second blow, this time to do it right. He willed his arms to bring the stone crashing down, to smash his enemy's face into oblivion. *Enemy? Oblivion? Where had that come from?* Blat furtively glanced towards the crevice, fearful of finding Krodan there. It was empty. Puzzling, but unimportant. He turned back to finish what he had started. His arms would not obey. Perhaps he could kick his adversary's head hard enough to kill. He swung his leg back as far as the space would allow. The limb refused to move forward. What was happening to him?

Time was wasting. Frustrated, Blat secured his foe with some of the blasting wire and stuffed a rag in his mouth in case he regained consciousness and shouted a warning. Blat really should kill him, but his mind skittered away from taking this most sensible action. Enough delay. He must focus on what was truly important: destroy the cylinders to free her. It was the reason that he was in the Brothers' Station in the first place; it was the reason that he had been born.

That didn't seem quite right. He recalled vague scenes of a family on a farm. How could such a life have prepared him for what he must do now? Shaking his head, he reached for Crag's backpack and the surplus explosives. While the Brothers were in the throes of their purification ceremony, he would affix charges to strategic cylinders and blow everything at once – entranceways and cylinders.

The drug coursing through the Brothers' bodies to enhance their religious experience had the side effect of making the outside world disappear. Blat

193

took care not to actually jostle any of them and, with speed and efficiency gained from his earlier work, had the cylinders wired in short order.

Blat squatted in the main entrance to survey his work. Pleased, he dashed to Mir's prison. She was as he had last seen her: beautiful and in pain. He rested his forehead on hers and was infused with the instant rapport they shared. She was proud of him; she would reward him; she would be his. Blat basked in the glory of her praise and promises, content to remain there forever.

"Destroy the cylinders! Do it now!" Her sharp command sent a stab of pain through his head, dropping Blat to his knees. His eyes watered and the sudden memory of another who had caused him great pain confused him. Hadn't it been a man that time? And hadn't he wanted some kind of information? Hadn't he wanted Blat to betray a secret?

"Do it now!" A second, sharper stab of pain lanced his skull.

Bewildered and in pain, Blat couldn't understand how he had displeased her. He lifted his head from where he cradled it in his hands. As his eyes cleared, they fell upon a discarded rag. He knew that rag. He knew the size of it. He knew the smell of it, even though it was too far away for its fetid odour to reach him. He gagged. That piece of filth had been in his mouth, choking him, leaving him breathless and weak. This was where Krodan had tortured him.

The veil of compulsion with which Mir clouded his mind receded. He raised his eyes to look at her.

Rage distorted her beauty into something ugly. Or had she always looked this way and he was only now seeing the creature that was imprisoned in the statue?

***

Mir was losing control over the human. She must act swiftly if she was ever to escape. She gorged herself with the dark power she had hoarded over the long years and aimed a potent command at the one who would not fail her: Krodan. He would not be as effective a minion as this one at her feet, but he would obey, of that she was certain. Even to destroying his precious cylinders.

***

Blat backed out of her chamber. Their link was much weakened, but in her agitation, Mir let slip a fragment of her plans. She would stop at nothing in her obsession for revenge. It was enough to terrify him. He raced back through the tunnels to Crag's side.

The scientist was conscious and extremely irritated. Blat debated for a moment about removing the gag, but decided that Crag would not likely vent his entire spleen with forty Brothers within earshot.

Crag spat a great gob of saliva onto the rock next to Blat's boot and grabbed the proffered water skin. He swished a mouthful around and spat it next to the saliva. Blat moved his foot a few inches.

"It's about time you came to your senses." Crag would never admit that he had let his guard down or that he should have incapacitated Blat as soon as he realised that the boy was compromised. But what was done was done; no need to let the minstrel know how he had failed them both.

For once, Blat struggled to find the words. He would have killed forty Brothers and unleashed Mir - whatever she was - onto the world. He explained what he thought had happened to him as best as he could. Crag listened with uncharacteristic patience.

"Some kind of mind control," Crag postulated when Blat had finished, "and somehow the cylinders are both blocking her return to flesh and blood and giving her mental abilities. But if the cylinders are destroyed how will she continue to use her mind control? I wonder if she's been controlling the Brothers all along? If so, why didn't she make them free her before this? Why did she have to wait for us?" Crag squeezed past Blat to enter the passageway beyond their hidey-hole. He had to think and in order to think, he had to pace.

Blat, too, considered the conundrum. The scientist was right about the mind control – he should know. But what was of far more personal consequence to Blat, and he came to the same conclusion whichever way he looked at it, was that Mir was at least as evil as Krodan and they had both been inside his head. Could he trust that his thoughts were his alone? Would he even be able to tell the difference? Could he still be Mir's puppet? Was a piece of Krodan concealed in his mind only to strike when the time was right? Blat felt a moment of empathy with Crag: it was a terrible thing to lose control of one's mind.

CHAPTER 9

Krodan slumped in a stupor of satiation while the rest of the Brothers shuffled in the general direction of the corridor that would lead them back to their quarters and the much-needed medication. There was no time - and Blat had no inclination - to sneak among them a second time to undo the charges he had affixed to the cylinders. He and Crag would have to wait for another opportunity or come up with a different plan. Crag was not happy but he didn't berate Blat as much as the minstrel had expected him to. Maybe the scientist was getting soft. *Ha.*

The last of the Brothers and, finally, Krodan left the cavern, and Blat surprised himself by welcoming the profound silence that descended. He got to his feet. "I have to remove the extra charges as soon as the way is clear."

Crag nodded from his watch at the peephole. He stiffened.

"What is it? Let me see." Blat and Crag exchanged positions. It was Krodan. He had returned and he was alone. The Elder strode swiftly and with purpose towards the cylinders. He stooped to examine the explosive paste that Blat had affixed to the underside of one of the cylinders. Horrified, Blat watched as Krodan returned to the main archway, knelt on the rock floor, and gently uncovered the blasting wire. Like a man possessed, which he undoubtedly was, the Elder stood and removed the nearest torch from its sconce. "No," Blat whispered.

Crag edged him aside. He took one look, turned, and grabbed their packs. He pushed Blat into the narrow crevice. "Move, you idiot."

They wriggled through to the main corridor and sprinted down its length, heedless of discovery. The blast knocked them to their knees. They scrambled to their feet and raced towards Willoughby's exit and into the light of midday. They kept on running.

"Wait." Crag's voice was hoarse from exertion. He was bent double, gasping for breath. "How much did you use, anyway?" he wheezed.

"All of it." Blat passed him the water skin.

"Oh." Crag took a sip. "That explains it."

They turned to see dust billowing from the myriad chimney and air vents, and, especially, from the direction of the main entrance. A deep rumbling continued; the noise inside the rocky warren must be deafening.

Blat sank to the ground. He covered his face with his hands and rocked back and forth. He was a murderer. A multiple murderer.

"None of that, now." Crag's rough voice was devoid of sympathy. "You weren't the one to set the stuff off and, mark my words, it wasn't Krodan either. It was that woman. That's exactly what she wanted, wasn't it? That's what she was trying to make you do, wasn't it? And you were strong enough to break free." His voice softened. "No, it wasn't you, boy, never you."

He heard the words; Blat always heard the words. In the logical part of his brain he understood them. But in his heart he would never forgive himself. If, deep inside, he hadn't wanted love so badly, would he have fallen under her spell? It was his weakness, this wanting, and she had exploited it. Sure, he had been strong enough to break free from her thrall but only after the rag had triggered his memory. He should have been stronger at the outset, he should have fought harder, she should never have been able to breach his defences. Love had nearly undone him before and, to protect himself from feeling that kind of pain again, he had built a barricade around his heart. She should never have gotten in, and now forty people were dead. All because he couldn't control himself.

"We should check for survivors. Maybe the Willoughbys will help. Come on, lad." Crag continued up the trail.

Blat watched him go. How could anyone have survived such a catastrophe? But if there was even a small chance, he would do everything he could. A flicker of hope was infinitely better than the blackness into which he plunged.

"Well," Angus spoke for his family, "we can't have the Brothers saying we never did nothing for 'em. Let's go lads." Angus and his four sons loaded their packs, kissed their womenfolk goodbye, and headed down the trail. The Willoughbys were anxious to help, equally drawn to assist the men in trouble as they were to have a close look at the fresh rock faces that would have been exposed in the blast.

Before they returned to the Station, Crag and Blat finished the thick stew that Mrs. Willoughby

200

insisted they have. They looked a might peaked, she'd observed.

"You tell that Angus we'll be along shortly with bandages and medicines. If you find anybody in there, they'll likely need a bit of doctoring." Effie Willoughby shooed them out the door and turned to her daughters and daughters-by-marriage, issuing orders like the head of the household that she was.

**

Krodan huddled at the base of Her throne. Her magic protected them from the chaos of the mountain breaking apart around them. She was so radiant that he could not bear to look upon Her for more than a few seconds at a time. She met his worshipful glances with a haughtiness that belonged to the Queen that She so clearly was. And he was Her loyal servant. He would do anything for even a fleeting touch.

Mir waited for the final tremors of the blast to subside. She had gotten very good at waiting.

But, oh, she felt wonderful! As the cylinders had shattered, the force that held her imprisoned was instead channeled into reviving her and she was filled with an ecstasy beyond anything imaginable. Hot blood coursed through her veins, her chest rose and fell in the bliss of a breath, her hands - free at last from the arms of the medical chair - flexed in the pure joy of movement.

It was a shame that these cylinders had had to be destroyed for her to live but she knew where to find more to sustain her abilities. Oh, yes, there were a great many cylinders on this backwater planet. Enough for even her great need.

Krodan fondled the hem of her gown, distracting her from her glorious return to life. She glared down at him. His cowl was thrown back to reveal the smooth skin of a well-shaped head. She would likely find some function for him at the main site, but perhaps he could have an additional use. She reached down and ran her fingers over his pate; he trembled under her touch. It had been far too long since she had possessed a man, body and soul.

***

The Willoughbys descended into the main cavern using the same technique that Crag and Blat had initially used. They found a smaller, intact chimney that led directly into the centre of the cavern where the Brothers' meals were prepared.

The devastation of the Station was a terrible thing to see. Blocks of stone as big as a wagon were strewn about like a child's play blocks. Benches were smashed flat and dividing walls had toppled into rubble.

The dust in the air made Blat cough and he dampened a cloth to wrap around his nose and mouth. He climbed over debris and searched in likely areas for injured Brothers. A fold of black material protruded from beneath a boulder. He scrambled closer. The outside three fingers of a Brother's left hand were visible. Blat stared for a moment unable to understand what he was seeing. His gorge rose in his throat and he swallowed hard.

The rest of the Brother was crushed beneath the rock except for spurts of blood that seemed to writhe in the unsteady torchlight.

That was the first of the Brothers they found that day. They worked methodically, searching wherever it was passable. No one spoke above a whisper; the Station had become a tomb.

In the not-too-distant past, Blat had been a man content with his life, a man for whom hardship and pain meant struggling with a difficult chording pattern or a few hours' walk in foul weather. That person no longer existed. Blat forced himself to move from cave to cave, looking and yet not wishing to see. A gnarly fist clutched his heart and it hurt to breathe. His mind wanted desperately to shut down altogether. Everything he had ever thought was good and true seemed trivial. The superficiality of his life shamed him. What was he, after all, but a scribbler of silly songs. It all felt so inconsequential in the face of such tragedy. Numbness settled over Blat like a heavy blanket.

The most direct tunnel leading to the woman's chamber and the cylinders' cavern was impassable. The Willoughbys were able to circumnavigate the worst of the damage but as they got closer to the centre of the blast the way became more difficult. So far, they had found twenty-four Brothers and not a single one had been alive.

Tired and grimy, the searchers returned to the main cavern for a respite. They sat on the floor and stretched cramped muscles. The women had arrived and in addition to medical supplies, they had brought food and drink. With a minimum of fuss,

Effie Willoughby and the girls had created a small haven of comfort amidst the wreckage of the Station.

Angus was excitedly telling his wife about the veins of silver that had been exposed by the blast. His eyes shone with pleasure. "And with the Brothers out of the way, we have our stake back to ourselves." His sons joined in the conversation and they made detailed plans to clear and excavate the choicest areas. It was a welcome diversion from the day's gruesome task.

Crag noticed the pallor beneath the dust on Blat's face, but they were all exhausted from the hard work and heartsick from their bloody discoveries. But the boy was taking this very badly and it would be just like him to get some harebrained idea about trying to fix what couldn't be fixed. It was a hard thing, seeing people dead and thinking you had somewhat to do with it. Crag, too, felt a smidgen of remorse - it had been his idea to trap the Brothers using explosives.

The Willoughbys returned to their homestead for the night but Crag and Blat declined the kind offer to join them. They would stay and keep watch; they hadn't accounted for all the Brothers yet and someone might need their help.

Blat couldn't sleep. The food and rest had revived him, and he needed to search a little more. Crag waved him on his way and rolled over in his blankets. The boy couldn't come to much harm in this mess of a place.

Blat grabbed his pack determined to try a few more of the children's passageways. He was careful not to dislodge any stones and to walk only where the footing was firm and stable. It was painstaking work but it soothed his conscience a little. He squeezed through a crack in a tunnel wall thinking it might be another of the secret pathways like the one that led to the peephole into the cylinders' cavern. It narrowed and lowered, and the smoke from Blat's torch stung his eyes.

His outstretched hand guiding him along a wall felt something odd. It was soft, not rock at all. He pushed at it and it gave way. He groped and found an edge to the material, moved it aside, and crept through the short passageway that had been hidden. Similar material covered the other end; he nudged it aside and entered. The room it led to was undamaged and easily recognisable as the woman's chamber. It should have been demolished this close to the blast. Blat swallowed hard - her chair was empty.

He returned to the spot where he had entered her chamber. The material that covered the opening of the passageway blended with the rock on either side; it was invisible if you didn't know it was there. Blat felt the walls around the entire room and found another of the disguising tapestries but the tunnel behind it was choked with fallen rock. Where was she? Had she escaped the same way that he had entered?

The archway to the nexus was at first glance buried in debris. When he looked more closely, Blat discerned a narrow but passable walkway twisting away into the darkness. It led towards The Map room. He inched along treading softly like he

205

had done all day. He heard voices. Elated but cautious, Blat crouched beside the entrance and glanced in. Mir and Krodan stood beside The Map. She was giving the Brother orders in a smooth-as-silk voice that caressed Blat's ears as no other voice had ever done. He yearned to be near her, to listen to that voice forever. Sweat popped out on his brow. He clenched his fists and bit his lip until he drew blood. The spell receded.

The Map room had gone quiet. Blat peered in again. The two were oblivious to his presence, engrossed as they were in some arcane hand waving. Suddenly, Mir grasped Krodan's hand at the same time as she placed her free index finger on The Map. They dissolved before Blat's eyes. A second later his ears popped.

He remained crouched in the entranceway trying to understand what he had seen. Blat rose and cautiously stepped into The Map room. He did not want to venture near the table where Mir and Krodan had been standing, but he couldn't see The Map clearly enough to tell where she had touched it. His mind skittered away from thinking about the part where they had dissolved. He took a deep breath and moved closer, belatedly wondering if he should get Crag. A layer of dust covered The Map except for one small spot. Without thinking, Blat reached and put his finger on it.

His head felt full of cobwebs and he shook with cold. The Map room disappeared around him and he wondered if Crag would be able to piece together what had happened. *Ha.*

***

Crag woke with Angus Willoughby staring him in the face - this was not a sight with which to welcome the day. The hot tea in the prospector's outstretched hand, however, was and Crag struggled out from his tangle of blankets to accept the drink. He could hear various members of the Willoughby clan tap-taping this rock and that rock in search of treasure. Two of the women were re-packing the medical supplies. Crag knew what that meant: they had given up on finding anyone alive.

As if reading his thoughts, Angus spoke. "We've found twenty-eight bodies and I reckon that to be as many as we're likely to find. The others'll be buried too deep. We'll look in the tunnels we didn't get to yesterday, but I doubt we'll get lucky." Angus shuffled off to let Crag prepare himself for the day.

Crag wanted to try once more to reach The Map room and he needed someone with him; someone young and strong. He wandered around the cavern but the minstrel was nowhere to be seen. *Drat that boy.* "Have you seen the young singer?" he asked to the room at large. Various Willoughbys turned in his direction and shook their heads. It was then that Crag looked at Blat's sleeping place. The makeshift bed had not been slept in.

With a shrill whistle, he got everyone's attention. "Blat may be in trouble. The young fool went out alone last night and it looks like he didn't return."

Angus quickly organised his family into search parties. "Where do you think he'd head to?"

The scientist didn't have to think long. "He'll try for the woman's cave." He briskly rubbed his face. He should have known that Blat might do something like this; that woman still had her vicious hooks into him. Gods, he would have to tie a rope around the idiot's neck and lead him around like a pet dog. But first, they had to find him.

At the end of several gruelling hours, one of the Willoughby boys found the crack that Blat had entered. The torchlight clearly revealed one set of footsteps in the thick dust which ended at a blank rock wall. Crag insisted that he be the one to have a closer look. As he moved his torch around the dead end searching for clues, the flame flickered just a little more than usual. He ran his free hand over the area and felt the material at the same time as he felt the smallest draft of air. He pushed the tapestry aside to reveal the passageway. He called the news back to the others and, single file, they entered the woman's chamber.

Blat's trail was easy to follow and in a few minutes, the rescue team stood in The Map room. Here, several sets of footprints led to The Map table before they simply stopped.

Crag put his arms out to prevent anyone from disturbing the scene. He gave the table a wide berth, peering beneath it and into every crevice around the room. There were no other signs of disturbance. He rejoined the others crowding close to the entranceway.

"If what you said about that woman is true, she might have done this. Cleared a way to this here map," Angus said. "But then what?"

Crag was asking himself the same question. He approached The Map and beckoned the others forward; he needed more light. A thin film of dust covered its surface. He bent and looked at it edge on and it was then that he saw the disturbed area. He dug out his glass for a closer look. It was in that inferno of a desert far to the west and, as far as he knew, there was nothing there but wind and sand.

He showed the location to Angus. "Do you know anything about this place?"

Willoughby looked at it for a long moment and sucked in his breath through his teeth. "Oh, I know a little about the general area. Not personally, mind, but I heard about it from an old traveller who heard it from a cousin. Reliable fella. It's said there's a strange look thereabouts and them that value their hides stay clear. It's said the air looks solid instead of wobbly like it does in the desert. And when there's a storm, why the sand piles up where it shouldn't." Angus pursed his lips. "I can't recall anything else."

There was a rumbling in the distance. "I don't like the sound of that. Best be off until the thing has settled. You comin'?" Angus tugged on Crag's sleeve.

The scientist looked up, his face was haggard and lines were etched deep into his brow. Angus knew the look of intense worry when he saw it. He put a hand on Crag's shoulder. "Wherever he is, he'll be fine. He's a smart lad." He tugged gently and Crag resisted at first, then with a sigh, turned and trudged back to the main cavern.

He would rest a little and return as quickly as possible to Quirindi's Station. It was the only thing he could do.

CHAPTER 10

The world spun lazily around in his head but he felt apart from it. Except for the granules in his mouth, it was almost pleasant. The granules did annoy him though and he painstakingly plotted a course of action to spit them out, unobtrusively of course. But his arm would not move his hand to cover his mouth and that, too, was annoying. With more and more insistence, Blat sent commands to his muscles and, as his efforts grew more desperate, a general discomfort that began as a nuisance exploded into shafts of pain radiating from the centre of his body. He tried to curl around his tormented belly, but even this small comfort was denied him.

He remembered that whenever he had been sick as a child, his mother would sit with him. She would apply cool cloths to his aching head and sing soft lullabies until he fell asleep. He still loved her with an intensity that scared him a little and it made him feel happy and sad at the same time.

Slow tears flooded his eyes and gently washed away bits of grit. After a time, he opened them and a panorama of stars filled his vision. He smiled. He recognised many of the constellations. Understanding gradually seeped into his brain. The warm memories of his mother vanished. In order to see what he was seeing he had to be far to the west - very far to the west. He hadn't travelled to Zayu that often; the desert city thought minstrels were amusing, nothing more. His trips there were more for his own education and to provide the

Conservatory with news from that far land. Regardless of how impossible it seemed, Zayu was where he was, or near enough as to make little difference.

His fingers twitched. Blat's attention was drawn from his dismay at learning where he was to the painful movement of his hand. Concentrating, he formed loose fists. He opened and closed his hands a few times dispelling the paralysis that had stiffened them. After a few gruelling minutes, he had limbered his body enough so that he could sit up and more completely assess his situation. It was not promising. Sand undulated in motionless waves as far as he could see. He looked behind him and stared at the disturbances in the sand where he had tumbled down the face of a dune. His pack had miraculously remained strapped to his back and he reached around to unhook the water skin. Half full. He'd better go easy. He rinsed the grit from his mouth and took a small sip.

With every moment that passed, his mind worked more clearly and he tried to piece together the last few minutes. Or had it been hours? He had no way of knowing how long the bizarre journey had taken or how long he had been unconscious. It was night - that was all he knew for certain.

Fatigue washed over him. There was no sense trying to find better cover when all manner of unsavoury beasts might lurk in the deep shadows and, besides, he would make fresh tracks if he moved so that anything - or anyone, and he felt quite justified in his paranoia - could find him. Better to let the slight breeze cover the traces of his roll down the dune and stay where he had landed. He took his pack off and rummaged through it. There were a few chunks of hard bread, various sizes of cloths for bandaging in case he had found any Brothers needing help, some rope, needle and thread, and his journal.

He hefted the well-used book in his hand. He hadn't written a word in days but now was not the time to catch up; his memory, though somewhat overloaded, would have to serve until he could get to it. The stories he had gathered so far would undoubtedly be the impetus for a dozen outstanding songs, more than Blat imagined possible when he had begun the search for an elusive mountain village. But that had lost all priority. What mattered was stopping Mir before she did more harm. Before she did more harm because of what Blat had done. Regardless of what Crag asserted, he held himself responsible for releasing her onto the world and he would fix it. Resolute, he wrapped himself in his cloak, shivering a little, and dropped into a deep sleep.

The heat was intense and sweat dribbled down his face. Searing light hurt his eyes. It took Blat a moment to remember why he was so uncomfortable.

His knowledge of the desert was largely from books. Whenever he had travelled to this part of the country before, it was via the Whitecap Island Road, which paralleled the coastline and its cooling breezes. It had never been this hot. He used his pack and boots to prop his cloak creating shade as well as a little air circulation. If he stayed in the lee of the dune and adjusted his makeshift shelter to match the sun's arc, he could rest until sundown when it was more sensible to travel in the desert.

Time crawled, or was it just the assortment of biting insects that found the tiniest of openings in his clothing? He itched and sweated precious moisture. He sipped now and then from his dwindling supply of water and the day passed in a swelter of unpleasantness.

As dusk approached, Blat got to his feet to stretch cramped muscles and eat some of the bread. He looked at the sky and, based on where the sun had set and his knowledge of the stars, should be able to sustain a westward course through the night. The shore might be somewhat closer in one direction rather than another but he had no way to know for certain; he simply couldn't be more precise without instruments. He had a long night of walking ahead of him.

He knelt to tighten the straps on his pack, telling himself that he was not procrastinating, when he sensed a disturbance. Not thirty yards away, a Brother of the Watch appeared out of thin air. Blat dropped to his stomach. A second Brother appeared. Then a third.

Brother after Brother materialised as if by magic. He counted them: twenty. They marched in the opposite direction of Blat's meagre hiding place, their heads bowed and in their usual silence. Blat remained motionless and watched until they disappeared behind a distant dune. He did not move for another hour, long after the desert had returned to its former tranquillity.

The point from which the Brothers had manifested seemed a natural part of the landscape. Still on his belly, Blat crawled towards it for a closer examination. Maybe they had travelled here as he had, only they were better at it and didn't land in a disoriented, dysfunctional heap. The thought of Brothers moving around in such a way sent a chill down Blat's spine. Could they appear anywhere, anytime? It did not bear thinking about.

At the place where the Brothers' footsteps began in the sand, Blat reached a hand out to gingerly touch the ground. It felt ordinary and held the same heat from the day as the sand around it. He crept closer. His fingertips sunk into a yielding substance - an invisible yielding substance. He jerked his hand back. Gingerly, he placed the flat of his hand on it; it felt slick and slightly greasy. He took a deep breath and slowly pushed his hand into the stuff. It disappeared. With a stifled yelp, he jerked his hand back a second time and clutched it to his chest. When the hammering of his heart slowed a little, he uncurled it, flexed his fingers, and examined them from every angle. There appeared to be no damage to his digits.

His stomach in knots, he reached out and pushed again. His hand vanished once more. Astounded, he wiggled his fingers. They moved easily. He wondered if anyone could see them. It would look decidedly odd – fingers waving in thin air. He smiled. With a start, he came to his senses. *What if someone really could see them?* Alarmed, he eased his appendage from the substance. Blat needed to think about this and retreated to a position of safety. Although what the protection of a mere sand dune could offer against this whatever-it-was, Blat could not imagine.

The night grew progressively colder. Stars glittered and seemed close enough to touch. Blat huddled to retain his body heat as his mind wrestled with the latest mind-boggling phenomenon that he had stumbled upon in such a ridiculously short time. Any line of speculation about these things moved into the realm of fiction almost as soon as it had begun, but he believed that it remained fiction only because he didn't understand yet. He had seen what he had seen and felt what he had felt. He trusted his senses. There must be an explanation however strange or alien. Alien. Now there was a good word to describe Mir. And what about the Brothers? They were Whitecap Islanders just like him, and yet they could appear out of nowhere through invisible walls. There must be an explanation however bizarre. Bizarre. Where was Crag when he needed him?

Dawn was a faint glimmer of light on the horizon when Blat saw movement. He hunkered down and waited for the details to resolve themselves. A cowled Brother stood out in stark outline on the crest of a dune. He was followed by a line of people. Brothers were interspersed among them. Blat heart constricted in his chest.

A hodgepodge of villagers and farmers - mostly men - were herded towards the invisible barrier. Their clothing was ragged and filthy. No chains bound them.

The first captive, a tall, stringy man, balked at the threshold. Some of the others fell to their knees begging for mercy; it was clear that they believed death or worse awaited them. A Brother snarled, low and menacing - *he must have learned the technique from Krodan*, Blat thought - and shoved the man through the substance. He roughly hauled one of the kneeling prisoners upright and she cried out in pain. The Brother casually backhanded her across the mouth and she sprawled in the sand. He grabbed her by the hair and pulled her to her feet. Slowly, he pushed her head into the substance. Her screams of terror ended abruptly when her mouth entered the wall. Her body continued to kick and flail. Soon tiring of the game, the Brother let go and kicked her the rest of the way through. Stunned, the other captives went docilely, resigned to their fate.

Before he allowed himself to think, Blat used the cover of the blinding sun as it cleared the horizon to scramble into the midst of the captives. He found himself beside a young woman, a girl really. She looked at him and hope flared in her eyes. In the next instant, she realised that he, too, was a prisoner and turned away.

Blat was better dressed and somewhat healthier than the rest; he would have to count on weariness or lack of attention by the Brothers to remain unnoticed. He needn't have worried; he was unceremoniously pushed through the wall just like everyone else. After all, who would *want* to go where a Brother led? He fought off the urge to wipe possible residue from his face. He did not want to miss something vital.

They were in a vast compound bathed in muted sunlight. He surreptitiously looked around from lowered eyes. There were several buildings constructed of stone even though the weather was kept at bay by the barrier that enclosed the compound like a vast translucent bowl. Much of the heat of the rising sun did not penetrate.

The prisoners were led across an open square and into a dimly lit hall. He glanced at the girl beside him and reached over to squeeze her hand in a gesture of encouragement. She did not react nor did she look at him.

The men and women were separated. Blat's group was ushered into a crude bathing facility and ordered to undress. In a moment of clarity before his mad rush to join the line of prisoners, Blat had buried his pack in the sand. He may or may not find it again but he felt quite sure that it would have been a very bad thing to have his journal discovered. Even incomplete as it was, he had made notes about Station Two and the twin's story. That would be more than enough for the Brothers to take a very special interest in him, something he most assiduously wished to avoid.

They were given cleansing sand and rough brushes. A blast of tepid water gushed from several spouts in the ceiling and the walls. Beyond the spray, Brothers monitored them closely to be sure they did a thorough job. Rough tunics and trousers were thrust at them and, barefoot, they were conducted to a second building furnished with a row of sleeping pallets on either side of a long, narrow room. The door was shut and they were left alone.

Unable to believe they were still alive, some of the prisoners simply stood there while others shuffled to a pallet and lay down. The room soon filled with the sighs and snores of exhausted sleep.

Blat chose a pallet close to the door. He lay down determined to remain vigilant.

He was roused by a kick to the end of his bed. A trolley was being wheeled down the centre of the room and those quick enough snagged a bowl of thin, greasy gruel. Blat saw a distinct disadvantage of his chosen location; he was barely awake before the food had passed him by. He would have to move faster next time. Of course, he hoped to discover what went on here and be gone before many more meals had been served.

The meagre repast finished, they were once again left to themselves. Blat paced up and down the central aisle. The others huddled on their pallets in sullen silence, not meeting his eye.

"Will you sit down!" The harsh demand came from a brutish-looking man. A long scar ran down the side of his neck and disappeared into the collar of his tunic. "You're getting on my nerves."

Blat chose to interpret this as an invitation for a little conversation and sat down on the conveniently empty cot next to the man. "Be happy to," Blat said. "Allow me to introduce myself. I'm..."

"I don't give a pig's sty who you are and if you don't move yourself away from me, I'll do it for you." He flexed his enormous biceps.

Not exactly the conversational byplay that Blat hoped for, but he had dealt with a great many hecklers in his day. He moved six inches further away and lay back with his hands behind his head. "Whatever you say."

After a few minutes, he began to hum a popular ballad. A sigh came from the pallet to his right and he distinctly heard an accompanying harmony further down the row. He launched into a second song, adding lyrics this time. The men began to sit up and smile a little when he reached the chorus; they knew the words and knew that the young man in the ballad tripped over his own feet in a bumbling attempt to impress a girl and landed in, what else, a pig's sty.

Blat's burly friend turned his back to the room and pointedly ignored the impromptu concert. During a lull between songs, a pleasant tenor voice took up a sad song of the sea. Blat added a low harmony on the chorus and another voice took the harmony line a third above the melody line. It was beautiful, and the three men nodded at each other in satisfaction at the end of it.

The dark mood in the room had lifted and soft conversations began among the men. It was obvious that a number of them knew each other. As any good minstrel would do, Blat edged closer to hear their stories. It seemed that the Brothers' had slunk into their village in the middle of the night. At some unheard signal, the Brothers barged into their homes and grabbed the first person they found, be it son, daughter, wife, or man of the house. It didn't matter who it was or how strong that person was, the hostage could do nothing though the paralysing pain. With a knife at the throat of the captive, the Brother made it clear that all the men

220

and the women of a certain age were to gather in the square and, if they did so quietly, the rest of the family would be left alive. No one had put this threat to the test.

"We'd heard about this happening to other villages, but who could believe such a thing? Some of them was left destitute without their menfolk, or so they said, and come begging for food. We shared a bit of what we had and listened to their tales, then sent them on their way. It was hard but we can barely feed our own selves." The man who spoke rubbed at his eyes. "But it's real enough, what those black-robed bastards have gotten up to."

"Aye. And even if you're on your own, minding your own business, they take you." The scarred man had joined them.

"How? How did they take you?" Blat asked.

He rubbed a hand down the white line on his neck. "It was mighty strange," he began. "I was camped along the Road. At first I thought something had gotten in my ear and was buzzing and scraping around. I poured water in thinking to drown the bugger, but it wouldn't stop. Got worse and worse. Fair drove me crazy. It was all I could do to stop from poking a stick inside my own head to make it go away. Next I knew, Brothers of the gods-burn-them-forever Watch," he paused to spit eloquently on the floor, "were shoving me in line with the rest." He gestured to the others in the room. "I tried to get away and each time the buzzing came back and worse. It was like needles driving through my head."

Blat saw a few nods among the men; some of the others had experienced the same thing. He spoke up. "I've felt it too." The scarred man looked at him. "When it happened to me, I concentrated hard on something else, on something I cared about. For me, it was music. It helped."

At that moment, the door was flung open and Blat scrambled to the end of his pallet for a share of the food. He was desperately thirsty - the Brothers' had left them nothing to drink - and he hoped to get a better look at what lay outside the barracks.

He didn't have long to wait.

As soon as they had emptied their bowls, Blat and his fellow prisoners were escorted into the main square. He studied his environs with a minstrel's eye for detail. It was easy to tell where they had entered the compound by the desert sand that sprayed out from a well-guarded section of the invisible barrier; the rest of the slate-like surface upon which they walked was clean and smooth. The structures to either side of the entrance housed the necessities of many a community: heat rippled the air above the launderer's tubs, the clank of metal on metal came from the blacksmith's anvil, and the largest of the structures held the kitchens in front of which was a neat corral separated into holding areas for pigs and chickens. The other buildings were long and two-storied with the look of barracks everywhere. Doorways opened onto the square in monotonous regularity and small windows allowed a little light to penetrate within.

The structure that formed the final side of the square and towards which they were herded resembled a keep or citadel. It was three stories tall and gracefully proportioned. Columns separated mullioned windows designed to draw the eye to the pinnacle. On it was carved an image. Two black swords bound together at the wrist guard with a blood-red band - the symbol of the Protector Order of the Brothers - were crossed in an X and impaled into a shape representing Whitecap Island. Blat had seen the red armband before, most recently on Krodan's henchmen, but never coupled with swords. This could not be good.

A pair of Brothers followed by two more strode out of the arched portal of the citadel and stood side by side facing the square. At some signal, they separated, two to either side, and a fifth Brother took his place in the middle. He was taller than any Brother Blat had seen. But that was not his most striking feature. The blanched pallor of his skin, the colourless eyes, and the complete hairlessness of his head including his eyebrows made it seem that he, in fact, did not have any features at all. His head looked like a large, soft-boiled egg on top of his shoulders. It was unsettling.

The prisoners were forced to their knees. Blat felt the tingling sensation begin at the back of his neck. He concentrated with all his might on the first song that came to mind. It was the one that he and his two fellow prisoners had harmonised to so recently. Sweat popped out on his brow and trickled down his face. Then it was over.

Relieved, Blat looked around. Over half of the captives in his group had crumpled under the onslaught. Those who had not were conscripted to carry the prostrate men back to their quarters. He noticed that the burly man had remained conscious, and when their eyes met over the body of one of their barrack-mates, Blat nodded to him. After a moment, the man nodded back.

This task completed, the twenty or so people still functioning in Blat's group were given ill-fitting sandals to wear and escorted to a nondescript door. They, along with other groups of prisoners, entered what Blat came to call the pit.

They descended into the earth for many minutes. It was cooler and that was welcome. The dressed stone degraded into rough rock walls and Blat was once again in a cave system. *Gods, when this is over I will never willingly go underground again.* At least he didn't have his eyes and sinuses abused by smoky torches. Light emanated from rectangular boxes set into the rock and was much like the light at Quirindi's Station only it held steady.

At the end of the stairway they were marched along a broad tunnel for several minutes. Blat could tell by the change in the sound of the footfalls ahead of him that the tunnel had reached an open area but he couldn't see over the heads of those in front.

The fellow ahead of Blat stumbled and Blat helped him regain his balance. This was when he got his first look at their destination. The earth had been gouged out as if by the hands of many angry gods. The crater that resulted went on farther than he could see and the entire bottom of the vast space was filled with cylinders, but these were different from the others he had seen. An image popped into his head of a school of fish on a sunny day, sparkling just beneath the surface of the water. The difference was that, here, in the bowels of the earth, instead of the sun, hundreds of prisoners laboured to create the glitter.

A stiff cloth was handed to him and he and five others were escorted to a grouping of cylinders. On the way there, Blat noticed that the sea of cylinders was everywhere divided into these groupings. Widely spaced among them and set apart in the middle of the main aisle were bigger and brighter cylinders similar to the main cylinder he had destroyed at Station Two. Blat fervently hoped he would not witness another of the Brothers' masochistic ceremonies.

With a minimum of direction, they were each assigned two of the dozen cylinders to polish. The well-muscled fellow worked on the pair next to Blat and they managed a few muttered words now and again when they were certain no Brother was within earshot. Blat learned that his name was Umbu. They made a pact that whenever either one felt the tingling sensation, he would warn the other.

Not long into the monotonous labour, Blat needed to relieve himself and wondered what to do. He looked around and saw a crude enclosure between this group of twelve cylinders and the next. He cautiously made his way toward it; no one stopped him. Sure enough, a fellow prisoner came out as he approached. Blat pushed the blanket aside and looked upon the malodorous facilities. It had a slop bucket in one corner and blankets over two other sides of the rickety wooden structure. The fourth side was the rocky cavern wall. This gave the occupant privacy at the ground level, but the roof was open and the Brother on a nearby platform could easily look in if he wished. Blat let the blanket drop behind him. It was the first time he had been alone since his arrival and he realised how much he missed his solitude. A prickle began at the back of his neck. *Oh, no!* He concentrated on music and the tingle passed him by. Wasting no more time, he finished and exited, looking around as he adjusted his trousers. These blanket-enclosed lavatories were spaced evenly along the wall of the cavern. A Brother glanced in his direction and Blat rushed back to his work area.

Blat polished until his arms ached and then he polished some more. The group of prisoners next to his must have been at this for many weeks. The sinews on their arms and shoulders were sharply defined. If they had not been so thin, he would have described them as being wiry with muscle. He nodded to one of them as they rounded the end of a cylinder at the same time; vacant eyes stared back. Whatever he had come here to discover, Blat decided he had better do it quickly.

A few hours into their labour, a prisoner shoved a trolley along the aisle between the clusters of cylinders. He doled out ladles of water and hunks of bread. Blat and Umbu followed the example of the team next to them and stood placidly in line, drank the water when it was handed to them, then sat on the floor to eat the bread. Blat noticed that there were no other new 'recruits' anywhere nearby. The Brothers must scatter them among the seasoned workers, or, rather, the demoralised workers. It was a smart thing to do; a quick look at the veterans and the new arrivals saw how things were done and any possibility of organising a revolt was greatly reduced.

It was during this break that Blat took the opportunity to examine the gigantic vault. He slowly rose to his feet and when a Brother looked his way, began to stretch his legs and arms. Under this guise, he was able to study his surroundings. Every fifty feet or so, wooden platforms had been erected from which Brothers supervised the work below. At the end near the staircase, a large gallery had been cut out of the rock wall. It was well-lit and Blat could see the outline of a woman. He stiffened. Mir.

"What is it? The tingling?" Umbu's anxiety was clear in his low voice.

Blat dragged his attention from the woman who had made a murderer of him. It wouldn't do to have her notice him and she might be able to sense him without using anything as mundane as her eyes.

He shook his head in answer to Umbu's question. He had to think. How could he get closer? He studied the activity around him. Some of the prisoners did jobs other than polishing. One fellow caught a folded package tossed to him from a Brother at a nearby platform. He then ran to the gallery and climbed a ladder to where he could hand the package off to a second prisoner whose job it was to wait there for just such a thing. If Blat could get *that* job, he would be able to hear what was being discussed and see what else was up there. But the odds of a fresh prisoner such as himself being assigned to that task were slim indeed.

The slop buckets must be emptied by a captive as well; Blat could not imagine a Brother doing such a task if there was another option. If only he could engage the team next to him in conversation he might discover what he had to do to be given such an assignment.

The short break ended. Blat and Umbu returned to polishing but now that Blat knew where to look his eyes were repeatedly drawn to Mir. She gesticulated and pointed to the pit. She stomped a slipper-clad foot and planted her fists on her hips. The Brother she argued with crumpled at her feet and she stormed off out of Blat's line of sight. It would seem that all was not well in Mir's world.

The work shift ended and they were escorted to their barracks. Tired and sore, they slumped onto their pallets rousing only to drain the bowls of thin stew that were circulated a short while later, after which most of the lights were extinguished. A solitary glow came from the area of the lavatory. This modicum of civility was a temporary affair that had been installed while they worked. Blat tiptoed to the washroom and splashed a little of the water that was rationed out on his face to revive himself; he needed to stay awake until all the others slept.

The air was filled with the sounds of men deep in exhausted sleep. Blat slipped from his bed and listened at the door. Nothing. He bent to examine the lock only to discover that there wasn't any. Of course. Why would the Brothers need to bother? Between the heavily guarded portal and the harsh desert, the chances of a successful escape were laughable.

The door opened with gratifying silence. A few wide-spaced lights illuminated the interior of the dome. Blat kept to the shadows and slipped towards the citadel. Brothers stood guard outside the main door.

A narrow alley separated the citadel from the barracks. Blat turned into it and inched forward. He probed the wall with his sensitive musician's fingers searching for a crack or a protrusion with which to lever himself up to the window casings he could discern protruding above his head.

A rough hand clamped over his mouth and an arm like iron crushed his chest. "It's me," Umbu breathed and loosed his grip.

The man moves like a cat, Blat thought.

Umbu pressed his mouth close to Blat's ear. "I'll give you a hand up. Be sure that if you find a way out of here, I go with you."

Blat nodded. It seemed he had a partner.

They positioned themselves beneath a window at the back of the building, as far away from the mouth of the alley as possible. Umbu knelt and made a cradle with his hands. Blat stepped into it and was lifted with apparent ease up to the casement. The shutters on the window opened outward; odd that it should have shutters at all. Habit, he guessed. Blat eased them open and peered into the room for a long moment. There was no sign of movement. He waited a moment longer, conscious of Umbu steady as a rock supporting him. With his hands pressed against the panes, he slowly

229

raised the window, reached inside, and levered himself into the room.

From a crouch, Blat listened. All remained quiet. He rose and leaned out the window, waving to Umbu who would be able to see the movement against the lighter background of the dome. He closed the shutters and the window; no sense leaving obvious clues for a passing Brother. Umbu would wait below for as long as he could. It would have to be long enough.

In most of the citadel-like structures that Blat had ever been in, the important chambers were located at the centre of the building so that they could be protected from all sides. They usually had only one door, further minimising exposure. The Brothers were Whitecap Islanders and would likely construct in the same way given the redundancy of the shutters. At least Blat hoped so.

The room Blat had entered was stacked with containers and broken furniture. He moved to the door and eased it open a little. A dimly lit hallway was dotted on either side by other doors. He stepped out and tried the nearest door. It opened easily at his touch. Blat could hear no sleeper's breathing, no sound at all. The room was filled with containers much like the room through which he had entered the citadel. He couldn't take the time to examine them; he needed a clue to Mir's plans, not an inventory of the Brothers' supplies.

A muffled gasp came from an adjoining room. Blat froze. On the wall to his right, partially hidden between two large boxes was a second door. Now that he focused on it, Blat could see its faint outline. He crept forward and knelt before the keyhole.

A cry from within had him scuttling backwards and rising into a fighter's stance. The door didn't open. He heard a second cry, this time much louder. He risked a look.

Mir arched her back, arms stretched wide. Her dark hair flowed down her back and the subtle curve of breast and hip were limned in the candlelight. Blat was smitten anew by her beauty. He felt a surge of desire. In the next instant, the familiar tingle of mind control drove all such thoughts from his mind. But it was not directed at him.

There was a Brother on the bed. His robe was bunched around his chest and its cowl drawn down over his face. He gasped for breath, thrashing beneath her. A sharper sting of pain grazed Blat's head. The Brother pumped harder and harder, then went still.

Mir lifted herself from her victim and swayed towards a figure huddled in the corner of the room. "That is how it should be done," she purred. The wretch in the corner lifted his face and Blat stared.

The ravaged, wasted features were those of Krodan. He raised bound hands towards Mir, the pleading in his face a pitiful thing to see. Mir's laugh was loud and harsh. "You had your chance to please me. All you are good for is your malleable conduit of a mind." Mir stepped closer and placed her hands on Krodan's head. He writhed in pain but could not pull away. He mouthed incomprehensible gibberish, slobber running down his chin. Shocked, Blat realised that he had no tongue.

At last Mir released him and Krodan slumped boneless onto his side. Sated in both mind and body, she returned to the bed and pushed the raped Brother onto the floor. She lay down and very soon began to snore.

In a rustle of fabric, the Brother gathered himself and crawled on hands and knees towards the door that led to the hallway. He pushed himself to his feet and glanced over his shoulder at Mir. His whole body tensed for a moment, then he turned and quietly left the room, careful to shut the door behind him.

For all that he had just seen, Blat had learned nothing of Mir's plans. He rose on somewhat shaky legs, opened the hall door the merest crack, and peered down the corridor. The abused Brother was no longer in sight.

Blat was unsure how much time had passed but he had no time to waste. He would risk the more protected interior suites. In fact, with Mir and Krodan out of the equation, he would take the biggest risk of all and seek the innermost chamber.

True to form, a side hallway led deeper into the citadel where, in a shorter and better lit corridor, there were only a few doors. These doors were solid and had no visible hinges. Blat chose the one that was marginally larger than the others and peered at the locking mechanism. From within his thick locks of hair, he drew forth a length of the very thin, very strong, very bendable wire that Crag had invented. His thoughts turned briefly to the cantankerous scientist and he smiled, visualising the mayhem that Crag was doubtless leaving in his wake.

Blat gently prodded the keyhole and felt the tumblers responding to his touch - a good Touring Minstrel needed many skills; one never knew what sort of predicament one might find oneself in. That fact was one of the real life lessons that Murzim had impressed upon him. The rude minstrel from Blat's first day at the Minstrels' Guildhall had become, if not a friend, at least an excellent source of all manner of tricks. In seconds, he was inside.

All it took was a brief glance to realise that he had chosen well and that his danger was correspondingly extreme. Parchment lay strewn on a sizable table that occupied the centre of the room. The walls were covered with maps and diagrams. Blat made a quick circuit of the room, trying to get an overall sense of what was there.

He halted in his tracks, his eyes drawn to the familiar. The name of a Conservatory Guild Master was at the top of a lengthy list. Shocked, his eyes raced down the rest of the names. There were many others he recognised: names of musicians, religious leaders, merchants, politicians, and even a few of the more notorious thieves. Each one had a letter or letters beside it and somebody had thoughtfully inked an explanatory legend at the bottom of the sheet: X for Protector, P for Priest, E(x) for an Elder of the Protectors and E(p) for an Elder of the Priests, A for Acolyte, and S for Server. The Acolytes and Servers did not have Elders associated with them although it appeared from the way that the names were organised that the Elders were

233

responsible for them. These were the orders within the Brothers of the Watch, and Minstrel Guild Master Dast was an Elder of the Priests. Blat had no time to ponder this devastating revelation; it was more important that he fully understand what he was looking at. He studied the lines and arrows and it took a moment more to see the awful truth.

The Brothers had infiltrated every level of society and this parchment named who they were and who they reported to. His head swam and he had the oddest sensation that he somehow knew of this treachery. How could he have? He shook his head. No time to ponder that either. He scanned the remaining documents and maps, furiously memorising details.

Blat slipped out of the room and made his careful way back to the window where Umbu, thankfully, still waited. He backed out of the window and placed his feet on Umbu's shoulders. Balanced there, he reached up to close the window and shutters then lowered himself silently to the ground. The dome was beginning to show the first blush of dawn. They hurried to their barracks and lay down on their pallets.

Blat lay still and concentrated on fixing what he had seen firmly in his mind. He groaned. One of the maps had outlined a massive uprising to occur during the next dark of the moon. If his sense of time was close, that was in less than three weeks.

During the next long, long day of polishing, Blat's mind whirled with what he had seen. Umbu sent him questioning glances throughout the day but any answers would have to wait until Blat had sorted out what to say.

One thing was certain: Blat had to escape very soon. Crag and Quirindi as well as the Assembly of Masters at the Conservatory and the City Council of Rivercrest must be warned of the danger. It wasn't so much how many Brothers there were - their numbers were relatively few - but rather who they were and the positions they held. Together, they controlled more of Whitecap Island than anyone could have imagined. They could only have done such a thing with mind-control. Destroying that infernal weapon was the key to their demise. If only Blat could figure out how to do it.

He had often wondered how Minstrel Guild Master Dast retained his status; he seemed somewhat short on talent in Blat's opinion, though he had never mentioned this to anyone, not even Talitha. It was not his place to criticise the Conservatory. At best, they would laugh at him, the farm boy, for thinking he was a better judge of talent than they were, but more likely they would have reprimanded him for his insolence. Maybe even expelled him and he would never risk that - he would never do that to himself or to Sarah. Though she would heartily deny it, Sarah would be humiliated if something like that happened to one of her recruits. Worse, she would be disappointed in him. So he had kept his thoughts to himself.

Blat had a fair idea where The Map room was likely located in the citadel. At least he and Umbu could travel quickly. The big man was in for a disconcerting experience.

That night, Blat told everything he had learned to the entire group in his barracks. He needed their help. Ironically, the mind power that the Brothers used to subjugate these men helped Blat to win them over. If something like that could exist, who was to say that other uncanny things might not exist? Like instant transportation.

"Well, I don't know so much as I'd like to move around so unnatural-like, but I surely want to get home to my family." Many heads nodded in agreement. A short, stocky man who had introduced himself as Opat spoke for the rest of the men of his village.

Opat went on to explain that he had exchanged words with a prisoner who had been here for some time. He learned that those few who still retained any willpower at all continued to dream of escape and had gathered valuable pieces of information. One of these pieces was that the portal to the desert was the only way into or out of the compound. If only the mind pain could be blocked.

Blat wondered out loud if any of the prisoners had actually tried to escape and Opat answered that, yes, some had. But the few who had made this attempt had been caught and their minds so destroyed that only fragments of information were consistent and were likely unreliable. However, it was possible that there were only four Brothers guarding it after the work shift. With so many cylinders to draw on, even a small number of Brothers had sufficient mental strength to repel any attack.

"I might be able to distract them and keep them focused on me while you sneak around and knock them out," Blat interjected.

Opat seemed keen at first. "It's worth a try." A frown creased his forehead and he shook his head. "And if you fail? Then what? They'd be certain to scour out our heads like so many dirty pots."

"We'd be as good as dead," one of the younger men added. The others in the room shifted uneasily and returned to their pallets. They had another long day of polishing ahead of them.

On that less than satisfactory note, Blat lay back on his pallet. He was exhausted from the foray into the citadel the night before followed by the day of hard work. He tried to compose himself for sleep but, as sometimes happened when he was beyond tired, his mind churned. He could use The Map to travel to Crag and Quirindi. They, in turn, could carry word of the Brothers' plans to Rivercrest. A Map might allow Quirindi to travel to Rivercrest and meet with the City Council and as leader of her people she would be able to convince them of the danger and of the urgency to act.

Blat mourned Moqor's useless death; if they had used a Map he would still be alive. He wished he hadn't thought about the taciturn Stationer; it reminded him of all the Brothers who had died in the cavern explosion. No matter what Crag said about it being Mir's fault, he was the one who had planted the charges and nothing could change that fact. And here he was, encouraging yet more people to endanger themselves by dangling the hope of escape in front of them. How could he do it?

He was tired of thinking. It only tied him in knots and was giving him a headache. He breathed in through his nose and out through his mouth. The right thing to do would come to him if he would only let it.

Relaxed and silent, the murmur of a new melody began inside his head. Struck by its simple beauty, Blat gently encouraged it, like a gardener tending a delicate shoot.

Blat had fended off the predations of Krodan's mind probe by protecting himself with music. Would it work as well for others? A catchy song might do it. Everyone knew that once such a song took root in your head, it would stay there - sometimes to the point where it became annoying. You had to make yourself concentrate on something else before it disappeared to wherever songs went when you weren't thinking of them. The song he had just created was such a song. He smiled, turned on his side, and began to doze.

A new thought niggled at him. Blat shoved it away; he needed to sleep. It niggled again. He sighed. It never did him any good to ignore a thought when it was this persistent and he let it clarify itself. *Committees never worked.* True, but rather useless information. He rolled onto his back and threw an arm over his eyes. The thought kept pushing at him, forcing his tired mind to work out what it was trying to say. The hierarchy of the Brothers stopped at the level of the Elders. There were many of them, far too many to ever agree on a single course of action, let alone do anything about it. Just like a committee. Blat's intuition did not have to make much of a leap: there must be someone above the level of the Elders who guided and controlled the Brothers and he must be here, at the desert Station. Perhaps the information he had memorised at the citadel pointed to it, only he had been too flabbergasted by what he had already learned to see it. Having such a tenacious mind came in handy when it wasn't driving him crazy, that is.

It looked like he and Umbu would have a second clandestine adventure. Blat finally slept.

***

Mir felt a spurt of hatred - quickly suppressed - as she entered the sumptuous chambers. Upelo certainly denied himself nothing and he revelled in flaunting this, especially to her. He always chose to meet with her here. She was forced to make do with plainer quarters, a pointed insult meant to put her in her place.

The Eldest was a truly evil man and for that she admired him. He suited her purposes for now and when his usefulness was at an end, he, too, would meet his end. A particularly nasty end. She had had such satisfaction breaking Krodan; Upelo would be so much better.

He was far too arrogant to entertain the possibility that anyone could usurp his position and Mir had to admit that he was strong, but not as strong as she was. She had been very careful to never let him suspect the full extent of her power and was content to watch him manoeuvre his minions into position. When the Brothers gained control over the land, she would pounce.

***

The next work shift passed much like the preceding two. Blat worried that he would lose the flexibility in his fingers from their constant grip on the polishing rag, and he took every opportunity to stretch his hand muscles.

The mundane work left his mind free to concoct contingency plans, but there were too many variables. What if Umbu was caught waiting for him in the alleyway while he searched for the leader of the Brothers? What would Blat do if and when he found this leader? What if no one else could learn to withstand the Brothers' mind power? Could he and Umbu do it by themselves? What if Mir sensed his presence? What if he had misread the plan of the Citadel and couldn't find The Map room after all? And, if he did, what if Crag and Quirindi were nowhere to be found? What if they couldn't convince the various councils of the danger? What if, what if, what if - Blat was making his head hurt.

Instead, he concentrated on something that he could do. He worked on the song. He hummed the notes that started the verse, repeated them, and added a seventh. Simple and easy; he liked it. The chorus should be fun and loud. He toyed with a few variations and settled on the one that made him smile the most. No need for a bridge; it would just complicate things. Blat pieced together the completed tune and made slight changes until he

240

was satisfied. It could be learned in a few minutes and was definitely catchy.

Next, he worked on fitting in words that would force people to concentrate. It had to be about something familiar to everyone, but with a twist to keep it interesting. He let his mind wander through his repertoire of children's songs and lullabies, and songs that formed part of a game. *That was it!* He would make it like a children's game! Who didn't remember those songs from childhood? It was the perfect method.

While his mind composed, his arms polished - circle in one direction, circle in the other direction. Everyone polished in the same way; it was hypnotic. The rhythm of the work wove itself into the rhythm of the song. The lyrics flowed naturally into that rhythm and were as easy to learn as the melody.

The bell sounded the end of shift and it was with a lighter step that Blat returned to the barracks for the evening meal. For dessert, he would teach his new ditty to his fellow prisoners.

Umbu was willing to return to the citadel, for which Blat was intensely grateful; he trusted the big man to watch his back.

Blat had two goals: one, to confirm the location of The Map; and two, to discover the identity and quarters of the leader of the Brothers. He and Umbu had discussed this second goal at length. Umbu felt it was too risky. The leader, if he even existed, would be very powerful and well-guarded. As much as this terrified him, Blat knew that no plan, however cleverly conceived, would succeed

241

for long without defeating the leader. They might slow the Brothers down but would not eliminate the threat. It would fester and grow. With revenge stirred into the pot, the next time the Brothers forayed for captives they would simply take entire families. Nor would they risk future breakouts: everyone would have their minds wiped. Blat couldn't fathom why they left them intact to think thoughts of escape in the first place, but Opat had set him straight. The brain-scoured prisoners lasted only a fraction of the time. One day they just stopped polishing and would not continue no matter what the Brothers did to them. They died soon afterwards.

Blat thought of little Louetta and how much joy she brought to everyone around her, especially to Sarah and Jamie-the-Cook. How could Blat not do everything he could to make Whitecap Island a safer place for her to play and for her to grow into womanhood? Blat had had only glimpses of the women the Brothers had taken. They were kept near the Brothers' quarters on the far side of the square but even at that distance, it was clear that the women were used for sex. He would stop this; such a thing would never happen to Louetta.

Escape would be the impetus for his fellow prisoners' cooperation. Blat understood that desperate need. He also understood that their escape would be a temporary reprieve if the plan that he had glimpsed was not crushed. The Brothers meant to subjugate everyone. They meant to have it all.

Blat and Umbu went down the same alleyway they had two nights previously and Blat scrambled through the same window into the storage room. He waited for his eyes to adjust, crept into the empty hallway, and entered the next room. He peered through the keyhole into the adjoining chamber. The snuffling sound to the left was likely Krodan, although the angle was too acute for Blat to see him. Mir's bed was empty; he would have to be very careful.

Everyone - Brothers and prisoners - kept to the same rigid schedule. For once, Blat was grateful for the Brothers' strict life of discipline. The corridors were empty and silent. He navigated his way to the inner set of rooms and pressed his ear to the first door. Nothing. He tried the handle. Locked. A soft footfall out of his range of vision had him scrambling for the wire in his hair. He worked with feverish haste. The footsteps drew closer. With a click, the door opened. Blat slid inside and closed the door. He breathed quietly through his mouth and stilled his thoughts. He felt the faint tendril of a probe wash over him and he called the song up to fill his mind. After a time, the footsteps receded and he opened the door a crack to see a Brother's retreating back. Blat cursed his luck; for some reason, the Brothers were more vigilant tonight.

He turned to examine the room he had entered. It was so un-Brotherlike that Blat was disoriented for a moment. His gaze flicked upon the exquisite brocade on the two chairs bracketing the marble fireplace, the delicate filigree on the four posts of the bed, the tapestries and paintings that hung on the

243

walls, the thick rug on the floor, and the ornate desk that took up a full quarter of the space. He approached the desk and ran his hand over its silky-smooth surface. It had several drawers, all of which were locked and would not yield to Blat's skill. He studied the room once more for clues to the identity of its occupant. Any personal items must be in the locked desk. This could easily be the leader's quarters but he was no closer to knowing who it was. Frustrated, Blat exited into the corridor.

A left turn, a right, up a short flight of stairs, and he entered The Map room. It was just where he supposed it might be. The Brothers were consistently predictable. Even though there were no guards, there was no other doorway into or out of The Map room and he was uncomfortably aware that this could quickly become a trap. Blat circled The Map table. He kept his hands behind his back; he did not want to inadvertently trigger its mechanism. A smaller chamber, not visible from the door, was off to one side and curtained. He glanced in and saw a raised platform. Perhaps this was where Mir and Krodan had 'appeared' when they travelled from Station Three. It was just as well that he had not placed his finger precisely on the same spot as Mir had; his painful landing in the desert was far more preferable to landing in the middle of the Brothers' citadel.

The night was waning and he had yet to learn who the leader was or seen Mir. He made his careful and quiet way to the planning room that he had found the other night. It would be the logical place for them to meet.

He approached the door and pressed an ear to it. There was the distinct murmur of conversation inside. Blat froze. He recognised Mir's sultry tones, now raised in impatience. A man's deep, baritone voice replied with dripping disdain. She would not like that. He could not risk opening the door but he must see who this man was who so blatantly defied her. Blat retreated into an empty, nearby room. He would stay as long as he could.

Shortly, the door of the planning room flew open and Mir appeared. She glanced back into the room and the glow from the lamps within lit her exquisite profile. She was beautiful in her anger. She turned and marched past Blat's hiding place, consumed with her own fury and oblivious to anything else.

Next, a Brother scuttled out, his arms filled with rolled parchments. He, too, hurried by, looking neither right nor left.

A third person in the room moved towards the door. Instinctively, Blat lowered himself into a crouch, his eye to the thin sliver of open doorway. A tall, gaunt man stepped into the corridor. Blat recognised the pasty complexion - he was the fifth Brother at the 'opening ceremonies.' He wore a black robe like all the other Brothers, but, at this close range, Blat could see that it was made of heavy silk rather than the coarse, scratchy fabric that supposedly helped purify a Brother's soul. As he neared, Blat discerned the intricate embroidery on cuffs and hem stitched with a blacker-than-black thread that glinted where the light caught it. The man continued past Blat's hiding place, his stark white hand like a dead thing against the inky fabric of his robe.

A dark wave of power lapped against Blat's consciousness. The song sprang into his mind. He squeezed his eyes shut and focused on maintaining that meagre barrier. The dark pounded at him, seeking the least weakness. As suddenly as it had begun, it abated. Blat doubted that the man even knew the pain that he had caused; it seemed like a natural state of malevolence. He would wager that the man's full strength could kill in an instant, a perfect credential for the leader of the Brothers. Blat opened his eyes in time to see the elegant robe disappear around a corner.

Blat crept across the hallway and into the planning room; he had to use a few minutes of his scant remaining time for one last look. The Brothers' leader or Mir might have left additional clues.

The table had been cleared of all documents, and most of the wall maps removed. Only the largest was left. Blat studied it. Several bright red threads had been sewn into the fabric where the larger towns and cities were located; the smaller villages and hamlets remained untouched. In one corner was a date. Beside it was a circle filled with black ink signifying the upcoming lunar eclipse. In the opposite corner was a stylised signature: 'Upelo,' followed by an ornately scripted 'Eldest.' Blat snorted; he should have figured that one out.

Blat had accomplished what he had come to do. "Time to leave," he muttered under his breath.

"I think not." The gaunt man filled the doorway, blocking Blat's exit.

Before the minstrel could bring up the merest defence, Upelo struck. The searing pain was but a gentle harbinger as Blat plummeted into the abyss.

***

Mir felt the wash of Upelo's power and briefly wondered who he tormented. Never mind. She had her own victim to consider.

Upon return to her unsavoury quarters, she had sensed the intruder in the alleyway and dispatched four of her large, devoted Brothers to bring him to her. They had done so with some difficulty apparent by the rips in their robes and the bruises on their faces. She smiled. He was a strong one. With Upelo otherwise occupied, she would amuse herself. Krodan gabbled in the corner - music to her ears.

"Umbu, is it? What an incredibly ugly name!" Mir stood before him, one slender finger touching the scar on his neck. "Tell me. However did you get this?" Umbu began to sing.

Mir winced. It was a terrible song and grated on her nerves. She tore off a piece of Krodan's fouled rags and stuffed it into Umbu's mouth. She squeezed his biceps, deeply gouging into the flesh with her sharpened nails. His hot glare changed not one bit. He was indeed a tough one. She would find out just exactly how tough.

***

247

Mir waited until she was certain that Upelo was in the cavern. She wished to make a spectacular entrance and timing was everything. Umbu looked wretched and bringing Krodan along would add a nice touch. She signalled to her guards that she was ready.

The stairway echoed with the industrious sounds of men hard at work. As she approached the cavern, the cylinders' power filled her with warmth and well-being - so very different from the power that had trapped her in stone. It was amazing what a slight difference in orientation could make. The properties of the ore in the cylinders were easily manipulated just like the feeble minds all around her.

Her party exited from the stairway and walked through the crudely chiselled tunnel that opened onto the observation gallery. She ran a hand along the wall; she would have it polished smooth. With so many strong arms at her command, it would be a trifling thing to have done.

The cavern quieted and Upelo's hated voice echoed off the far wall. He was making a little speech. Mir sneered. It betrayed weakness that Upelo felt the need to communicate with these savages.

She stepped to the front of the gallery and all eyes turned toward her. It was not just that she was the most beautiful woman any of them would ever see. They sensed her power and wanted it. She relished their desire, especially knowing that they would never satisfy it.

Umbu was shoved forward and pushed to his knees; Krodan cowered beside him. She closed her eyes and waited for the gasp of shocked, indrawn breath that she had so anticipated, but it never came. Puzzled, she glanced around the gallery. Upelo's mocking grin was not unusual, but she had fully expected a glint of admiration for what she had done to the brawny prisoner at her feet and perhaps a surge of anger to be reminded yet again of what she had made of his strongest Elder. Then the Eldest stepped back.

That wretched minstrel lay sprawled on the stone floor. His light-coloured hair spread around his head like a corona, contrasting with the dark slate of the floor. His eyes were closed and his breath came in short gasps. She remembered him. Oh, how she remembered him, and how he had betrayed her.

"You... you...," she sputtered, unable to form words through the red haze of rage. She lashed out, but Upelo's mind-guard around the minstrel was impenetrable. She whirled around, her wrath bubbling like an erupting volcano. Her moment of triumph, when she would reveal what she had extracted from Umbu, shattered around her. Umbu. She wrapped her fingers in his hair, tightening them until she felt thick hanks break free, and threw her head back. Her rage sizzled into his head.

Umbu screamed. He shuddered and slumped forward. In slow motion, he toppled from the gallery ledge hitting the cavern floor with a thud.

For long seconds, the hundreds of prisoners in the cavern were still, frozen by what they had witnessed.

A ragged, weak voice barely broke the stillness. Blat. The singing was erratic and the minstrel coughed weakly every few notes. A murmur began from some indeterminate point in the multitude of prisoners. It began to swell like a wave, but unlike a wave, it travelled in all directions at once. A single voice rose above the murmur and sang in a strong clear tenor. A second voice joined in, then a third, and within moments the cavern reverberated with dozens of voices raised in song. The minstrel's song.

Upelo and Mir exchanged a glance. They had learned of this so-called song of protection during their separate interrogations of Blat and Umbu. Upelo shrugged his shoulders and raised his eyebrows as if to ask, 'who could ever understand these peasants?' Mir agreed.

The song gained in volume and was beginning to become uncomfortably loud. Mir waited for Upelo to use his much-vaunted might to quell this minor rebellion. She looked over at him and saw by his clenched jaw that he was doing just that, but the song continued. She smirked. She may have to graciously offer her assistance.

The prisoners in the back pressed into those ahead of them; they rippled forward, singing all the while.

She watched for a few moments more, then sidled next to Upelo. "Are you having a little difficulty controlling this rabble?" she asked, in her sweetest voice.

Upelo spared her a glance. There were droplets of sweat on his brow. Feeling the first vague tendrils of alarm, Mir gathered her strength careful to conceal its full extent. She would help and the Eldest would be in her debt. That might be useful.

She joined her power to his. Together, nothing could withstand them.

A dull, vibrating wall halted her. She pressed against it and sunk in. It seemed to wrap itself around her, sucking her into its pulsating mass. She probed, sharpening her attack. Excruciating pain seared through her head. Her attack had ricocheted back on her! Upelo would have to stand or fall on his own; she wanted no part of this. With infinite care so that the Eldest would not suspect, she retracted her power. He would think she was just another weak woman unable to handle the strain, as he thought of all women.

Mir's senses returned to normal. Pandemonium. Prisoners dragged Brothers from the supervisory platforms and their black robes disappeared beneath the angry mob. Others forced their way up the staircase. Over it all rang that abominable song. Umbu had told her about it, as he had told her about everything. She had even had him sing another bit of it for her and laughed in his face. But now, it was transformed into a weapon. She refused to be defeated by a child's song. Worse, much worse, it had been written by that minstrel. Blat, another incredibly ugly name, had much to answer for.

The Brothers guarding the gallery had hauled the ladder up from the cavern floor and stood in a protective ring around Upelo. Other Brothers were positioned in the tunnel leading to the staircase. The Eldest continued to struggle; his hands shook and he wobbled on his stick-thin legs. The strain on his body would soon be too much for even one of his stamina.

Blat remained prone on the floor, a slight smile on his face. Mir's rage returned. She ordered her guards to bring the minstrel and they muscled through to the stairs. The Brothers guarding it did not hesitate to let her and her entourage pass. They knew of her twisted penchant for causing pain.

The front line of prisoners saw people escaping the pit and they surged forward. Intoxicated by the freedom that lay within their reach, they did not notice who ran with them into the open air. Mir and her small party kept to the edge of the square and entered the citadel through a concealed side door. All was quiet within.

Warned by a sense of unease, Mir looked back towards the cavern entrance. In the flood of prisoners, Upelo's bleached pate stood out like a beacon. He was surrounded by his guards, and was steadily making his way to the citadel.

Mir ran to the transport room. She would get away from this place for a while, at least until order was restored. This was a setback, nothing more.

Upelo's party was gaining on hers. For all that he was an emaciated, ancient man, he was fast. She turned into the short stairwell and took Blat's arm in a vice-like grip. He was the cause of all this trouble

252

and he would pay. With a final spurt of energy, she was in the room and around to the other side of the table. Upelo was just a few feet away. Her guards would hold the entranceway as long as they could

The song had nearly drained her power, but she had enough for one transport. She slapped her hand on the map regardless of the destination - anywhere was better than here. As she disassembled, Upelo rushed into the room and saw where she was going. He smirked. She still had enough substance to glance down. Station Three. There were no whole cylinders at Station Three. She would not be able to renew her power. She would be trapped. Blat had seen to that.

CHAPTER 11

Crag badly needed a drink, but there was no alcohol to be had.

These Stationers just didn't know how to properly imbibe. With them it was always 'healthy food for a healthy mind' or 'proper nutrition for proper thinking.' Gods, he was sick of it. He paced along the corridor, oblivious of the Stationers who scurried out of his way.

The Station's Healer had smoothed the aberration in Crag's brain and it had helped, but he was simply too tense to allow the healing to fully restore him. He worried about that fool minstrel, he worried about Tang's devotion (what if he let the boy down?), and he worried about ever being able to figure out the device and how it affected the cylinder - if it even did affect the cylinder. Would these people die just because he was too dense to see the answer? He pounded his fist on the rough rock wall and winced at the pain he inflicted upon himself. All of this would be more tolerable with a drink.

The people of the Station were worse than useless. They had so long revered the machines, even one that they had never seen assembled before, that Crag's experiments bordered on the sacrilegious to them. Quirindi kept the more zealous off his back so that he could work but even she winced at the way he casually manhandled the components. They were only bits of metal, he told them, but he might as well have saved his breath.

He had tried inserting combinations of combustible liquids and powders into the orifice of the device. Some of the results, although quite spectacular, did nothing to activate it or affect the cylinder in any way. He knew in his gut that he was close, the answer just out of reach, tantalising him.

Not surprisingly, he found that he had paced to The Map room. He often came here to think; the Stationers pretty much left it alone. Although he did not understand how, Crag was certain that The Map had carried Blat to the desert in the west. When he had asked Quirindi about this, she shook her head. The Stationers had never done such a thing nor had even thought to try such a thing.

Crag crawled beneath The Map table. He had studied it many times from all angles but he might have missed something.

***

Tang found him there and quietly placed a tray of food on the floor beside the entranceway. He had seen Uncle Crag - as he had come to call him, but only in the privacy of his own head - in this kind of mood before and it was best not to disturb him. He lowered himself onto a cushion and waited to be noticed. Tang had an idea and now that his telepathic ability had finally manifested itself, he wanted to test it.

When Tang had arrived at Station One, he reassembled the device and was very proud of his accomplishment. The job had taken some time and he had had to coax a couple of his friends into helping him; the adults wouldn't touch it. He then read and re-read the Readings. He could see the outline of a pattern but didn't know what it meant. It had something to do with the land or with the dirt in the ground but he could barely hold the shreds of the vague picture together. One thing was for sure: no one but Crag would listen to something so farfetched.

He had tried to tell his sister but she was tired of his mad ranting, as she called it. Besides, she was much too distracted by that guitar. *Gertrude*. Every time he saw Tina, she showed him how the tips of her chording fingers had developed fine calluses. This is a good thing, she'd say. Blat will be pleased, she'd say. Listen to what I wrote, she'd say. And off she'd go, playing yet another sad melody. Tang had to admit, though not to her, that she was getting pretty good. The other young girls trailed after her, hoping Tina would let them try the instrument. Not much chance of that happening! She guarded the guitar like it was her very own cylinder. Tang didn't mind. It helped her to not think about their parents just like his work helped him. It was better not to think about them.

The dishes rattled on the tray; another tremor. That was happening more and more often lately. He remembered the very first one even though he had been young at the time. It had sent the entire Station into a panic - people crying and rushing about - it had scared him. There was talk of leaving but it was decided that it was safer inside the mountain than outside so they stayed even when some of the farthest corridors collapsed. No one had been hurt. Yet.

When he told Crag of the growing number of quakes he grunted and said that it was the same everywhere and not just in the mountains. Everything was topsy-turvy. The tides were bigger, the storms more frequent and fiercer, and in some places, huge cracks had appeared in the earth. No, the outside was not a safer place.

The Brothers had attacked his home and killed his parents, and now the whole world was falling apart. It just wasn't fair.

**

Crag emerged from beneath The Map table and placed his hands planted firmly on its surface. He unfocused his gaze until the minute detail before him became a hazy blur. He let his mind wander where it would. Sometimes his best ideas came when he just let go. It was very difficult to do, especially with nothing to drink, and, when he did let go, the moment of lucidity he hoped to achieve was a fleeting thing, gone before he could make much use of it.

The device was a machine, of that Crag was certain. He could see how it went together; he should be able to make it work. There was just some trick that eluded him.

His brain wasn't working the way it used to. For that matter, the world wasn't working the way it used to. What could have caused the change in the weather patterns? What could have caused the very bones of the earth to become so agitated? Those idiots at the Conservatory had no idea, although their plodding had eliminated several possibilities. What was left? Crag wondered if the Stations were part of the answer. The difficulties in the Stations had begun at about the same time as the first severe weather changes had been noticed. It could be coincidence. Crag hated coincidence; it was unscientific.

His stomach growled at the same time as the aroma of stew filled his nostrils. Crag turned towards the entrance and there was Tang gently wafting the steam rising from a bowl in his general direction. The boy was intent on his mission and Crag had a moment to study his face. Tang had grown up in the past few weeks. No surprise there. The tiny furrow in his brow deepened as he concentrated on getting the aroma of the food into the room. His concentration was intense. He made an excellent student. Tang's lips curved into the slightest smile. *Ha. The little cave rat is reading my mind.* Somehow, this didn't bother Crag at all. The smile grew wider.

"All right, all right. I'll eat." Crag sat and dug in.

When the worst hunger pangs were subdued and Crag had slowed his eating to a more civilised pace, he queried his young charge. "So. What's on *your* mind?"

Tang's ears reddened at the sideways rebuke. "I'm sorry; I promise I'll get better at control."

258

Crag waved the apology aside. "We have no secrets between us. Tell me what you're thinking while I finish this food."

Slowly and with more than a few backtracks and stumbles, Tang told him about the picture that had begun to form in his brain. About how the cylinders might have changed how the Stationers' minds worked and about how the cylinders might have changed how the world worked. And how the two might be connected.

Crag ignored the wrinkled apple that was his dessert and his tea cooled in the pot. He reached for his writing things and began making notes, gesturing for Tang to continue talking. He plied the boy with questions. The cool tea eased their throats and they finally had to call a break when Tang could no longer put off using the facilities.

They rose, stretched cramped muscles, and made their way down the corridor surprised that it was so empty and quiet. They must have talked for hours; the Station was asleep. They, too, would have a short rest and resume their discussion with fresher minds.

The tremor that night was the most violent yet. Ancient stalactites, suspended for hundreds of years, were shaken loose from their anchors and crashed to the ground with thunderous reverberations. Rock dust sifted into the living quarters and the terrified Stationers fled to the main cavern.

Quirindi assigned cleanup duties and the busy-work calmed her people. It gave the Council a few hours to discuss once again the contingency plans they had already formulated - hard choices for an untenable situation.

Crag had slept through the excitement and it was only when a passing Stationer awakened him that he learned of the latest disaster. Time was running out. The theory that he and Tang had been working on floated around in his mind and would have to be tested sooner than he liked but wasn't that always the way of things? There was never enough time and you just had to go with what you had.

The thought of a drink niggled at the back of his mind. It was beginning to annoy him. Why would he think of alcohol at a time like this? Better to dump it into the device for all the good it would do him.

And there it was. The answer had been pushing at him for days. Alcohol. Gods, he wished his mind would learn to clearly spell things out instead of this roundabout way it had.

He found Tang with the other Stationers milling about in the main cavern. The boy raced towards him. Crag explained what he needed and Tang broadcast the message with his telepathy. *Handy, that*.

It was not long before a few red-faced Stationers deposited their various stashes of homemade liquor at Crag's feet. Quirindi was busy elsewhere and what she didn't know...

Using a funnel Tang borrowed from the kitchens, they poured a small amount of the purest of the spirits into the device. They waited for a few minutes and when nothing happened, poured in a second quantity.

Some of the young Stationers gathered around to watch and took a collective step backwards when the device began to hum.

Crag and Tang hugged each other, grinning like idiots, and did an impromptu jig.

The hum from the device rose to a whine, sputtered a few coughing gasps, and died. Still in their victory embrace, Crag and Tang stared at it and slowly released each other.

One young Stationer, embarrassed by his cowardly reaction, dared to smirk. Tang was grateful that Crag did not see and could not read the snide remark that the boy's mind muttered. He and his friends turned on their heels and wandered off into another part of the cavern, doubtless looking for better entertainment, all the while avoiding any adult who would surely give their idle hands a task to perform.

Crag was insensible to it all. He stood with his arms folded across his chest, head bowed in thought. He shrugged. "What have we got to lose?"

He motioned for Tang to help him and, together, they poured the rest of the spirits into the device, topping it up with some of the lesser vintages.

Nothing happened at first, then the low hum began again. It continued to build until it reached a steady drone. There was no audience to witness this time; the young people were elsewhere and most of

261

the adult Stationers were busy gathering necessities for the evacuation.

Crag and Tang had always been puzzled about where the device attached to the cylinder, if it even did so, and now that they had it running, that particular conundrum was still a mystery.

The change, when it came, was barely noticeable. The cylinder was covered with a thin layer of dust from the latest tremor and the people had had no time to clean it. Ironically, it was the movement of the dust that caught Crag's attention. The small particles seemed to dance across the surface and some of them shot to the ground as though they had been expelled. Crag sent Tang back to the Map room for his bag. He needed his glass.

With the greater magnification of the glass Crag watched in fascination as the dust particles that remained on the cylinder performed with military-like precision. The motes were not round as he had supposed but rather had an elongated shape and were all oriented in the same direction.

Crag had seen this sort of behaviour once before with an especially dense rock that he had found. The rock seemed to attract anything which contained the least bit of metal and would cause all the bits of metal to point the same way. He had thought it an unusual property but hadn't come up with any practical use for it. It seemed that he might have overlooked something.

It wasn't long before the lighting in the cavern was as bright as the noonday sun. It made the chaos in the cavern more terrifying.

Quirindi rushed to his side. "What have you done?" she whispered.

A tremor shook the floor and Quirindi stumbled into him. They held on to each other. Crag squeezed his eyes shut to protect them from the grit that rained down from the weakened ceiling.

"We must leave!" Crag shouted to be heard above the tumult of the shifting mountain and the panicked Stationers. He pulled her toward the corridor that led to The Map room. She pulled with equal strength toward the corridor that led outside.

"*What are you doing?*" In her panic, Quirindi sent the message right into Crag's brain and the pain of it broke his hold on the Station leader. He shook his head. She must understand.

Tang was beside him. "Tell her," Crag hissed.

The boy focused his thoughts and the theory that they had arrived at the night before was announced not just to Quirindi but to the entire Station.

Quirindi stared at Crag and Tang. Her people stopped in their rush to the Station exit.

The choice was not difficult: the Stationers could take their chances in the valley outside where they knew that the adults would die once they were away from the life-sustaining properties of the cylinder, or they could use The Map to go where another cylinder was located. It could be equally dangerous. There was no telling if or for how long The Map would work or what the condition was of the destination cylinder. But it could mean salvation.

Quirindi had not lived nearly three hundred years by making bad decisions but she had always had the time to consider all aspects of a problem. Although Crag could not read her mind, he could see the indecision on her face.

The cavern shook again.

Several of the younger Stationers hurried into The Map room including Tina with Blat's guitar clutched to her chest. Tang turned to Crag and Quirindi, the certainty on his young face shone like a beacon.

Quirindi's people knew what awaited them outside and had heard Tang's alternative. She mind-broadcasted that, this time, she could not tell them what they should do. This time, they would have to choose for themselves. It was time to make her own decision. She stepped towards The Map table.

In the end, more than three-quarters of the Stationers used The Map to travel to the desert. Crag insisted on going last and Tang stayed with him.

They looked at each other and Crag could see the exhaustion in the boy's face. Another shudder rippled through the rock of the mountain. Tang gripped Crag's hand and firmly placed his free hand on The Map. He closed his eyes and his brow furrowed in concentration. The last thing Crag noticed before the world disappeared was how the rock dust had settled like cinnamon sprinkles on the boy's eyelashes.

Cold seeped into his bones. He was in a black void, deaf and blind. Crag despaired. Had they been wrong about The Map and its purpose? Had

264

they been wrong that the cylinder powered it and that telepathy focused it? Had they sent all those people to their death? He could no longer feel his body, and his mind felt like a rickety house in which the windows were closing one by one. He tried to hold the last window open. He needed the feeble light that shone through it. He didn't have the strength. It closed and he was dead.

The warm liquid made him cough.

"He's coming around."

That sounded just like Tang. It would make sense that the boy would feed him in the afterlife just as he did before.

A damp cloth gently wiped his face.

"That's better. He had so much sand up his nose and in his scruffy beard that it's a wonder I could recognise him at all."

Scruffy beard? Why that little imp! Crag shoved the cloth away and pushed himself onto an elbow. His eyes watered and he blinked to clear them. When he could focus, he saw Tang grinning at him.

"No, you're not dead. And, yes, we are in the desert. At the Desert Station, and it has lots of cylinders." Then his face fell.

Crag cleared his throat. "And the bad news?"

Tang looked away. "And lots of Brothers."

265

CHAPTER 12

Crag took in his surroundings. They were crowded into some kind of barracks. "How long have we been here?"

"Not long. About two hours."

There was more and Crag waited for Tang to tell him.

"Quirindi was taken by their leader."

"Alone?"

Tang took a moment to reply. "Yes, alone." He chewed his lip. "There was something very odd about that Brother."

This could be good news or bad news; there was no way of knowing. But with the Brothers, it was probably bad; it remained only to discover the matter of degree.

Crag slowly sat up and stretched his arms, working out the kinks from the frigid cold of The Map travel. He stood and shook his legs. Everything seemed to be in working order. He walked to the door and tried to open it. Barred from the outside.

One of the adult Stationers had followed Crag's progress. He came forward. "There are many cylinders here to sustain us," he said, "but the Brothers are able to block their minds from us." Other Stationers nodded confirmation.

Brothers with lots of cylinders and we don't know what they're up to, Crag thought. Very bad news indeed.

***

Quirindi had suffered during the transport and her fragile body still felt the repercussions. Her hand shook as she brought the cup of hot tea to her lips. At least this leader of the Brothers had some modicum of courtesy while he kept her waiting.

She studied her surroundings, so very different from the caves which had been her home. It surprised her at how quickly she became accustomed to the soft chair in which she sat and to the warm, dry air of the desert. Her newfound comfort would doubtless be short-lived; the Brothers were not known for their hospitality.

It remained for her to negotiate the best possible outcome for her people and it seemed that she would be forced to do so without the benefits of telepathy. It was difficult to lie with mind-to-mind speech, but she thought that it could be very easy with the spoken word. She would have to listen carefully to every nuance and watch the face closely for signs of deception. Blat and then Crag had given her some practice and for that she was grateful. She was also grateful for Crag and Tang's help with evacuating her people from the disintegrating Station. They had bought her people a reprieve and she meant to make the best use of it.

***

Upelo had had the Stationers' leader escorted to his own chambers and studied her from the peephole hidden in an adjacent room. She could not sense him, weak-minded as she was. They were all

267

weaklings. It had been a simple matter to place a barrier around their minds.

She disturbed him though; there was something eerily familiar about her. It could be that he was remembering the short, painful time when he had called a Station his home. She had the same look of all those who chose to cower in the ground like the worms that they were. But he felt that it was more than that and he would not speak with her until he knew the source of his disquiet. He never ignored his instincts.

She was old, far older than any other Stationer he had taken. It revolted him. His taste was for young flesh. Even then, he had of late grown weary of their thrashing about. His blood was cooling and his mind had been taxed by that insidious song. His jaw ached from the strain and he was tired.

His Protector Brothers had quelled the uprising. Some of the prisoners were tortured as examples of what happened when they defied the Brothers. But some had managed to escape to the outside. The desert would likely finish them but Upelo would not risk any hint of this stronghold being revealed. The last escapees had been caught and returned to their abandoned posts at the cylinders, their minds burned clean. There would be no more rest and there would be no withholding of punishment. They did not need to last beyond the eclipse.

A smile rippled across his lips. Mir and the minstrel were trapped in a rocky tomb, alive he fervently hoped, so that they could die the slow death of dehydration and starvation. That is, if Mir survived the shock of her worst nightmare happening again. He only regretted that he would not witness it. She was a stupid woman and stupid people deserved to die. Her destruction of Krodan had made this clear to Upelo. To throw away a useful tool was just not smart. The minstrel, on the other hand, was very smart. Upelo should have killed him when he'd had the chance. He would not make that mistake again.

Movement drew his attention back to the old woman. She was moving around the room, examining but not touching. What would she have learned over such a long span of living and would any of it be useful to him?

He grew weary of waiting for some insight into his misgivings about her. Perhaps it was nothing but residue from the past few days. He would interrogate her now.

Upelo slipped into the room through one of several entrances secreted behind or within objects in his room. He chose the door behind his most exquisite tapestry.

The woman stiffened when she sensed his presence behind her and turned slowly to face him. Her eyes opened wide and rolled back inside her head. Upelo caught her before her head struck the floor. He didn't want her damaged just yet.

In her unconscious state it was easy to slide a probe into her mind and rummage through her most recent thoughts. He sneered. How very noble - she was dedicated to her people and would sacrifice herself to help them. Upelo would have to wait until she awoke to delve into her past. He lifted her into a chair, surprised at how light she was.

Her eyelids fluttered open and he held a cup of water to her lips. "Drink."

She pushed his hand away. "No. I want to look at you." Her eyes filled with tears. "You have hardly changed."

Upelo sighed. She was mad; she would be of no use to him. He summoned a guard to take her to a nearby cell. Perhaps another of the Stationers would provide information and be better sport.

The guard arrived to do his bidding and took Quirindi by the arm. She turned in the doorway. "I have always regretted losing you." The door closed and she was gone.

Memory can flail you and tear you apart. It can destroy your life and it can remake it. It can be buried in the deepest hole and suddenly leap to the surface. Upelo crumpled to his knees and held his head in his hands, swaying back and forth. It hurt. It hurt and it wouldn't stop.

Upelo was uncomfortable, and he made it a point to never be uncomfortable. He pushed himself up from the floor and sat at his desk. His mind whirled with plans for vengeance. The people who had cast him out, who had thought to murder him, were in his grasp. And the worst offender of all, his own mother, was in the next room.

He had been far too occupied, at first, building the Brothers of the Watch, to return to the home that had discarded him. He couldn't think why he subsequently ignored it after he had amassed the power to crush it. She had forced him to see this weakness; she would pay for that. His hand shook

270

as he poured brandy from a crystal decanter. She would pay for that, too.

***

Angus Willoughby gently prodded the rubble aside. The gleam he hoped for winked back at him. The silver was the purest he had ever seen. This was it! He had found the seam!

He rolled his head on his shoulders easing the infernal cramping that had begun to plague him a couple of winters back. He grinned. With this find, he could stay home a bit more; maybe work on that fiddle tune he had started way back. He would probably drive Effie crazy but that was nothing new. His grin widened. It would be fun to tease her day and night. Especially at night.

He marked the spot and gathered his tools. No sense starting the delicate extraction work at this time of day. It would wait until tomorrow, and he would bring the boys with him. This find would make all their fortunes.

A low rumble from the vicinity of the north end of the cave system stopped him in his tracks. He marked time for a good five minutes; there was no other sound. He had been fairly certain that all activity had ceased from the blast, but this could have been another of the increasingly frequent tremors that shook the range. They had best get the silver out quickly.

"...will tear the tongue out of your head." The snarling threat echoed around the rock walls. "The

271

last thing you will ever see is its bleeding piece of meat."

The woman's voice had risen to a shriek. Angus hesitated. It sounded like something he wanted no part of, but whoever it was, was on his stake and he had had entirely enough of people encroaching on what was his. He chose a pickaxe from his rucksack and slowly approached the direction of the altercation: the room where the statue of the woman had been. Angus pushed aside the first of the tapestries and crept down the dark and debris-strewn passage.

"Be reasonable, Mir. I can help you get away from here."

That was Blat's voice. Angus crouched behind the material that disguised the archway into the room. He eased it aside a bare fraction of an inch and peered inside.

Mir stood over Blat who lay on his side before her. He was curled upon himself and appeared dazed. Blood slanted across his forehead from a wound above his left eye.

"Help? From you? I remember the last time you promised your help." She levelled a kick at Blat's groin. He turned at the last instant and took the blow on his hip. Still, it had to have hurt.

Angus hoped they would keep talking; it covered the small sounds that he made as he moved up behind Mir.

He was still a few feet from her when she turned. In silence, she launched herself at him. She was far stronger than Angus would have believed possible and, as he doubled over from the blow to

272

his stomach, she kneed him in the face. He fell to his back and lost his grip on the pickaxe. It clattered away. She didn't notice, intent as she was on kneeling on his chest and getting a firm grim around his throat. Silver stars filled his vision. *Silver*, he thought. He would never see that lovely stuff again.

Her grip abruptly lost its strength and Angus sucked in a small stream of blessed air. His head pounded and he was pretty certain that she had broken his nose. Her crazy green eyes, so close to his, look startled for a moment, then looked at nothing.

Angus shoved and she toppled to the cave floor. He rolled over and got to his hands and knees, coughing out the blood and mucus clogging his throat. He turned his head and stared at his attacker, only then seeing the handle of his axe sticking out of her back.

Beyond her body, Blat trembled, head bowed, taking deep breaths. His arms hung down at his sides. Angus had never seen a more welcome sight.

***

Quirindi was taken to a nearby room. It had no windows. A crude pallet made from wood and straw filled most of it. There was a bucket in the far corner that had not been emptied recently and its stench made her eyes water. When the guard slammed the door shut, she was enveloped in darkness. A lifetime in the Station had erased any fear of the dark and given her the ability to discern

273

shapes and shadows in all but the most profound gloom. She moved to the pallet and sat. She had much to think about.

She felt a faint twinge of pride. He had not only survived, he had thrived. It must be the very same anomaly in his mind that had forced him to do those unspeakable things so long ago that had given him the gift to live beyond the cylinder's protection. But it did not take telepathy to see that it had exacted a heavy price and that her sudden appearance had caused him great pain.

It was not in her nature to ignore suffering. She would help him in whatever way she could. After all, she was his mother.

CHAPTER 13

Umbu watched from beneath half-closed eyelids. He didn't trust these new prisoners and listened closely to their conversation. Much of it was nonsense about devices and dust motes and he thought that the Brothers must have burned a little too deeply into their brains.

He wasn't all that certain if his own brain was working properly. How could he know? That woman had used her mind-control to abuse him and it had hurt. Little did she know that even her inventiveness paled against what he had already been subjected to in his life. The scar on his neck was from the very last time one of his 'guardian's' guests had approached him in the night. That was when, at the tender age of ten, he had killed his first man.

Mir's interrogation had extracted everything that Umbu knew, much good it did her. He smiled a little. She had inflicted the worst injury right there at the end when she pulled his hair out. Though it shamed him, he must have fainted and fallen from the platform. The cavern had been empty, except for a few very dead Brothers, when he returned to consciousness and no one noticed when he exited the pit. The only activity in the square was prisoners on their knees scouring the slate so that it shone. The Brothers had regained control and the only way to stay out of their clutches was to return to his barracks.

"Ha. A song you say."

Umbu opened his eyes a little wider. A tall, lanky man gesticulated with abandon.

"That crazy minstrel beat them with a song? They have a hundred cylinders and Brothers everywhere and he beat them by humming a tune?" The man slapped his hands against his thighs and doubled over in laughter.

This was too much. Umbu slowly raised himself from his pallet and slunk along the wall to where the new prisoners had gathered around the weathered farmer. Ches had been laid up with a broken ankle on the day of the revolt. As hard as they worked their prisoners, even the Brothers recognised when a man could not stand.

Ches huffed. "I heard it with my own ears and saw what it did to them Brothers. I saw it from that door right over there." He gestured towards the barracks' door. "It was the same as when you cut the head off a chicken and it runs around some. They didn't have no control over themselves nor us. For a while, leastways."

"So where is the minstrel now?" Crag asked.

"He was in no great shape, y'see. That leader fella had took him and tortured him some." He scratched his chin. "It was hard to see with so many people running around but I think it was that woman had him dragged back to the big place. Ain't seen him since."

Umbu had manoeuvred his way to a position behind the tall man. He could reach out and, with a quick twist, take him down. This fellow, whoever he was, had no call to mock the minstrel.

"If I know Blat, and I know him pretty well, he'll be conniving or sweet-talking his way out of whatever pile of trouble he's landed in. That boy can do more than sing and pluck a tune on a guitar, though he's mighty good at both. Now don't tell him I said that," he hurried to add, "it'll go straight to his head."

Umbu hesitated. Only a friend would say that last part. He let his body relax and cleared his throat. "I know where he might be."

Crag spun around, his eyes narrowed. "Well, let that be a lesson to me. You were just pretending to be mind-wiped." He extended his hand to the stranger. "Crag Bithoone, Inventor and Scientist Extraordinaire, at your service and I would very much like to hear where you think Blat has gotten himself to."

Umbu did not like to be the centre of attention but this was important. He cleared his throat again and told of how, at first, he had watched the minstrel as he did all newcomers. He deigned to mention that, at first, he had found the minstrel a nuisance at best, but soon learned that Blat was driven to thwart the Brothers and that was good news indeed to Umbu. The others in the barracks dared not risk the retribution that might befall their families if they challenged the Brothers and Umbu couldn't blame them.

He told Crag of how he was assigned to work alongside Blat and suspected the minstrel was up to something. He had followed him later that same night when the minstrel crept out of the barracks. The rest of the story was quickly told: how Blat entered the citadel and discovered the Brothers' plot and where The Map room was located; how Blat knew that focusing your mind could deflect the Brothers' control and composed a song to help everyone do this; how Blat suspected that the Brothers must have a leader and was determined to identify him; and how he and Blat were caught and tortured on their second foray.

***

Crag was trying very hard not to think of Blat once again in that woman's thrall and buried his anxiety by asking a plethora of questions. Umbu was a fount of knowledge about the workings of the Desert Station and about the layout of the Brothers' citadel.

"From what I was told," Umbu continued, "the song worked and everyone made it to the big yard. But in the scuffle and confusion and mad dash for the hole in the invisible wall, people stopped singing, and it wasn't long before the Brothers rallied and either subdued with mind pain or killed any prisoners that were slow to return to their barracks.

"So now you newcomers must learn to protect yourselves. You must learn the song."

The Stationers were already adept at focusing their minds. The song, however, was another matter. To the people of the Stations, singing was just not done. Crag surmised that the early Stationers who had made music taboo knew of its ability to affect their cylinder-enhanced minds.

The scientist, however, had no time to ponder the significance of musical vibrations and their relationship to cylinders and mind control. A half dozen well-armed Brothers barged in and herded them to their first work shift. He kept Tang close by his side; Umbu stepped into place behind them. They entered the doorway to the pit.

From Umbu's description, Crag knew they would soon pass the short tunnel to the gallery. He stared. There was not one but two fully assembled devices along the back wall. He was passed the opening before he could see if there were more. Perhaps Tang had had a better look.

Although the cylinders' cavern had been described to him, Crag was stunned. Row upon row of cylinders gleamed in the steady artificial light that seemed to emanate from the walls and roof of the cave. At equidistant intervals, immense cylinders rose above their lesser brethren. He ignored the sharp sting of a whip striking his shoulder. A second, harder blow broke the spell and he hurried down the final steps.

It was some time before there was a respite in the monotonous labour so that Crag could ask the boy if he had seen the devices. By then, Tang drooped with exhaustion barely understanding the question. None of the Stationers were used to this kind of continual labour and the guards were liberal in applying their whips. It seemed that the recent uprising did not sit well and they were determined to quell any nascent thoughts of insurrection by inflicting pain as often as possible.

"Did you see the devices?" Crag repeated, a little louder.

Tang looked at him, dazed. A guard's quick lash caught Crag on the brow and a warm trickle of blood dribbled down his face. To make the point clearer, the Brother lashed out at Tang. The boy winced in pain as the tip of the whip lacerated his forearm.

Crag saw red, not from the blood on his face but from the anger in his heart. But there was nothing he could do and he squashed the intense desire to take that whip and shove it down the guard's throat.

***

Blat gingerly removed the strapping from around his chest. Freed from the constricting bands of material, he could almost take a full breath.

After two days of Effie's ministrations, he was feeling more himself. But the best healing had taken place when he had spied the guitar in the corner of his sickroom. Certain that Angus had put it there for him to find, Blat gently picked it up and caressed the warm wood. It was very old and it was a beauty. He ran his fingers over the strings. Someone had even tuned it. He ignored the pain of his cracked rib and the aches of his healing bruises, and lost himself in music. Fleeting images of Talitha inspired him to the more gentle songs in his repertoire.

His body was healing and the music soothed his mental trauma. Ironically, he had Krodan to thank for his continued existence as more than a mindless polisher of cylinders. Krodan's lengthy torture had forced Blat to build a high threshold of resistance to Upelo's onslaught. The new, raw places that the leader of the Brothers had gouged into his brain were already not so tender and the scar tissue of time would eventually dilute the ugly experience into an unpleasant memory.

When his fingers began to cramp and his shoulders to wince, he laid the guitar in his lap and bowed his head, content for a moment, the first in a long time. Blat looked up at a deep sigh from the doorway. Crowded in the small space was the entire Willoughby clan.

"That was fine," Effie said for them all and turned to her family. "Now off to your chores." She shooed them along, except for Angus, on whom she bestowed a significant look.

"I expect you'll be wanting to head out," the prospector said.

Blat nodded.

"Young Jord has been going on about Rivercrest ever since I made the mistake of telling him about it some years ago. It would do me a great service if you would take him with you when you go. He's no good to me right now the way he's all caught up. You need to have a calm mind when you tackle a silver job. And he could do the heavy work for you. He's a good lad."

Blat nodded again.

Angus looked at the guitar in Blat's lap. "That belonged to my father and I would be proud if you called it your own. The travel case is still sturdy though it's seen a few years and a few miles." His eyes took on a faraway look. "Dad would rest easier knowing that someone played it." He turned and left the room.

He and Jord left early the next morning, saddlebags packed to bursting with victuals and other necessities, as Effie called the generous portions of the healing concoctions that she included. The addition of copious quantities of honey to her potions did little to disguise the foul after-taste. He and Jord exchanged a covert glance. The stuff would soon become part of the countryside.

The first couple of days jolted every muscle in Blat's body and his rib caused some aggravation, but he soon regained his ease in the saddle and his journeyman's endurance. They would make Rivercrest in good time.

***

"So," Crag began in his best lecturer's voice, "first, we rescue Quirindi. Second, free the prisoners - if we do this first, the Brothers might kill Quirindi before we can get to her - and third we must find their leader - Blat was right about that part. Upelo, is it? - and take him to Rivercrest so that we can put a stop to his nefarious plans." He had raised a finger at each item and now wiggled them in Umbu's face. "Look. There are a lot of fingers left. While we're at it, why don't we also repair the brain damage done to these poor bastards?" Crag indicated the men who lay on their pallets, eyes vacant. "And - I know! - we could try to make it rain in the desert at the same time!"

Umbu put his massive fists on his hips and glared at Crag. "I didn't say it would be easy," he growled. "What kind of master inventor-scientist are you? Surely you have overcome difficulties before this."

"Difficulties? Difficulties? Not getting enough heat to melt a rock, that's difficulties. Trying to convince a bunch of bureaucrats that I need more funds, that's difficulties." Crag began pacing up and down the narrow aisle that separated the two rows of pallets. "This, on the other hand, is impossible. Look at us. A few Stationers scattered among a dozen barracks. Stationers with no fighting experience and some of whom are children. And then we have fishermen and farmers who may have fought a fish or a plow but have never even seen a real battle. This is our army. And I don't care how loud they can sing; look how it fell apart the last time." Crag turned on his heel and strode down the aisle away from Umbu.

The others in the room watched the interplay, careful to not bring attention to themselves.

Tang sat in a corner, brow furrowed in thought. He had seen Crag go on like this before and knew that it just meant that he was thinking out loud. His Uncle would soon surprise them all with a brilliant plan. So he was as shocked as anyone to find himself speaking. "If we could empty the devices, we could disrupt the entire place without having to fight."

Crag stopped in his tracks. His shoulders started to shake. It took a minute for the scientist to turn around so that Tang could see his face. A wide grin split it in two. He was laughing. "My boy, don't ever stop amazing me," he said between chortles. Crag sat down next to him and squeezed the breath out of him. Flushed and embarrassed, Tang awkwardly returned the hug.

"We'll need to find their stash of hooch. They must have a stash somewhere." Crag turned to Umbu.

"You mean alcohol?" the big man asked.

Crag nodded.

Later that night, Crag and Umbu repeated the clandestine approach to the citadel that Blat had found. Crag surmised that the Brothers would keep the devices' fuel in the coolest part of their most protected building; the gods forbid that the Brothers themselves should be able to get at it and have a little fun.

They used some of the grease they had skimmed off this evening's excuse for a meal to lubricate the hinges in the grate that protected a basement window. As soon as they had it open, a musty odour emanated from within. Crag's teeth gleamed in the faint light. He knew that smell; the Brothers made their own libation. Umbu lowered him into the room. Barrels were stacked along the walls of a long room and the apparatus for making more of the same glinted at the far end. Satisfied, he reached up to grab Umbu's hands and the big man hoisted him from the room. They closed the window and grate and retraced their steps.

The various components of their plan had to be executed simultaneously. They must empty the alcohol from the devices and foul the extra supply. They must extricate Quirindi and take control of The Map room if only for the time it would take to activate The Map. They must overcome any Brothers that got in the way, either in the cavern or in the citadel. The Protector Brothers were big and were armed; it would do no good to thwart their mind-powers only to be skewered by their swords.

The next morning they marched to the cylinders' cavern to put in another day of polishing. Crag was at a loss as to the purpose of this mindless activity - first polish one way then polish the other way. There must be a compelling reason, though, or the Brothers would not go through so much effort to have it done. Maybe it had something to do with how dust particles dance on a cylinder's surface. Crag couldn't take the time to speculate about that now; he would stash it in the back of his mind along with the hundreds of other puzzles to ponder someday. He had more urgent things to think about.

The entire plan hinged on a single premise: that the Brothers did not have machines like the ones that formerly powered the Stations' cylinders to keep this facility functioning but rather relied solely on the devices to do so. De-activating the devices would then turn the cylinders to useless hulks and though he didn't much care if the Brothers suffered, Crag was torn about what it would do to the Stationers. He would have to work on that later. First, they must stop Upelo. Blat's discovery of the wide net that the Brotherhood had cast made Crag's blood turn cold. If they didn't stop him, it wouldn't matter if the cylinders worked or not.

***

Crag fretted about their lack of first-hand information regarding the layout of the citadel, but Quirindi must be saved and soon. She was not a strong woman. Even with Umbu's assurance that he could find The Map room and guess where Quirindi would likely be held, they had a slim chance of success.

One team would destroy the liquor by the simple expedient of emptying it onto the floor - quiet and efficient. A second team, six Stationers with the strongest minds in the group, would clear the path to the devices. Tang had to be with that team to show them how to empty the liquid from the devices. It was a dangerous job but the boy glowed with pride at having such responsibility. Crag sighed. He did not like this worrying business at all. It was what he imagined being a father was like. His stomach clenched at the thought. Father, indeed. More like stupid idiot. But there was no choice; he couldn't be everywhere at once and Tang was the only other person familiar with the device.

Crag's task was to extricate Quirindi and proceed to The Map room. With all those cylinders nearby, she should be able to provide the mind-power to transport them. If this Map was similar to the others he had studied, Rivercrest should have at least two places to which they could travel. Upelo's Map room would likely be guarded, especially since the arrival of the Stationers. Crag needed the most able-bodied men with him but instead chose only one other. They had to be quick and quiet in the citadel. Umbu was strong and the closest thing they had to a fighter. His skills had been learned in dockside brawls and he fought dirty. Perfect.

All was as ready as it could be and in the middle of the short sleep shift, the teams set out.

Umbu boosted Crag into the citadel. The scientist secured the knotted blankets they had brought, lowered the makeshift rope out the window, and the big man climbed up to join him. In seconds, they were crouched in the dark chamber.

Umbu led the way. For someone so large, he could move as quietly as a light breeze. The leather rope he had fashioned from a worn sandal silenced the first guard. A quick tug around the neck, a small bit of thrashing, and it was over. He dragged the body into a storage room and liberated the slender dagger from the sheath strapped to the guard's calf. He held it with expert skill. Crag wondered what other talents Umbu would reveal.

Quirindi, when they found her, was weak but conscious. Her translucent skin seemed to provide scant cover over her jutting bones. Crag wrapped her in the thin, stinking blanket from the pallet and lifted her into his arms. They continued to The Map room.

***

The two devices were larger and in far better shape than the one Tang had assembled at Quirindi's Station. As they emptied them of alcohol, the light flickered. The disruption in the cylinders' power was much faster than he had imagined. They quickly finished and exited the cavern.

Alerted by the variation in the light, Protector Brothers poured from their lodgings, strapping on swords as they ran. Tang's team kept to the deep shadows that were growing deeper by the minute as the light continued to fail. Tang could sense his mind power weakening ever so slightly. He wondered what it was doing to the older Stationers.

The more debilitated prisoners could not be included in the breakout. Their bodies were sound, but what was left of their minds could not comprehend a change from their simple routine. Crag had sworn that he would return for them and Tang believed him. Tonight, though, the priority was for as many as possible to escape in one piece. This would leave cylinders untended and the Brothers with a reduced source of power in the event they had a secondary source of alcohol hidden somewhere.

The light changed. Could the Brothers have replenished the devices already? One of his team members nudged him in the ribs and pointed upwards. The dome was dissolving; it was the starry desert night that now illuminated the Brothers' compound.

The citadel was just ahead and they hurried down the alleyway grateful that the blanket rope still hung from the window. Tang motioned for his companions to ascend while he held the rope still. Against Crag's wishes, he had convinced his team to try to reach The Map room. What if Crag needed his help to complete the mission? Although the desert was a much safer escape route, it would take entirely too much time to reach the nearest town. Tang had to make sure that the outside world was warned in time.

There was a shout. Tang watched the last man scramble through the window before he turned to face the Brother racing towards him.

He was small and he was fast and he side-stepped the Brother's grappling lunge. He kicked out at the man's right knee as he dove by and was satisfied with the grunt of pain as the Brother went down. A dark shadow loomed above him and Tang rolled frantically out of reach banging his elbow on the building's stone wall.

Blinding pain filled his head. If he could have he would have kicked himself. In the fray, he had let his mind-guard drop.

***

Upelo looked at the ragged boy and wondered how many more insults he would have to endure. With the power he commanded, how was it that a small child could worm his way into his sanctum? He would have to punish a great many of his so-called Protector Brothers.

His mind flitted to Krodan. Mighty Krodan with his visions of godhood. He had been a useful puppet, though, and Mir had destroyed him. A female. Women and boys were an affliction that must be eradicated.

The lights flickered. Upelo ignored it.

He looked at the boy over steepled fingers. So small, so helpless. Much like he once was. And look what he had accomplished. No, he would not underestimate the abilities of anyone so young.

He thought of that noxious old woman. How could he ever have needed the approval of such a weakling? She had lived many years and should be brimming with power. Instead, she had given up almost immediately.

Such a contrast with this child who exuded defiance from every pore.

He gazed at the flickering lights. "You say you did this? All by yourself?" The boy had been telling him this preposterous tale of tampering with the holy repositories. But just in case, Upelo had sent a Brother to verify the story.

A light tap on the door signalled the Brother's return. "Enter," Upelo bade him.

The Brother bowed in obeisance.

"Speak."

"It is as the boy says." The Brother remained motionless, awaiting the Eldest's next command.

Upelo considered. The devices, as the child had named them, had been there since the Brotherhood had first discovered this stronghold. How could a young boy have learned what it had taken so many of his Priests so many years to achieve? Upelo brushed the question away. He only had to look at his own life to know that great things can be accomplished regardless of age and experience.

The Eldest felt the first twinges of his mind power weakening. Perhaps he was more tired than he thought. He would finish this quickly. He smiled at Tang. "You will undo what you have done." He twisted his command into the boy's mind, puncturing through the flimsy defences with ease. Upelo breathed a sigh of satisfaction as he plunged deeper and deeper, scraping strips from the tender underbelly of Tang's mind.

The sound of running in the corridor jolted Upelo from his delicate work. He scowled.

"See to it," he ordered. The Brother backed to the door and stepped into the hallway.

Upelo saw that Tang slumped in his chair, pale and shivering. Upelo felt a little better about the rude interruption of his work.

The Brother re-entered the room.

"Speak."

"Intruders."

Rage, hot and deadly, boiled in Upelo. He would suffer no more inconveniences. This would be stopped. Now.

He rose and strode to the door. "Bring the boy."

Brothers were scurrying everywhere like the mindless minions that they were. They were worse than useless. He stormed down the corridors, burning minds as he went.

The transport room was just ahead. Where were the guards? Upelo lashed out at whoever was inside and was blocked by that infernal song. He clamped down on his power and extracted a miniature crossbow from within his robes, careful not to touch the poisoned tip of the quarrel. *Let's see how well they sing when they're dead.*

A trio faced him from across the map table. One of them was in the protective embrace of a tall man. She raised her face and looked at him, continuing to sing in her feeble old-woman's voice all the while.

His arm shook as he raised the crossbow. "You should never have let them exile me, mother." The voice that came out of his mouth was shrill and pitiful. He hated that she could reduce him to the sniveling youth he had been. He pulled the trigger.

"Nooo!" a man's voice shouted from a great distance.

She stopped singing, her eyes wide and startled, continuing to stare at him as Upelo watched the life drain from her.

Moving through air that felt thick, Upelo stepped to the map and carefully placed his hand on the table. He dropped the crossbow and reached behind to snag the boy. Together they dissolved.

***

Crag remained motionless, unable to absorb what had happened.

"We should go after them," Umbu said into the silence. "I saw where he put his hand. Rivercrest."

Crag looked at the tiny woman in his arms and gently placed her body on the floor. He knelt and adjusted the blanket around her. She was the

292

Stationers' leader and she was dead. Nothing could be done about that now. But Tang was very much alive. Umbu was right; they must continue. He nodded.

"Can you make it go?" Umbu gripped the Brother that had accompanied Upelo. When the Brother remained silent, Umbu shook him until his teeth rattled against each other. "I'll take that as a yes."

CHAPTER 14

The hot, noisy, messy Guildhall had never looked so good. Blat stashed his saddle bags and guitar in a corner beside the doors and took a deep breath. Home.

It was near the end of supper when the musicians sat back and relaxed for a few minutes. Soon enough, they would return to their duties. At the moment, though, the dining hall was full and at the height of its cacophony. It took a truly powerful shriek from the other end of the room to pierce the tumult. Sarah. She approached at a run, joined by various members of her family along the way.

Blat was crushed under the pleasant weight of hugs, laughter, and excited babble. He nodded and laughed along with them, no one understanding a word that was said. Jamie-the-Cook put a massive arm around Blat's shoulders and deftly guided the cluster of bodies through his domain and to the relative quiet of the kitchen.

Talitha stood at the pastry counter and wielded a tiny spatula with delicate precision. The masterpiece before her looked exactly like the spectacular mountain peak near the centre of Whitecap Island's glacier. She added one final sweep of snowy frosting, placed her tool in the rinsing bowl, and flung herself into Blat's outstretched arms.

"It's good to see you, my friend," she said into his ear.

Friend. For the first time, it sounded like enough to Blat. It sounded good.

When they were seated around the table, Blat turned to beckon Jord forward. The young Willoughby boy had been drawn along in their wake. Introductions were made and, giggling, Leonora and Louetta made room for Jord between them. In spite of his flaming red face, Jord performed a reasonable bow to the two girls and sat with as much grace as he could, given that he had to climb over the bench.

Blat watched the proceedings with interest. He had gotten to know the lad quite well on the trek to Rivercrest and liked him very much. Jord had proven his skill at any number of tasks but was particularly clever when it came to horses and the Guildhall was always in need of competent hostlers. He would put in a good word for him if Jord should decide to stay. Blat smiled. He would never forget the look of wonder on Jord's face when they had topped the last rise and the city spread out before them like a crystal goblet filled with bright jewels.

When Louetta's most recent pranks were discussed in detail, Leonora's competence at everything was described, and Talitha's new signature desert devoured - a delicate pastry filled with chocolate and cream - all eyes turned to Blat.

Like any good minstrel, he waited for complete silence. Blat closed his eyes and began to hum his song. He added the words and in a few short bars, Sarah joined in with a delicate harmony. Jord had learned it on the trail and added a very-passable tenor to the mix. Soon the entire table had joined in as well as most of the kitchen staff. The song wafted out into the main dining area. Heads poked in through the kitchen door. Minstrels were always ready for a new song, especially if it was a good one. Someone pulled out a set of pipes, another added the plink of cutlery on glassware, and yet another clapped on the backbeat.

Everyone in the Guildhall would soon know the song. If the Brothers attacked, make that *when* the Brothers attacked, they would have at least one weapon at the ready. Blat repeated a final chorus and filled the brief silence at the end with his storytelling voice. "I travelled deep into the mountains," he began, "in search of material for a song. I found much, much more…"

The questions, when they came, centred on the power of Blat's song to affect the Brothers' mind control. Every musician knew that music could soothe or cause anger or make you weep, but they had never considered the possibility of it being able to cause something so dramatic. That such mind control existed in the first place was momentarily overshadowed by the fact that music could affect it. This was so momentous that it could not be left until morning. A contingent of senior minstrels left immediately to inform the Masters at the Conservatory.

Blat's eyes felt gritty. It had been a long day in the saddle and a long, exciting night. His young charge had been guided off to bed some time ago and Blat thought that an excellent idea. He was permitted to leave only after he promised many more tales to come, and climbed the familiar stairs to the dormitory. His old room was much as it had been. Some wonderful person had brought up his saddle bags and guitar. He tugged off his boots, shrugged out of his clothes, and crawled into bed.

***

"I don't care if he's been sleeping five minutes let alone five hours. I will see him! Now!"

In his years at the Guildhall, Blat had trained himself to sleep through almost anything: the thunder of students racing off to class, the discordant squawks of a novice horn player, the piercing wail of a descant soloist. But this roar in the corridor was different from the everyday sounds and that difference woke him. It was a good thing that he decided he might as well check it out and had at least put on trousers when the door burst open and a more-dishevelled-than-usual Crag Bithoone strode in.

"Good. You're up. We have work to do. Here, put on more clothes." He opened a cupboard and threw a tunic at Blat.

Blat caught the garment that was tossed at his head. "Good to see you, too," he said as he pulled on the garment. "I can't help but notice that your time away from my good influence has sorely degraded your manners." Blat sighed dramatically. "And you were making such progress."

The scientist pulled his head out of the closet where he was rummaging for who knew what. "What's that? Bad manners? Why you insolent pup…" He strode the two steps that separated them and grabbed Blat into a fierce, brief hug. "How's that for manners? It's good to see you, my boy, but as I said, we have work to do. Now, are you coming?"

Sarah leaned on the doorjamb and shook her head. "I'd forgotten just how pushy you can be, Crag Bithoone."

The scientist's entire demeanour softened. He turned slowly, and with a grace that Blat had never seen in him before. "And I'd forgotten just how lovely you are," Crag said.

Blat watched the interchange, keeping as quiet as possible. This was the first time he had seen Sarah and Crag together; he had been either in school or on the road whenever the infamous Crag Bithoone visited. Blat knew a little about their history and how they had once been lovers. The attraction between them still sizzled. They held each other's gaze a moment longer.

Sarah turned and walked down the hall. "They're assembling in the main Concert Hall. You'd best hurry. Oh, and there's hot food in the kitchen. Your friend's there already."

Crag stared after her until she disappeared around a corner. "No time," he muttered, "never any time."

Without another word, Crag and Blat, guitar case in hand, headed toward the kitchen.

When they reached the end of the dining hall, Crag had regained his composure. "So. Now you have to play for your breakfast?"

"I just like to have it with me." Blat was inordinately fond of the old guitar. *Gertrude* would not be pleased.

Much surprised, Blat recognised Umbu in the far corner with his back to the wall and a huge platter of eggs in front of him. He stopped shovelling them in long enough to clap Blat on the shoulder and returned to his food. Blat took the hint that he would only learn the story of how the big man was here and in the company of none other than Crag Bithoone after the plates were emptied, and sat down beside him. One of the kitchen staff placed more food on the table and they all three ate their fill in silence.

When they had finished, Crag recounted how he and Quirindi's Stationers had transported to the desert and sabotaged the devices. He didn't know if any other prisoners had escaped and the only fatality he knew of for certain was Quirindi's. Her death was a huge blow; she had been a vital link to the Stationers.

Blat shook his head at the loss of such a gracious, peaceful woman. It was nearly beyond comprehension that Upelo was her son. He shivered. Who knew what killing his own mother would do to him?

Abruptly, Crag crushed the sweet roll he held in his hand. In a quick, fierce motion, he threw it at the wall. It slid to the floor, leaving a trail of syrup and crumbs. It was safer to wait until the scientist decided to speak - Blat had learned that the hard way during their travel together - and it wasn't long in coming.

"And Upelo..." Crag made a fist and pounded the table. "He took him. That bastard took him."

Blat's stomach knotted around the ample breakfast he was beginning to regret. His first-hand experience with the Eldest was all too sharp in his memory.

"Who? Who did he take?"

The anguish in Crag's eyes gave Blat his answer: Tang. Upelo had Tang and they were in Rivercrest.

Blat quickly related what he had learned and done since he and Crag had last seen each other. When he got to the part about Mir's demise, Crag's eyes brightened.

"Some good news at last. But the rest of it is a dog's breakfast." Blat scowled at him. "Except for your song, of course."

Sarah rushed in. "Well, come on then. They're waiting!"

Filled with misgivings about naming Masters as conspirators with the Brothers, Blat had nevertheless decided to hold nothing back. Their reactions might reveal something, and Umbu along with a few minstrels would shadow any that left the building.

The Concert Hall overflowed with students and teachers. Nearly the full complement of the Assembly of Masters was present on the dais, something witnessed only on the most important of occasions. Word of Blat's experiences was mildly interesting but remained just some unsubstantiated tale until proof could be produced. The appearance of Crag, a rogue but brilliant scientist, was barely worth noticing. But the fact that he had a Brother of the Watch in tow had caused a near panic the previous evening. It was the Brother that had brought this august body out and had filled the Hall. Few had ever even seen a Brother and none had ever had the opportunity to question one.

They would be told everything and could ask the Brother whatever they wished, Blat promised the agitated crowd, but first they must learn the song. The Assembly nodded its permission; its jaded membership was curious about what it was rumoured that this song could do. This was accomplished in short order. Their acquiescence to learn the song didn't mean that the Assembly would credit anything that was subsequently said and, sure enough, both his and Crag's tales were met with disbelief. Umbu was not acknowledged. Some of the more fantastical claims, like a statue coming to life and the ability to move instantly from place to place triggered by telepathy no less, were met with raised eyebrows and muffled snorts of laughter.

Frustrated, Blat recited names - the ones he had memorised from Upelo's planning room, the ones who were members of the Conservatory - flinching slightly at the outrage he expected. The reaction, however, was strangely muted. It seemed that the members named had gone missing the previous day; Upelo must have already gathered his Rivercrest Brothers to him. This gave a small amount of credibility to Blat's tale but the Assembly was far from accepting that any danger was imminent.

When the Brother of the Watch was ushered in, the sensitive acoustics of the Concert Hall resonated with the collective intake of breath. The Brothers had long struck fear into the hearts of all Whitecap

Islanders and, to make matters worse, this was one of the Protector Brothers, the red armband a sharp contrast against the black of his robe. For a moment, no one in the Hall spoke. The Lute Master put the first question to the Brother. It was barely audible but had the power to unleash a whole barrage. The Brother stood where he had been told to stand and said nothing, his pale face devoid of expression. When it became clear to even the most persistent that he would continue to say nothing, the Brother was taken from the Hall and returned to his cell.

Notwithstanding the Brother's obstinate silence and the general disbelief of Blat's story, the Assembly agreed to have the transport locations guarded, especially since The Map room in the Desert Station had clearly depicted one in the Conservatory itself.

It had been coincidental that a senior magistrate had witnessed Crag, Umbu, and the Brother materialise in front of him, in his wine cellar no less. He had dropped the dusty bottle he had been examining and cursed loudly at the loss of a particularly fine vintage before it occurred to him to be alarmed at their sudden appearance. They explained who they were and where they had come from. The magistrate didn't believe a word; he had heard a great many prevarications in his courtroom. These were doubtless the scoundrels who had taken several cases of a premium brandy from his premises earlier in the year. Nevertheless, he reported to the Assembly what he saw. Security Guards were also dispatched to his home with orders to secure the cellar. If there were more transport locations... well, there was nothing they could do about them.

The Assembly of Masters' spokesperson rose from his seat. "Return to your Guildhalls and keep silent about what you have heard this morning. We must determine the veracity of these claims," the slight mocking tone was not lost on the sensitive ears of the musicians in the Hall, "and we do not need the populace in a panic. We will take it upon ourselves to inform the Rivercrest City Council of what we feel they should know." The Masters retired to an adjacent meeting room. Blat and Crag were not invited to join them.

Blat could see that Crag's patience was at an end. They had done all they could do here.

"We can't wait for them to digest all of this," Blat whispered. *Just like any group of bureaucrats, they couldn't make a quick decision even if the entire world depended on it. Ha.* Especially *if the entire world depended on it.*

Crag nodded. "We'll just have to do what we have to do, my boy."

As the volume of discussion and argument rose to fill the hall and distract those around them, Crag and Blat sidled to one of the side entrances, Umbu at their heels and Sarah close behind.

The four of them stood blinking in the bright mid-morning light. "Where to?" Crag asked.

Sarah knew of a small, dingy room in the cellar of an alehouse where they could make plans, and come and go unnoticed. Secrecy was a good thing, they decided, when you didn't know exactly who was a Brother and who wasn't.

***

It was dark in the closet and Tang stank from the sweat that had dried on his body. His legs had grown weary from standing but he could only sit or lay on his side with his knees tightly tucked into his chest which was also tiring. *But this was better than looking into the crazy eyes of that Brother,* he thought. The man had transported them to wherever this place was and shoved him into this prison. Uncle Crag had surely seen where the Brother had put his hand on The Map and would rescue him. If he could find someone to work the transport before he got caught.

Footsteps sounded outside. He stiffened. The door was flung open.

"Bring him."

He recognised the voice of the Crazy Man, as Tang called him in his head. Big hands grabbed his arms and hauled him from the closet. The harsh light hurt his eyes and the confinement in the closet had cramped his muscles. His attempts to struggle free were futile. They put a smelly sack over his head and tied his hands together leaving a piece of the rope dangling which they used as a leash. He was half dragged down a hallway floored with strips of wood, this much he could see through the gap at the bottom of the sack.

They turned into corridor after corridor until Tang was totally disoriented and descended a stone staircase that was damp with moisture making the footing treacherous. Tang concentrated on each step; if he fell and hurt himself, it would hamper his rescue. The staircase ended at a flat rock floor, just like at the Station.

One of his captors shoved him forward and he fell to his knees. He yelped in pain and was cuffed on the back of the head.

"Silence!"

His knees hurt and his head ached. He would give a lot for a drink of water.

The sack was pulled off his head and he squinted up at the Crazy Man. Not a good thing to see. Tang looked to one side; his eyes widened. In the dimness beyond the Crazy Man, Tang could make out row upon row of Brothers. Armed Brothers.

He did the only thing he could think of and started to hum Blat's song. The last thing he saw was the Crazy Man's fist swinging towards his head.

Tang had overheard Blat talk about his ordeal with Krodan. But minstrels told stories for entertainment, didn't they? Tang always thought that Blat exaggerated what he had gone through to make it a more gripping story. He knew better now. He was ashamed at how quickly he babbled everything he knew; he couldn't speak fast enough to get it all out so that the Crazy Man would stop the hurting.

The new cell he was thrown into was a little larger than the closet. He could sit on the floor with his legs stretched out before him. Best of all, a cracked bowl had been pushed through a slot at the

305

bottom of the door. It could be poisoned; Tang didn't care. He drank the water in one long swallow.

His head still hurt and he couldn't seem to use his mind-to-mind skill. Maybe there was no one nearby to sense. He hoped the reason was as simple as that.

Tang tried to piece together how much time had gone by since he had been taken from the Desert Station. He was hungry but not that hungry. That meant about four hours.

He grew weary and, try as he might, could not keep his eyes open. He was pretty sure that he wasn't drugged. Too late to worry about that now. He leaned his head against the wall and slept.

***

Despite the danger, there was no keeping the Tucana family from helping.

Jamie-the-Cook was the first to appear at the door of their not-so-secret-after-all hiding place. "You think you get to have all the fun? In my city?" He glared at the quartet seated around the rough table. "I think not." He dragged a stool that had been shoved into a corner and planted his considerable bulk upon it. It creaked and groaned but held. It wouldn't dare defy the Master Chef.

Sarah showed no surprise that her husband would leave his duties and be able to find her. Blat had the suspicion that it was Crag in their midst that had precipitated Jamie's speedy arrival.

306

"Now I'm not saying that I can sing those Brothers into the beyond, but I know this city and I know everyone in it. That's got to be of some help."

At Crag's sour look, Blat jumped in. "And we're grateful to you. Information is exactly what we need. Detailed maps to be precise, especially of the locations and floor plans of the larger buildings. Upelo needs a place to gather his flock. Can you do that?"

Jamie looked at Sarah for the first time. "Consider it done. I'll be back." He left as quietly as he had arrived, swinging a dark cloak around his broad shoulders and pulling the hood low on his face.

Blat spoke. "We need people who can reconnoitre without attracting attention to themselves." He looked at Crag.

"Now what would I know about sneaking around?" Sarah and Blat waited. Crag harrumphed. "All right, but you should know that the Thieves' Guild doesn't work for free. It's not in their nature. But I'll see what I can do."

"I'm a better choice to go." He had been so quiet that Blat had forgotten he was there. Umbu slipped out the door.

"I like a big man who moves well," Sarah interjected into the silence. "When we have more time, I would like to hear his story."

Crag rose and began pacing, muttering and grumbling, pounding his fist periodically into a convenient object - the wall, the table, his other hand.

307

Blat gestured Sarah to the far end of the room. "Not a patient man," he whispered. "Best leave him to it and hope he doesn't hurt himself."

Sarah nodded. "He'll think of something, though. He always does."

"It's young Tang that has him fretting. I'm surprised he can bear to stay in this room at all. He must be mellowing." Blat hoped that they wouldn't have to test that theory for much longer.

The maps of the town streets and buildings that Jamie procured proved to be a marvellous distraction. Crag took out his writing implements and his glass and proceeded to mark the locations of likely meeting places on each one. Jamie added a few marks of his own, defunct structures that might still be serviceable.

The number of places to check was staggering. They did their best to limit the locations by those most likely to suit what they knew of the Brothers: monasteries, churches, and halls that were large enough to hold a substantial crowd. There were still over forty places to check. If the Thieves' Guild refused to help, it would be a lengthy task.

Jamie left shortly afterwards. He needed to return to his kitchen. Talitha had doubtless kept things running smoothly, but if the Minstrels' Guildhall was being watched, things should appear normal. With that in mind, Jamie would also arrange for Blat's room to look lived in.

Blat looked down at his hands, hands that should be playing an instrument not planning an attack. What was he thinking? Somehow he had gotten the idea that he was some kind of hero. He thought that he had outgrown such fantasies. Apparently not. If Upelo sensed him, the Eldest would not stop until Blat was dead, whatever the cost. Blat had embarrassed him and Upelo could not let him live. But this time Blat might not be the only casualty. Nearly everyone he knew and loved was at risk. He simply couldn't let that happen.

Inspiration struck. In every good battle there was a distraction or two. Blat decided that he would make a great distraction.

Umbu returned after nightfall; two children straggled in behind him. Every few minutes, one or two more arrived until the room was filled with their small, dirty faces.

Blat's expression mirrored Sarah's look of dismay. "They're children!" he exclaimed. "How much help can they possibly be? Don't the Thieves' Guild chiefs realise that if the Brothers take over, they will be just as much under their control as everybody else? What are they thinking to send these, these... babies!" Blat glared at Umbu.

Umbu's scar twitched and he actually smiled a little. "These so-called babies are the best sneaks in the city. Why I imagine that anything of value that you had on your person is now in the possession of some enterprising 'baby.' Isn't that right?" His gaze flickered to the small girl next to Blat.

Her teeth flashed in her face. "Jus' practising." She dumped her booty on the table: Blat's coin pouch, eating dagger, and the tin whistle he had recently borrowed from Sarah just to see what he could do with it.

"You see?" Umbu said. "Very good at what they do."

Blat nodded, bemused, as he gathered his things from the table, and turned to stare at the little girl.

"Beg pardon, sor," she said and belied the apology with a grin.

Sarah raised her not insubstantial voice to be heard above the giggling. "If you find any Brothers, make a note of their locations. And if you see a captive boy in their midst, make a special note." The elbow-height heads nodded.

In short order city sections were divided among the children and they dispersed quietly into the night.

Umbu also left to see what else he could discover among his 'network of associates' as he called them.

"More waiting," Crag grumbled. "I hate waiting."

***

"I hope we can trust him."

Sarah's voice washed over Crag like a soothing balm and it took him a moment to respond. "Trust him? If he meant to betray us, we would already be caught. Or worse. He hates the Brothers as much as any of us. More, probably. That Desert Station was the worst kind of prison. No hope of escape. Brothers on the inside and desert on the outside. Impossible. Umbu may have other motives but he certainly won't help the Brothers of the Watch." He met Sarah's gaze and was transfixed by her eyes.

He realised that they were alone in the dank cellar, except for Blat who amused himself in the far corner with that ever-present guitar of his. The delicate notes he plucked from it lent a surreal quality to the disreputable room.

There was nothing he could or would do about the powerful attraction that drew him and Sarah together. For some things it was simply too late. He had done some shameful things in his life but he would not add family wrecker to them. He cared too much to hurt her that way. Bad enough that he had disappeared from her life without a single word of explanation those many years ago. Even then, he knew that his mind wasn't quite right and he couldn't bear to become a monster in her eyes.

He had nearly lost his resolve when he heard she was to marry Jamie-the-Cook. The news had precipitated one of his worst drinking rampages, and for that particular episode he had been banned for life from some dingy little town whose name he couldn't remember. It was located in the middle of the eastern swampland; the stinky sludge had suited his mood. After that, he wandered aimlessly for a few months and eventually returned to his work. When Sarah's first child came along, he was far away in Zayu, the desert capital, busy designing a water system for the regency. The scorched earth and dust-filled air also suited his mood. He stayed away for many years and ever so slowly the gaping hole in his heart scarred over, though it still ached from time to time.

"What will we do when we find them?"

Sarah's question brought him back to the problem at hand. It was almost a relief to think instead about an invasion of Brothers.

***

Blat observed the interplay from his dark corner and sighed. He could sense their mutual pain, and was quite well acquainted with unrequited love. Talitha. He still dreamed of that one perfect kiss. That one disastrous kiss. He could wish all he wanted for more but it was not to be. Wasn't it just yesterday when being her friend was enough? He shook his head. No time to rehash old regrets yet again; he was sick of it. It was time to move on.

It was also time to plan.

"If we subdue Upelo the rest should be easier," Blat said as he stood and joined them at the table. The Eldest was the key. It was Upelo's will that compelled the Brotherhood. It was true that even with him out of the way, the senior Brothers might prove difficult; Upelo needed them to be able to think for themselves and their minds had been left mostly intact if Krodan was any example. As this went through his head, Blat jotted names and positions on a scrap of parchment. Some of these people were very influential in the city and could command not only the City Guard but also, Blat was loathe to admit, the Conservatory Security Guards.

The greatest number of Brothers was at the Server level. These were the rejected, the ones who did not have the kind of mind that Upelo required.

They performed mundane duties for the Brotherhood and obeyed any command they were given. The Eldest would use them as a battering ram of bodies.

Blat thought about these innocents who would be hurt and about the citizens of Rivercrest who were unaware of the darkness building in their midst. It would be far better to strike the head from the serpent before it was ready to strike.

Crag and Sarah leaned over his shoulder. Blat drew a squat pyramid with Upelo at the apex, the Protector and Priest Brothers one level below, followed by the Acolytes (hopefuls from whose ranks the Priests and Protectors were chosen and who dealt with the Servers), and lastly the Servers. He added the names from his previous list to each of the levels.

"The Assembly may be ready to listen to a plan by now and it should be easy for them to convince the City Council to act," Sarah said. "Between them, they are in the best position to subdue this level of the Brothers." She pointed to the Priests who were mostly merchants and other businessmen.

"Agreed," Blat and Crag said together.

"Upelo will keep many of his Protector Brothers close by and the Acolytes will likely be with him as well so that they can pass on his orders to the Servers. We can hope that the Servers will simply forget their commands once the others are taken." Blat had seen and heard enough at the Brothers' Stations to believe that many of the Servers had had their minds ruined to such a degree that this was likely true. Without continuous direction, especially in a situation so different from what they were used to, they would be harmless. Maybe.

The difficulty lay in distinguishing one order from another. Except for the Protectors, they all wore the same thing. The only way to tell a Server apart from the others was by what he was actually doing, like scrubbing a floor or cleaning out a refuse pit. He explained as much to Crag and Sarah. It was quickly decided that there was nothing to be done while the Servers remained under the control of the Acolytes; they could be dangerous and there were a great many of them.

The Thieves' Guild children began to return. Groups of Brothers ranging in number from a few to several dozen were seen in churches, public buildings, and alleyways. They knelt, heads bowed. So far, there had been no sign of Tang. Crag stalked to the far end of the cellar.

Blat watched him go and touched her arm as Sarah made to follow. "Leave him be," he whispered.

Sarah stared at the stooped shoulders, yearning to offer comfort. He'd had so little love in his life; it would be such a shame if this, too, was taken from him. But she knew Blat was right. Crag did not wish to have his emotions witnessed, he never had.

They turned their attention to a large-scale map of the city and marked the locales where the Brothers gathered. A picture began to emerge.

"This is not good. This is not good at all." Blat stared at the pattern they had drawn, revealing the Brothers' strategy. The critical systems of the city were surrounded: the water, the fuel, and the refuse disposal. A multi-pronged attack would bring the city to its knees in short order. Especially if the Brothers compromised the water.

Something niggled at the back of Blat's brain, taunting him. He was forgetting something.

Crag had begun pacing. Up, down. Up, down. His boots thumped on the old wooden floor. Normally, Blat ignored the scientist's quirks but tonight it was driving him to distraction. "Would you stop that?" He hadn't meant to sound so cross.

Crag slowed and turned to face Blat. "Something bothering you?" The menace in his voice was clear.

Great. Our dearly beloved scientist would choose tonight to have an episode. He would choose the blackest night of the month to show just how black-hearted he could be. Crag would drag them down with him into the blackness... That was it! Blat leapt to his feet. "You're a genius!"

Sarah and Crag looked at him as if he had lost what remained of his brain after the Brothers had scoured it.

"How could I have forgotten? Whatever they're planning will happen tonight. At the dark of the moon. It was on Upelo's planning map." Blat thumped his forehead with the palm of his hand. "How could I have forgotten?"

"Tonight?" Sarah's soft question brought the reality of it crashing down.

They looked at each other. They needed to stop the Brothers right now and their army consisted of a motley group of youngsters and the three of them. Four, if Umbu ever returned.

Jamie-the-Cook chose that timely moment to thump down the wooden staircase. "Now don't be alarmed," he said as minstrels and kitchen staff paraded in behind him. The hubbub of sound in the confined space was more than Blat could handle and he covered his ears with his hands. As though the motion was some kind of pre-arranged signal, the room quieted.

Jamie looked somewhat abashed. "It couldn't be helped. They're a nosy bunch and wouldn't be put off." He glanced down at the map of the city. "And by the looks of things, you could use the help."

The throng chimed in with its many offers of what they would like to do to a Brother if they ever got their hands on one. No one tortured a minstrel and got away with it. Blat should have known. And as serendipity would have it, the uncalled for reinforcements were just what was needed.

He felt a tug on his sleeve and looked down into a very young face with very old eyes. Disconcerting.

"Found a big bunch of 'em." The small Thieves' Guild urchin stuck a grubby finger on the map. "Right there."

One of his comrades pushed in beside him. With an even dirtier finger, he traced the best way to enter the cathedral.

The first boy spoke again. "In the catacombs. You have to be real careful when you go down. A bit slippery." Both faces looked up expectantly at Blat.

He fished around for his money pouch, which should have been firmly tied to the inside of his tunic. It landed with a dull thunk on the table in front of him. The boys feigned angelic innocence.

Blat took out two silver pieces and placed one in each of their outstretched hands. They turned and slithered through the crowd. He tried not to think about how many of his friends would be missing an item or two.

He looked at the expectant faces of his fellow musicians. "Right. We need people to go to the Conservatory and tell them about each of these places." He indicated where groups of Brothers had been found. "They'll need to divide up the Conservatory and City Guards and send a contingent to each."

Crag elbowed his way next to Blat. "I still have some of that blasting paste we used at the Station. It would severely discommode the big group at the cathedral. It could also be a very good distraction."

Distraction. Blat would be the true distraction, but Crag could certainly make it easier. Upelo would be with the largest group in the catacombs, commanding his minions like a spider from the centre of its web. The stairwell was too narrow to allow enough people to enter simultaneously to make any kind of assault effective. But one or two people might be able to sneak in and, with a Crag-style diversion to help, they just might be able to stop this thing before it got started. Umbu would be a good candidate and as if thinking of him had conjured him, he appeared at Blat's side. He had a bundle in his arms that turned out to be several black robes - Brothers' robes.

"Right," Blat said again. "Umbu and I will use a couple of these. and I don't even want to know how you got them, to sneak into the catacombs." He held up his hands to quell the protests that erupted. "We have experience protecting ourselves from the Brothers' mind pain. Crag. Take however many people you need to set the charges. Try not to bring the whole place down on our heads." Crag aimed a mock punch at the minstrel. "Sarah and Jamie, you have the difficult task of convincing the Assembly that they must take action immediately." He paused and looked at his friends around the room. "The Brothers strike tonight, at the dark of the moon."

The scientist was first to leave, selecting half a dozen minstrels to accompany him. "Give me one hour. I'll need to study the place so that my charges are set perfectly, as usual. I'll only bring the place down on your heads as a last resort." With a grin, he turned and slipped out into the night, his assistants close behind.

Sarah was next to move. She rolled up the map, and with Jamie and several senior minstrels to help strengthen their case, made for the door.

The remaining group milled about, full of determination to do something, anything.

"Go to the taverns," Blat suggested. That got their interest. "Go to the other Guildhalls, go anywhere there are people, and teach the song to everyone you meet."

Blat and Umbu were soon alone. "We have two tasks: stop Upelo and rescue Tang. I will deal with Upelo; your job is to find the boy and bring him to safety." Umbu nodded.

Blat emptied his pack and stuffed two of the robes into it; Crag's team had taken the others. Umbu busied himself secreting various knives and other paraphernalia about his body. The minstrel gaped. "Ready?" Umbu gave the whip lashed around his waist a final pat and nodded. "Let's go then, if you can still move without skewering yourself that is." Umbu glided past him and exited the cellar. "I guess so," Blat said to the empty room.

The fresh night air was welcome after the stuffy, musty basement. Blat breathed it deeply into his lungs wincing slightly at the pain of his nearly-healed ribs. 'Deal with Upelo' might easily translate to 'Kill Upelo.' What had he become? The guilt he carried from the disaster at Station Three continued to weigh heavily on him, not to mention the gruesome fact that he had plunged an axe into Mir's back, even if it had saved Angus Willoughby's life. Here he was, about to add to the burden.

Perhaps another solution would present itself. Blat doubted it; Upelo would not go down easily. The Eldest was evil beyond anything Blat could comprehend. He had created the Brothers of the Watch by subjugating young boys to his will and had destroyed who knew how many in the process. He had taken young women and given them as playthings to his favourites. Those he could not make into usable Brothers or use for sex, he turned

319

into slaves. Mir had shown him these things and more. Blat would be able justify his actions to anyone, to anyone but himself.

Umbu knew the city even better than Blat, especially the back alleyways. They arrived undetected in the vicinity of the cathedral and hid in nearby shrubbery to study the area for several minutes. They detected no movement either by Brothers or by Crag and his team.

Crag's hour was nearly up. Blat and Umbu donned their robes and crept towards the remote doorway that the young thief had described. It opened into a vestibule that was as black as pitch. They stopped to listen. Nothing. Step by careful step, they skirted the stone walls of the church and approached the entrance to the catacombs.

As they went down the slimy staircase, a murmur rose from below - the sound of many voices in soft supplication. Blat had only heard the Brothers vocalise in unison once before, at one of their ceremonies, and it disturbed him more than he could say.

The back of his head began to tingle and he concentrated on the melody and lyrics of the song he had written. He put his mouth close to Umbu's ear. "Sing the song at hard as you can inside your head."

Surprisingly, they met no guards on the descent. Upelo was getting cocky. And cocky people made mistakes.

They approached the final bend in the staircase. It exited in the middle of the back wall and opened onto a low-ceilinged crypt. It was long and narrow and filled with supplicant Brothers. At the far end Upelo and his Elders held court on a makeshift stage.

Blat and Umbu immediately assumed a kneeling position, heads bowed. They waited, expecting to be discovered, but no one paid them the least attention. Umbu nudged him with an elbow and began to sidle left along the wall. Blat watched from beneath his cowl for a moment and then moved in the opposite direction. He inched sideways and forward, toward Upelo.

A deep rumble seemed to come from all directions at once. Many of the Brothers looked up, their eyes immediately blinded by the dust and small debris dislodged from the ceiling.

Blat took his cue. He rose to a crouch and rushed to the front of the room, unnoticed in the growing chaos. Upelo stood in the midst of his Protectors and Priests, hands clenched at his sides. Several Brothers in the front rows collapsed. Upelo was indeed making mistakes.

Another rumble shook the rafters. Blat glanced back toward the stairway; it was clogged with fleeing Brothers. Whatever Crag had done, it was working well. He would be sure to tell him when he saw him again. If he saw him again.

Blat turned toward the Eldest and noticed a bundle at Upelo's feet. Tang. A large, dark form slipped in behind Upelo and his entourage. Umbu.

Blat made his move. He rose to his full height, threw back his cowl, and took a deep breath. He sang like he had never sung before. The acoustics of the room funnelled the notes directly at Upelo.

The Eldest's shock lasted only a few seconds but it was long enough for Umbu to grab Tang and for Upelo to focus on him. Blat smiled as the pain took him.

***

As much as he would like to spend many days punishing the minstrel, Upelo had no time for niceties. He took Blat's mind in an iron fist and squeezed. He would be rid of this nuisance once and for all.

Upelo was aware of his Elders watching. Good. This would also serve as a demonstration to them should they dare to defy him.

He squeezed harder. The minstrel writhed at his feet, his body snapping back and forth. He would do himself an injury. Pity.

Why wasn't he dead yet? Upelo had no time for this. He brought his full attention to the task. The minstrel clung to that infernal song like a starving dog with a bone. It was starting to annoy him. That was when he heard it. The song was outside of his head too. It came from the stairwell.

He pulled a little of himself from Blat's mind to scan his surroundings. He was alone on the stage. His Elders had deserted him and the boy was gone. Brothers lay strewn about on the crypt floor like the mindless beasts that they were. No matter. He had overcome worse odds.

Upelo focused a lance of power and aimed it at the singers entering the vault. They dropped like stones. More came behind and he struck again.

322

They staggered and fell. The song faltered for a moment then regained strength as yet more singers pushed forward. Seething with frustration, Upelo knew he must renew himself; he would transport back to the Desert Stronghold.

In a swirl of black robes, Upelo turned towards the transport map secreted in the bowels of the catacombs.

The minstrel blocked his way. Impossible. He should be a vacant husk on the floor. The minstrel made a fist. The blow caught Upelo directly on the nose. He heard it break. The most exquisite pain shot through his face. He brought his hands up to feel the damage and bright, warm blood spurted onto his palms. He was transfixed. He couldn't remember when he had last experienced physical pain. He marveled that he had never thought he would enjoy receiving pain even more than he enjoyed inflicting it.

He waited for Blat to hit him again; he yearned for Blat to hit him again. But the minstrel cradled his hand to his chest, a look of alarm on his face. Had he broken his hand? That would be good. Pain was good.

Upelo chortled in delight when his arms were wrenched behind his back and his hands tied viciously together. Someone forced him to walk and they skirted around Brothers that lay every which way on the rock floor. *What was wrong with them?* No matter. His face hurt. His arms hurt. His wrists hurt. It felt good to hurt. He needed to hurt.

Many of Upelo's Protectors and Priests were captured as they attempted to flee Rivercrest. The remaining pockets of resistance were unearthed by the resourceful children of the Thieves' Guild. The Servers were easily contained. These poor souls were placed in any home that would feed them in return for the menial work they could do.

Over the next few months, the remnants of the Brothers of the Watch scattered over Whitecap Island were captured by Guards accompanied by singers from the Conservatory. Although the Guards physically restrained the Brothers, it was the singers who subdued them. They sang a peculiar series of notes whose vibrations disrupted the changes that had been forced onto the Brothers' minds. Their power to control others ceased to exist. It would, however, be some time before they returned to normal lives; their incarceration under Upelo had forced them to do many depraved things not soon forgotten. With the help of medicines, music, and counselling, it was hoped that many could be helped.

Upelo remained under close guard. He had not responded to any healing ministrations and, when he wasn't commanding that he be served, mostly raved about needing more pain. Whatever happened, Blat sincerely hoped that he would never see the man again.

***

Tang sat in the sunny room and admired the weaving of his bedspread, although the colours were a bit bland by Station standards. Tina sat on a stool by the window and played her guitar. Blat had given *Gertrude* to her, which she was sure to proclaim several times a day. She was getting good, too, and had started novice classes at the Conservatory. He was secretly proud of her but would never tell her that; her head was swollen as it was.

His head, however, was still sore and parts of his memory were cloudy. The healers said that the pain would go away and his memories would become clear again. He didn't much like the treatment, though. He couldn't imagine how the healers, or should he say healer-musicians, could stand to sing and play such terrible music. Even though he knew that the sounds could fix people's heads and bodies, it was too bad it had to sound so awful.

It had all started with Blat's song, but Blat's song didn't sound bad. Tang shook his head and winced a little. He just didn't understand how it all worked yet, but neither did the Conservatory people. A whole new building was being planned just to study musical healing. They were going to call it The Raike Institute after Blat's family name. Blat said his father would be proud.

Father. He turned his head away from Tina, hiding the sudden glisten in his eyes.

"It's about time that boy had some fresh air." Crag's booming voice filled the hallway.

"But sir! It's too soon!" Tang could have told poor Francis that he didn't stand a chance. The only one who could slow Crag when he was on a mission was that scary Doctor Ilyam with his gravel voice, not to mention his huge arms.

"Bah. Out of my way." Crag strode into the room filling it with his exuberant presence. Tang's heart lifted.

***

Blat contemplated the tree's reflection in the lake. It was good to be out of the city; all the attention and bustle had become overwhelming at the end and he had just needed to get away.

His mind drifted over the recent events in his life. Umbu hadn't escaped unscathed from their night at the cathedral. Upelo's Protectors had tried to stop him from taking Tang and had attacked Umbu's mind for a, thankfully, brief time. Blat didn't doubt that the big man would make his way whenever he was ready toward whatever goal he chose. In the meantime, Umbu remained in Rivercrest, a city that he knew inordinately well. Blat would have to ask him about that sometime.

Jord Willoughby had also chosen to stay in the city. Blat suspected the decision had a lot more to do with the lovely Leonora than with his new position at the Guildhall's stables. With Jamie-the-Cook keeping a close eye on the boy, there was little to worry about. Perhaps he would wander by the Willoughby's homestead to let them know how their youngest was getting along. But he would not, no matter what Angus said or how he tried to coerce him, go into the stake. Blat's days of any and all things underground were over. He would travel above ground and sing songs, like a proper Touring Minstrel.

Tina was a true marvel and it was no wonder that the Conservatory had offered her a spot in the novice class. Her Station upbringing lent a certain ethereal quality to the music she created. Sarah had taken on the role of mentor; Tina would do very well under her tutelage. Blat felt a twinge of regret that he had given *Gertrude* to the young Stationer, not because she didn't deserve a fine instrument, but rather because it had been a gift from Talitha. Talitha assured him time and again that the guitar was his to do with as he wished. He realised that he had cherished it because it was from her. And he had given it away. Blat had a small epiphany. Giving the guitar away was a symbol, a symbol that he had moved on. He was pleasantly surprised to feel relief.

And Tang. As soon as the boy had been well enough, Crag extracted him from Ilyam's care - not an easy feat - and had Tang firmly under his wing. Tang was overjoyed that his Uncle Crag had chosen him, the ignorant Station boy, as his official Apprentice. Blat believed that there would be no separating the two of them regardless of what decision the Station Council made regarding Tang's future. It helped that one of the Conservatory's top priorities was the welfare of the Stationers and that Crag was chosen to lead the research on the cylinders and devices at the Desert Station. The devices, it seemed, were a last resort to power the cylinders if the machines should fail. The newly appointed Guardian of the Readings from Quirindi's Station had made the radical suggestions that Upelo's manipulation of the cylinders might have caused the unusual weather and the other disturbances in the land, and that Mir's entrapment in stone was also somehow related to the vibrations within the cylinders. Crag loved radical ideas and in his zeal to work long and uninterrupted hours, the scientist had let himself be subjected to the 'musical healing racket.' Blat smiled at a recent image that sprang into his mind: tall, lanky, dishevelled Crag and small, neat Tang in a close huddle over some odd piece of equipment, so engrossed and happy that neither had even known he was there. That was true music to his heart. If they fixed the weird weather, that would be good too.

At the thought of music, he opened the battered guitar case beside him. He would have to call it something other than 'my guitar' soon, but it hadn't revealed its name to him. It would.

He loved the beautiful old instrument. Its mellow tones seemed to awaken a matching resonance within his body. Whatever he played, he felt, not only as a song but as a true projection of himself. He had just begun to explore this new phenomenon.

He strummed; the tuning was good. He settled his back against the tree and began to play. The notes floated out, resting here and there on a branch or a blade of grass, before continuing on into the woods around him.

Blat sensed that he was being watched. He opened his eyes.

The short hairy creature that studied him from large yellow eyes twitched its ears, or should he say 'his' ears. The diagonal strip of crude leather across his chest did little to hide the obviously male genitals. The ears twitched again. Blat heard a twig snap and instinctively looked in the direction of the sound. There was nothing there.

He turned back in time to see the yellow eyes turn to lavender. The creature shrank to the size of his hand, jumped into his guitar case, and vanished.

Blat blinked. It seemed his adventuring days weren't over just yet.

Crag was going to love this.

THE END